And There Were Giants

By Hazel Lezah

Copyright © 2017 Hazel Lezah

All rights reserved.

ISBN: 9781520639048

Contents

Chapter 1 'The End' 5

Chapter 2 'A Journey' 9

Chapter 3 'The Crossing' 14

Chapter 4 'Elias' 19

Chapter 5 'Home?' 25

Chapter 6 'Birne' 35

Chapter 7 'Spring' 39

Chapter 8 'Early Summer' 46

Chapter 9 'The Sheep Shearing' 50

Chapter 10 'Anye' 54

Chapter 11 'Harvest Moon Festival' 60

Chapter 12 'Things are not always as they seem...' . 65

Chapter 13 'An end to silence' 69

Chapter 14 'The Curse' 73

Chapter 15 'Born to be a warrior?' 80

Chapter 16 'New Life' 83

Chapter 17 'Mira' 87

Chapter 18 'Marte' 91

Chapter 19 'The beginning – of another end?' 93

Chapter 20 '… over time…' 103

Chapter 21 'Within the wall' 110

Chapter 22 'Am I still alive?' 120

Chapter 23 'An Unexpected Visitor' 123

PART II 127
Introduction.. 128
Family Tree 128
Chapter 24 'A step too far' 129
Chapter 25 'Moving on…' 135
Chapter 26 'An Unprecedented Event' 141
Chapter 27 'In Sickness and in Health' 148
Chapter 28 'The Root of Evil' 153
Chapter 29 'The Secret' 156
Chapter 30 'Self-destruct' 163
Chapter 31 'A Change of Fortune?' 166
Chapter 32 'Watching and Waiting' 170
Chapter 33 'Our Friends from across the Sea' 174
Chapter 34 'A New Way' 182
Chapter 35 'A Burden Shared' 189
Chapter 36 'Revelations' 199
Chapter 37 'Possessed'... 206
Chapter 38 'Unrest' 214
Chapter 39 'Denial' 222
Chapter 40 'A Storm Brewing' 226
Chapter 41 'Portents of Evil'................................... 235
Chapter 42 'A Free Spirit?' 244

Chapter 1 'The End'

Why here? Why leave me here, of all places? I can scarcely breathe now; my breaths are coming thinner and faster as I feel that familiar sensation of panic beginning to envelope me. In the darkness I can make out cobwebs and other unidentified shadowy objects, but it is not enough to distract me. I try to concentrate on the horrific events that are unfolding outside but my mind keeps dragging me back to my all-consuming fear. The walls of my hiding place loom high and impenetrable in the darkness, shielding me, yet shrouding and stifling me with their strength. Father's words keep repeating in my head:

"Never forget child: your family and your people come first. Your wishes come second to theirs, your needs come second to theirs. You exist for them, and you must never let us down."

But I can't stay here, I can't bear this, I simply must get out…..

Oh no, they must be getting nearer….. that was louder, I'm sure of it….. but Father said they could never breach the outer wall! …… Dear God, that sounds even closer than before!….. And momentarily my consciousness is dragged away from my confined hell and out to the ordeal of my family and my people. They are not safe like I am, they have come second. I know that I am preserved so that I might live though they might die. How can that be? How can that be? And now the irony of this hits me: how could Father have put me first?..... Another cry of agony, but silence never follows like when an animal is slaughtered for the table, just cry upon cry and fierce roars as if of beasts – can these be men? Then I realise, with horror, that they must have breached the outer wall and must surely be by the Keep or Main Square. What can I do here? I must break free, I must, I MUST…..

"Your mother told me to hide you here Roslin. You will be safe. Our hopes rest with you now….."

And with that he was gone….. Leaving me imprisoned within these walls ….. Yes, this was her doing - she never understood me….. I must get out, I must get out, I MUST GET OUT!

"… Our hopes rest with you now….."

I must get out, I must get out, I MUST GET OUT!….

"never let us down.…. You exist for your family and your people, never forget, …. never forget, …."

But I will die if I can't get out! my heart is thumping in my ears, I cannot breathe, it's too hot, I must run, I….. What was that? Despite the din outside, I know I am no longer alone in this room…… A door has opened. Is it Mother? I must cry out and tell her to get me out. NO those are men's voices …… Then who is it? Steps….. now more…… now that is Mother's voice, but she is pleading, sobbing….. I have stopped breathing now. I know I am close to the grainy stars…… I have been here before, that time when Edgar and Jonas pushed me in the trunk and shut the lid. The memory flashes before me, and I hear them again, laughing and smirking at my trembling; they knew what feared me most, more than spiders, more than worms, more than father's anger or the stories of vicious giants from a foreign land….. but this is not boys' laughter I hear, this is men's. The tone is the same though, mocking and sadistic, and I realise that this has finally eclipsed my terror and I may actually be able to do something after all - for my people, for my mother:

"Leave my mother alone!"

But I am appalled by the sound of my own voice. It is a feeble, ineffectual whimper, in complete contrast to the battle roars and raucous laughter, utterly weak and pathetic. Still, everything in the room stops for a moment and my attention is drawn once again to the sounds outside – ever nearer – ever louder – and strangely chorus-like now, triumphant. They have won. We are lost.

And There Were Giants

Suddenly there is a crash, and light floods into my gloomy hiding place behind the wall. I am discovered. BUT I AM FREE! I gulp in air. I must act..... for my family..... for my people.

And then I see her. She is crushed beneath the most enormous ogre I have ever seen. He has hair like matted straw jutting from a helmet of steel and his sweat-drenched skin is streaked with blood. His arms and legs are as thick and gnarled as tree trunks and he is pounding on my mother as if to crush the life out of her whilst all the time he is bearing a jagged sword at her throat. And then I glimpse another, lurking in the shadows close by – this was my liberator. His features are masked by the gloom and yet his eyes seem to glow icy blue with their own demonic light.

Then I understand...... I have failed. I have failed my father, I have failed my people, and I most certainly have failed my mother – because I am powerless. I have no weapon, no army, nothing. I am a girl – a mere girl – a disappointment to my family, my people. And now that I have given myself up, even my mother's hopes have been dashed. I too will be crushed to death.... But I am FREE. (I can't believe that at a time like this such a thought can still enter my head)!

Paralysed for a moment that seems to last for ever, we all stare at each other and then.... that laughter! I shall never forget it. But, more memorable still, is what my mother does next. I feel a blow and I am down on the ground and beneath a crushing weight. My terror is too much, and I am falling away now into blackness; the pain is unbearable. Then I hear my mother screaming something incomprehensible and I realise that she is directing these alien words at our captors. Suddenly the pain stops. To my astonishment, my aggressor shrinks back and is cowering over me for a moment. Time stands still and I can almost hear them thinking, but then my captor is shouting at the other in his foreign tongue. The other roars back – he is beside himself with fury! What has happened? What has she said? But there is no time to think; in a flash, his sword is up and down, and my mother's life blood is pouring from her and gushing over me as I drag myself over to hold her - for the very last time. Now I know I am truly alone in the world......

Chapter 2 'A Journey'

In those early days, I did all in my power to block out the horror of the raid and focus instead on what was to become of me. However, try as I might, I found that any train of thought would lead back to it eventually. Until now, my life had been mapped out, determined and predictable. All that was gone now. I had no idea what was in store for me, so all I could do was try to survive and hope that my misery did not get any worse. We had been trudging through mud for days and the weather continued to deteriorate. All around was thick, impenetrable forest but for the soggy paths beneath our feet. Every now and then, little flecks of snow would drift slowly down from a leaden sky. In truth, the warm, summer moons were only just past, but they seemed like a distant memory now. And with the change in weather, more disputes flared between my captor and 'the other'. It was as if the chill and rain were a bad omen and it seemed to me, struggling to keep up, that they were hurrying more and more to get to our destination.

Every part of my body ached with exhaustion, for I had never walked so far in my life. I was cold, sore, and still bleeding a little, but I cared little for the physical ordeal. While my body laboured, my mind raced - with thoughts of what lay ahead and of what I had left behind. Where was I going and what was in store for me? Could it be any worse than I had already endured? After a while, when I could walk no further, they bundled me onto one of the horses, already laden with plunder. I should have been glad of the ride had it not been for the fact that every jolt increased my pain.

Up ahead, I spotted that I was not the only human cargo from the raid on our homeland. The horses were stolen, as were the bundles they carried, but there was also one other girl I recognised. I wondered how she had fared at the hands of their brutality. She was one of the younger women who attended to my mother. I felt my thoughts drifting back again over the life that had been snatched from me. Aisla, that was her name. Yes, I remembered her, she was a beauty – not as my mother had been – she did not share her green eyes, chestnut brown hair, or length of limb, but she did have a beautiful face, was youthful and, unlike me, had a voluptuous figure. Mother had always been tall and graceful; I, however, had inherited none of my mother's beauty. I was tall for our people but thin, almost boy-like. My 13th, 14th, 15th and 16th birthdays had all passed without my really changing shape at all or developing any curves. Mother's maid, on the other hand, was surely what all men were supposed to desire, and she had indeed been admired.

It struck me again, as we journeyed on and on, that I had never travelled this far and for so long before, even when taken to see prospective suitors from other kingdoms. These endeavours had all come to nothing of course. I had not been what they were looking for (perhaps my quick tongue had had something to do with that as well)! Yet I was not ashamed of my body or mind. There had been times, as children, when Jonas and I had ventured out and escaped the restraint of our royal upbringing. Then I had always been equal to his pursuits, whether it be swimming against the current in the river, or running with the deer in the trees. I could easily track and find them. Not only that, but I had been cleverer than him at letters, learning to read the scriptures from the monks long before him, even though he was a year older than me. I was his superior physically and intellectually, which he resented. Occasionally, he would punish me with jealous tricks like the time he and his friend had sent me to search in the trunk, only to then push and lock me in. Immediately, my mind was drawn back to the confined hiding place of the raid, and once again I tried to shut out the memory of it. While we were growing up, my brother, Jonas, could not do wrong in my parents' eyes, and was never chided for his treatment of me. He had been the son and heir and the favoured one, until a fever took his life just on the cusp of adulthood. It occurred to me that, had he still been alive, it would have been he who was placed in the nook behind the wall rather than me. I turned quickly away from that thought too.

We were not allowed a childhood, Jonas and I – play was for peasants' children, not the highborn. Jonas was heir and I – well, I was born to serve. Not as a servant of course. On the contrary, the fact that I had never needed to do menial work was a crucial part of my dowry. My duty was to serve my kingdom by my alliance – no more. I was born to serve my future husband and people as my mother had done. Though mine should always have been a privileged life, I had always felt sure it would have been lonely and confined. I would have been shackled to a loveless marriage with no aspirations, no freedom and above all few pleasures. I was trained for this role from as soon as I could remember. So, Mother never knew how well I could run and swim, Mother didn't care that I could read and write. No, all she saw were my struggles and failures – right until the end. We could never be close, Mother and I, I could never be what she wanted me to be, and I could never understand her. Yet nothing could rid me of the sight of her terrible death at the hands of that monster! And what of Father? I dared not imagine….

For a moment, I was distracted from my reminiscences by a strange smell that I hadn't noticed, nor indeed ever smelt before. Not a bad odour, just alien: fresh, yet paradoxically rather rancid. Where could we be? The trees were definitely getting thinner now too – perhaps we would be settling near here for the night…..

My thoughts were not diverted for long, though, as they were soon back at the raid again. This time I fell to wondering about Mother's strange rant. Had she been trying to protect me in some way? Was this why they still did not come near me, but why Aisla seemed to disappear each evening into their camp? I didn't trust them at all and yet I sensed that perhaps they were keeping their distance from me?

We were climbing a steep hill now, and the path was rocky and winding. Also, the wind was getting ever keener, and I sensed we were approaching something.

Then, over the brow of the hill, I saw it in the distance. The most enormous expanse of water I had ever seen – as far as the eye could see –and this was not behaving like any water I had seen before either. It was not a running river or a still pond; it was heaving and swelling and crashing against the shore, and was such a colour! A kind of muddy brown, transforming slowly into a pale green/grey and finally into a dark blue. And the noise! It was so windy here, it was tearing my hair this way and that, and the roar, combined with the crash of the waves on the stony shore, was deafening. So, this was where that pungent smell was coming from. Strange birds were circling up ahead, huge white birds screaming and calling to each other in their unearthly tongue. It was truly incredible!

I could have stood there taking it all in for ages, but since we had stopped, the two leaders were arguing with each other again whilst the others looked on nervously; I could only assume this sight was not what they were hoping for? Were they really not expecting to see this water? Had we come the wrong way? Then a group of men started to run off up the shoreline and out of sight into the trees.

What happened next was just another of the extraordinary events that were turning my life upside down. My hitherto sheltered, predictable, withdrawn life under the protection of my parents was well and truly over. There before me appeared three boats, but these were nothing like the little wooden craft used to cross our river at swollen times. No, these were enormous and with a most striking shape and majesty. They were long and perfectly formed, and of a timber craftsmanship I could only wonder at; yet I shivered as I imagined how terrifying their arrival would be glimpsed from afar, for on each prow was carved the fiercest of creatures. Could such beasts actually exist? I trembled at the thought but then fell to wondering how these vessels could look so powerful and substantial, yet be light enough to be carried by these men down to the water's edge.

Immediately I was trembling again, for I had realised, with horror, that we were to cross this swollen and heaving water. Could that be possible? The men were on their knees, no doubt summoning their god for strength. I wondered if I should do this too but then quickly discounted it – what had my God done for me? These heathens had destroyed everything I had ever known and loved and left me in peril and the unknown. No, I must trust to my strength in the water. If the boat capsized then I could swim back to the shore, I knew I could.

Chapter 3 'The Crossing'

It was of course the sea. Back then, I had never seen it before, but I soon recognised it from the terrifying stories the monks told us about ogres who crossed it from far away to steal and plunder. Those stories had now become my reality. What they hadn't told us was that the sea was an enemy too: it was a wild and merciless creature full of putrefying debris, and the icy stinging spray that spewed from it bit into you with its salty white teeth. Now my fear of these men transformed into a bitter sort of admiration as they battled and won against this beast time and time again.

The first day it had been restless, heaving us this way and that, but the second day was a true fight for survival as we lurched over great mounds of foaming water. At first, I was terrified, feeling that each mount and descent would be my last, but after a while, I began to trust in the ability of these men to keep us above the waves, and fell to wondering how they had learnt to do this? Was this where their strength had been wrought – against the elements, against storms such as these and day upon day of rowing? I could not believe how far this water stretched; beyond the horizon and further still; there was no way back now - it seemed interminable, inexhaustible, endless.

Mercifully, after the ordeal of those first two days, the sea then calmed and became less angry. There was always a keen wind which cut through us, as did the spray if it hit us, but apart from these discomforts I became quite used to the constant chafing of the waves. We ate, slept and rowed, then ate less, slept less and rowed more, for days and days on end. Little was said, though I could see the men at the front were navigating us through this maze of sameness. How they could possibly know their way, I had no idea.

It was on this journey that my skin and gums began to crack and bleed, and my eyes were dazed by the glare of the light on the sea. I took to covering myself in whatever material I could find from head to foot and soon blended in with the cargo and became like another bundle of plunder. But the salt and wind got into everything. I felt I was almost forgotten in this race for survival, this race to get to their destination whatever and wherever it may be. I was never asked to contribute anything to the labour of that journey. I would be shivering in a corner whilst they were sweating and heaving away or falling on what food we had. I ate and drank sparingly. I couldn't face the thought of bodily functions, though provision was made even for this, and I kept myself as warm, still and quiet as I could in this jolting, swelling world.

There came a day when I was woken from my frozen stupor by a shout and was witness to the most incredible sight. A shaft of light was coming from on high and beaming down on the sea from an otherwise leaden sky. I took it as a sign from God and I could tell I was not alone in so doing. Perhaps there would indeed be an end to this journey after all. Perhaps one day there might be land again; oh, how I longed for that day! And so, I once more put my faith in God and prayed for the souls of my mother and father; I prayed for my people and that something still remained of my homeland; and I prayed that I might be spared the wrath of these evil giants.

After that, there would be times when I was convinced we were coming in to land and my hopes would rise only to be dashed once more, as no sooner did we seem to draw near to some distant shore, then we would be torn away again, on and on, searching, and I began to wonder whether we had indeed lost our way. It had been getting colder and colder as the days wore on, and I felt we must be nearing winter now – the journey had certainly seemed long enough.

Finally, one interminable day, when I had been trying to sleep, though the wind was howling around the boat, there were shouts and whoops of joy. It must be land! I gazed out, desperately trying to glimpse this new haven, but could scarcely fathom anything at all. Whatever they could see was concealed from me by a rapidly thickening fog, and I wondered how they could decipher anything in that ethereal world. At last, a slit opened in the swirling grey blanket, and I briefly caught sight of - a mass of forbidding rock! As we drew closer, cliff upon cliff rose up before us, with not a landing place in sight. To my amazement, they continued towards this impenetrable fortress, undeterred by the apparent lack of landing place. I closed my eyes, again certain we were rowing to our deaths. Then opened them again. Somehow, we were passing through a narrow break in the rocks towards a little wooden jetty. I sat transfixed (as I could scarcely move by now) a stiffened, useless ghost of my former self, and I gladly succumbed to the strong arms that hauled me out onto the jetty.

Those that greeted us from the gloom were as huge and burly as my captors and were heavily armed. I was dumped unceremoniously on the slats, and my body continued to rock and sway as if the wood were heaving with the swell we had left behind. Looking up, I was suddenly aware of how the walls of rock bore down on me on either side, high above my head, and I felt a slight panic rise within me – my old trouble again. I tried to look up at the sky, and amongst the higher crags, I could just about decipher that men had built bastions and lookouts there. Was this how we were to live then, like goats hopping from one outcrop to the next? It was indeed a hostile place; the cold was palpable, no doubt from the fog which was still increasing in density and swirling around us, its fingers clutching at us with a chilling, yet featherlight touch. I thought of the green, fertile land and gentle hills I had left behind. If this was all they had, then perhaps this was why my captors had dared to venture so far and so perilously over the sea.

Our welcome party led us up steps cut into the rocks, me stumbling and staggering to find my feet all the while after my enforced confinement, until we came upon one of the small settlements I had glimpsed, built into the rock. It was then, whilst arrangements were being made for the night, that Aisla was carelessly bundled in beside me. Suddenly together like this was our first tangible reminder of home and we hugged each other tight, no barrier of status between us now: we were survivors. She too had known the cruelty of these men, she too longed for an end to this misery. That night we slept like babies in each other's arms.

The following morning, we were rudely awoken and to our dismay, Aisla and I were parted. It happened so quickly that we had little time to protest. I never saw her again. The seemingly endless journey resumed, this time over land. Once more, I was stumbling along a rocky path that led us from one craggy summit to another, no beast to take the burden of my weight now. And so, I was forced to resign myself to this new, barren, frozen world with its huge, vicious men.

I did begin to wonder which would end sooner – my life or this travelling. I felt my lifeblood draining away from me the more we trudged over the harsh terrain; surely it was only a matter of time before I was no longer of this world? But somehow, I made it – maybe it was just my innate curiosity spurring me on to find out where we were going, or maybe I was just hardier than I thought.

It was beginning to get colder still, when I began to notice murmurs amongst the ranks and a quickening of pace, despite the incline of the slope, and I began to think there may be something other than stone beyond the horizon. Finally, as we reached the summit of that rock and stepped over the ridge, there before us was the first greenery and the first trees I had seen in that godforsaken land. It was there too that I first set eyes on the grandest and most imposing stone dwelling I had ever seen, great plumes of smoke spiralling up from it as if heralding our arrival. All my suffering and exhaustion were momentarily forgotten as I admired this majestic structure, acknowledging to myself that I had not expected my captors capable of such a feat of architecture. How could these savages navigate the sea and build structures such as this?

The men had paused and soon I could see why. A mighty door had opened and a welcome party, far statelier and more striking than before, was heading slowly towards us. As they approached, and I could see them more clearly, the sheer bulk of their voluminous robes and great height in their fur-lined boots reminded me of how small and defenceless I was. Not a woman amongst them, their beards hung down like fleeces. I could scarcely see their eyes through all the mass of hair, though I could just make out, in the dim light, that they were of the same pale blue as my captors' – like gems set in stone and covered in pale grass.

They soon lost interest in me as they hailed each other in their foreign tongue, so my gaze turned once again towards the building down below me. I gasped at the scale and beauty of it. It stretched far into the distance. So, they aspired to this! I couldn't help but be impressed. However, one thing struck me about this great hall, and father's words echoed again in my head, "They cannot reach us here Roslin….." This mighty castle had no stronghold at the top of a hill, no mighty surrounding wall. On the contrary, it nestled in a defenceless valley! Proud and rich as these people were, they obviously feared no-one.

Chapter 4 'Elias'

We were thus greeted with ceremony and torches. It was plain that they revered their leader and his companion, who were given horses – great shaggy creatures which I had never seen before - but their welcome soon became raucous and loud, where our people would have bowed in humble respect. I waited, practically deafened by the noise, expecting to be brought to the fore and exhibited as part of their prize, but it seemed that I was forgotten in their celebration. Well, at least that was the end of our journey, I thought, perhaps I might now be given shelter, food, and a bed for the night.

But if I had believed that this was to be my new home, I was wrong again – unlike the humble Aisla, I was not destined for that magnificent building at all - but was diverted onto another track leading off in another direction entirely. With a shock, I realised that my only travelling companions were to be the leader - the brute who had murdered my mother - and the other, my 'liberator' and their attendants. I had already endured what they were capable of; what was their intention now? Would they never rest? At first, I thought they must be leading me to a grander home still – they were, after all, the leaders, and I was, after all, of royal blood. This thought comforted me for a while, until new fears began to creep into my already crowded and baffled mind. How could I possibly believe either of them would want me in their household as they had barely acknowledged me since we departed? More likely they were leading me to some horrible death, perhaps as a sacrifice for their safe passage, or as revenge for whatever my mother had screamed at them! I had already been shivering with cold, but at the prospect of my imminent death, I began to shudder uncontrollably.

We were now on horseback again and passing through sparse woodland with strangely fragrant trees that were covered in tiny dark green spikes – obviously a more fertile region of this otherwise seemingly barren place. On and on we travelled, my trepidation growing with every step, and the mist only seeming to thicken more and more. Finally, I could just about make out some dwellings ahead, though no sign of any imposing buildings as before, and for a moment, I caught myself questioning that they should be bringing me, the daughter of the Lord of all our land to such a lowly place? But no – what was I thinking of? I was obviously worth more to them dead than alive, and I tried again to stem the fear that threatened my consciousness.

We had been moving downwards on a slight incline all the way and were now in another tree-lined valley. As we stopped, I could hear trickling water and bustling movement as our presence was made known. Strangely, these sounds were so reminiscent of my old home that I felt almost reassured. But when more torches were lit, in an attempt to cut through the deepening gloom of fog and dusk, my previous anxiety returned and intensified. For now, I could plainly see, great devilish ghouls lumbering towards me out of the swirling mist. I tried to let out a scream, but no sound came. Instead I stood there, literally petrified, as behind them two final figures appeared, one much larger than the others. And now I knew that my time had come for here was the true 'giant' from the monks' stories – so far I had only seen the ogres - but this was indeed a giant! The trembling started again; I was so cold, wet from the damp fog but above all terrified of this new realisation – that after all I had survived, all I had been through, I had been brought to this end….. for I remembered their words quite vividly: 'the giants were the worst, the cruellest of torturers …. ' and here, in this desolate land, there could be no escape.

~~~~~~

As his stepbrother approached on horseback, with a band of his men and what appeared to be a dishevelled child, Elias felt that sick, uneasy feeling he always felt…..

And There Were Giants

I had been expecting him to have returned long before now – they were late, judging by the turn of weather. Still there was no surprise in that, Edvard was always too full of his own ego to worry about the danger of a storm at sea – he thought he was invincible and his greed for loot took precedence over anyone's safety; no, what concerned me was that he had come straight here fresh from his journey. It could only mean one thing: that he had something to crow about or to deride us with. Birne and I exchanged glances as we hurried out to meet them – this did not bode well. In truth, any visit from my stepbrother did not bode well.

There they were, triumphant - sea-ravaged but nevertheless glowing with the success of their spoils.

"Brother, I am returned, and I have much bounty and glory to bring my kinsfolk." He said this as proudly as usual, as if expecting me to gush back with enthusiasm and awe. Instead I remained silent. I could not bring myself to say anything at all. The truth would incriminate me and anything else would be falsehood and sycophancy. Then he turned and summoned something to be brought to the fore – I looked on, wondering what mischief my brother had thought up this time. The little girl on horseback was brought forward into the half-light. I could barely make her out, but I could see she was quaking with fear – I knew that fear.

"Brother, I know by now that you care not for riches and jewels, but I feel I never bring you anything at all….. so, I have brought you a wife. Take good care of her – I have reason to believe she is of royal stock and likely to be….. 'delicate'." There were sniggers and smirks. I felt their eyes on Birne and myself and we instinctively moved together – side by side as always. We knew this was our weapon – we knew this kept us safe here. The laughter and scorn were nothing in the scheme of our daily lives. Then she was taken down from the horse and brought close before me. She was wide-eyed, and cowering. I was suddenly reminded of the tiny bird with the broken wing I had found once, as a child: how its eyes had stared up at me in terror, totally unable to escape, and that feeling I had of power. I could have crushed that tiny bird to pulp with one hand – which of course Father had done the minute he discovered my cherished new foundling. I blotted out the memory at once as I had learnt to do so well….. And now this. Instinctively I took a step back, I could see my size was intimidating her. I did not have to speculate what he could have done to her and indeed what she was thinking I would do….. But she would be safe with me.

"Thank you, Brother. I will indeed take good care of her." This was obviously all the reply my brother wanted and seemed to please him enormously. With that he turned and pulled his horse away, his men scrabbling to remount and follow him back into the darkness.

I looked down on her again in the light of the torch, this time seeing her green eyes, her dark hair, her pale young face (though I could see now she was not a child as I had first thought). She was mysterious, indeed quite bird like, so slight and with those curious eyes, and raven black hair. But she was mine! I had never had to care for another human being before. Her fear was still apparent, and I tried desperately to think how to appease her. I knew she would not understand me if I spoke but nevertheless, I took another backwards step away, this time towards my homestead and said as gently as I could, "Come, eat," beckoning to her. She didn't move a muscle and continued to stare at me warily, but I sensed a slight relaxation in her stance. This time I turned my back, walked a little further and turned again, "Come, you must be tired from your journey, come and eat with me. I will not hurt you."

Slowly the others melted away, gossiping amongst themselves. Only Birne remained. Suddenly he intoned,

"I will see you in the morning, sleep well with your new 'wife'….." and with that he was gone. He seemed irked in some way, and I thought about his choice of words for a moment. Was he angry that I was to have a new charge? Surely not. I carried on as before. This time she stirred and ventured a step towards me – I had won a measure of her trust! The pleasure rushed over me. I could take care of her. She would be safe here with me.

~~~~~

Roslin dragged herself towards the 'giant's lair'......

Despite his immense size there was something, something in those eyes that spoke to me – could it be pity? I had witnessed such cruelty and violence, but there was nothing like that in his face. Struggling with my fears and memories, an instinct deep within me told me to follow the giant; after all, what could be worse than what I had already endured? I was near death anyway.

To my surprise, it was deliciously warm and cosy in the dwelling. I was used to tall ceilings and a raging fireplace in some distant wall, not to a fire in the middle of a room so that all around benefited from its warmth. As I wavered in the doorway, I began to feel lulled by the heat. Somehow, I managed to slowly draw myself near to the fireside where sheep's fleeces and throws were scattered. The giant moved to the other side of the fire and beckoned to me to sit down on one of the fleeces. The comfort was overwhelming after the hardship of the journey and if I had not been on high alert, I would have fallen asleep there and then. And still he kept a distance from me, moving slowly and deliberately as if I were a deer he did not want to scare away. There was something else about the room that was enormously comforting too – the smell – there was the most enticing smell of something good to eat. He moved over to a table and arranged something, then came over to the fire, stirred the contents of a steaming pot set over it, and poured some of the delicious smelling food into a bowl. As I stared at those enormous, rough hands, it suddenly occurred to me that this huge man may be a mere servant after all! I drew further comfort in this surmise, for surely only a servant would prepare and serve his own food like this? Then, to my relief, I saw now that the food – the bread, stew and some berries - was intended for me! He came closer now, and I felt my breathing quicken, but he continued to leave some distance between us and laid the food down before me. He gestured and spoke again, and despite myself, I couldn't help feeling that there was a gentleness and thoughtfulness in his booming voice and actions. Could I have been wrong about this giant? And suddenly I began to feel overwhelmingly tired and hungry. He did not eat but watched me silently from the far side of the fire, whilst I devoured the food, which was as good as it had smelt. I then felt exhaustion sweeping over me once more. What else could I do now? – I simply had to sleep. The moment I sank into those deep soft coverings I had indeed surrendered myself to sleep……

Chapter 5 'Home?'

When I woke, I knew I had been sleeping well into the next day. There was no sign or sound of anyone. I had certainly not been held captive then – but where would I have run to anyway? It was time to explore my new 'home'. I was in a small chamber in a large comfortable bed thick with drapes and beautifully soft fleeces. If I were to be a prisoner, this was surprisingly good treatment! As I ventured out into the main room of the dwelling, I noticed food by the spent fire. I decided not to touch it; how could I expect it to be for me? Yet somehow, I believed it was. After my treatment last night, I had begun to hope I might be safe here. I moved cautiously as far as the doorway of the humble building and peered out, momentarily blinded by the bright sunlight; nothing barred my way.

Standing on the threshold, I was struck by how cold it was despite the bright sunshine – my ragged clothes would never keep me warm in these temperatures – winter had certainly arrived. An extraordinary landscape stretched out before me. The modest dwellings were all of stone with wooden roofs, and beyond the clearing in the valley, I saw slopes of green and silvery-grey interspersed with glittering tiny streams, and a thousand flat and shining rocks splintered over the grass. Even the trees in the distance were alien, their shape strangely angular against the horizon as if they had been carved by a sharp tool.

Gathering up one of the fleeces about me, I ventured out a little more. There was still no sign of anyone, but I could hear sounds not far away, and soon I began to see the people of this village. Bustling about, or at work, everyone had a purpose – this was indeed the world of servants – rough garments, tools in hand, working at whatever they were doing – I did not know. I recalled my idle past and wondered if I would be expected to work here too? But I was tiny in comparison to these giants – what use could I be here? The nearest I had ever been to work was my study of the scriptures or needlework for a tapestry.

True, I had mastered both easily, so the thought did not daunt me.

My host was nowhere to be seen, but presently a woman spotted me and came forward and gestured to me to go back to the dwelling. I felt the conflict of the night before when the giant had beckoned to me, and yet her face again betrayed a different look to my captors', and I felt compelled to trust and follow her. To my relief, I was indeed encouraged to eat the food by the spent fire, which I did ravenously, her eyes watching me all the while. Then she handed me rough clothes, of a texture I had never felt against my skin before – obviously meant for outdoors – and so much more suited to the biting cold. They were of course far too big, and she practically had to bind me into them, but I was grateful for the warmth they gave me. Now I was ready to repay my hosts' welcome and learn my new trade, but the woman made no attempt to begin any training. Instead she gazed upon me for a moment, then felt my hair – so dark compared to her wavy, flaxen hair, laced with grey. I would no doubt be a novelty to them – so small in comparison, with my hazel-coloured eyes. They were all fair or red-haired, fair-skinned and tall. I was glad I had taken my parents' height, though I still felt so tiny compared to them – even this woman. Suddenly, she gestured to herself and said in their strange, lilting tongue 'Martha', then pointed at me. I replied with my name, smiling at her with gratitude, and to my relief she smiled back. A feeling of warmth spread over me as Martha's face creased into the most beautiful of smiles. Next, she fell to examining my hands. Certainly, compared to her hard, calloused hands mine were soft and supple and my fingers long and slender. I had never admired my hands before, nor thought that my figure or features might ever be of interest to another human being. In fact, I had never compared favourably with others of my sex, and yet I felt, by this woman's gaze and exclamations, that she was not simply curious but possibly even envious?

Though I welcomed her kindness and her touch, the whole

experience was so strangely intimate, that I felt again like I was in an alien world. I could not remember anyone touching me with such gentleness before, yet I welcomed it and yearned for more attention. She was looking after me – as if I were a child........her child.......

Mother. How I had wished to be like her. Why could I not be like her? Why could I not sit and smile and work with a needle all day long. Why could I not glide like a swan, my gown flowing behind me as she did? Why could I not sit quietly and listen to the men talk and lower my eyes in that alluring way of hers? Why did I want to run and tussle with my brother? Why did my hair not lie like hers, but fell in tangled, tousled locks this way and that…? Well, I knew I cared not for the hours of grooming….. But my biggest question was this – if I was not born to that grace, why did she not teach me? Why were we so seldom together? Did she not know how quick I was? No, she didn't, and it was not important anyway. I was not born to be quick and clever. I was born to be obedient and still and beautiful like her. And I was not…..I was a disappointment, and so Mother only ever seemed to look on me from a distance – a distance she was no doubt glad to preserve.

The woman smiled again gently at me, brushed my face with her fingers and muttered something to herself which did not sound unkind. I smiled back and thanked her with all my heart. That gentle, tender way about her, it was so warming, and the way her eyes crinkled into those familiar lines when she smiled. Like the others she was tall, and she had a sort of faded beauty about her maybe worn away by her harsh outdoor life. Perhaps I could find a new beginning here in this village. Perhaps I could learn and do something to please them and repay their kindness.

I did not see my giant host again until dusk. As before, my heart leapt in fear at the sight of him, but as he approached, I saw that he, too, was smiling down at me. My fear abated once more. That great mop of hair on his head and the beard masked his face, but he had soft, grey/blue eyes which spoke of a kindness that was mirrored in his actions. I couldn't help but relax the longer I remained in his presence – his attitude towards me was a kind of deference, which I had certainly come to expect from our servants, and he ensured that my every need was met. However, he treated his fellow servant Martha with a jovial intimacy, which I found quite touching. Indeed, I had never witnessed such familiarity and warmth.

By the time he had returned, Martha had created a bed by the fire and had made another kind of stew as I looked on. She never once asked for help but took care that I should see each step of the work. She talked to me incessantly, and I realised that I must indeed learn this new language like a child. That day, I learnt many household words, and undertook there and then to be a model pupil and learn as fast as I could.

Naturally, I expected this new makeshift bed to be mine. Martha left shortly after my host arrived, and alone with him once more, I felt my original uneasiness return. However, it was not as intense as the previous night, and though a heightened silence reigned once more, I did not feel as if I were in any imminent danger. If anything, I detected a certain weariness about him now, which belied his obvious strength and stature. He had brought back a load of logs and had set them down beside the dwelling. After we had eaten yet another wonderfully satisfying meal, he stretched out by the fire – gazed at me for a while, said a few words gesturing to the bed chamber where I had slept before, then lay down on the makeshift bed and instantly fell fast asleep! I did not dare to wake him, so after watching him for a while and reassuring myself he could not harm me in this state, I went back to the little room and fell, myself, into another deep, restorative sleep.

The next morning was as before. He was up and gone before I awoke and had left me food by the fireside. I dressed in the outdoor clothes once more and made my way out into the bleak sunlight. As I walked towards the sounds, I caught sight of the friendly Martha again and my heart lifted. This time she led me to what must be her dwelling. It was slightly bigger in size to the giant's and split into three rooms. I noticed a man's belongings and deduced that this woman must have a husband. She again showed me how to prepare food and this time took out what I saw to be wool and tools and showed me that she was making some sort of clothing. I watched in admiration as she used the tools to weave the garment. The repetitive motion seemed easy to me and not dissimilar to my tapestry work, and I soon mastered it, though painfully slowly compared to my teacher. She was obviously pleased with my progress and gave me my own to work on there and then, and so I began my first ever piece of useful work. This was not simply to decorate the wall or bed of my chamber; I would wear or sleep under this, or someone else would. This was to be my craft, I thought. Yet the next day there was something different to learn, and the next and the next, and I began to realise that survival in this land did not depend on one occupation per servant – as it seemed to in my land – but that here you must be proficient in all. I learnt to carve a bowl that would carry my soup; how to tend to animals that were kept in buildings nearby; how to make strange potions, which I would later learn were to heal a number of common ailments; how to clean; weave; cook; and also how to sew; and tend plants in the soil. I took my turn to collect water from the springs for our dwelling and immediate neighbours, and washed clothes in the river, shivering from the icy water. All this work left me physically exhausted yet gave me a new strength, and all the while I wondered at this new way of life. In the continuing absence of my captors, who was directing this work? Who was the leader? How was it ruled and managed? I supposed that there must be some contact with my captor and his men - but we did not see nor hear from them for days, weeks, what must even have been months. I put this down to the snow.

Oh, what snow! We'd had snow in my homeland but neither

the depth nor the misery of this. Clothes washing ceased, and we took to gathering bowlfuls of the snow as our water instead of venturing out to the frozen streams. Up until the snows, my new life had suited me perfectly: I was happy and occupied and somehow accepted into my new community (despite my 'difference'). True, people stared and whispered at first, but this soon stopped as they grew used to my presence and, perhaps most importantly, learnt quickly to earn my crust. But the harshness of that winter was miserable. I had never been so cold in all my life, not even on the journey to that faraway land. Every venture into the big white world was dangerous, and I feared for the men whenever they did this. Before the snows, my host had just managed to complete another 'room' and bedstead, with the wood that he had cut, and had taken to sleeping in there. Of course, I questioned that he should give up his bed for me, but then he was only a servant, and in those halcyon days I was stupid and naïve and had little concept of men. Only that some were to be feared, as my dreams would constantly remind me.

There was one night, in the depths of that terrible winter, when he returned frost-bitten and grim. By now I thanked God each time for his safe return, for I feared not only for my own but for all those people's safety in these cruel times. Even with the fire the dwelling felt cold, and there was a howling wind outside blowing an icy draught through us, despite the fact that we had lined the walls with every spare fleece or blanket. That night we did not move from the fire but huddled closer and closer for warmth. The nearer we got the more I marvelled at how comforted I felt by his presence so close to mine – as if he were my protector – when only a moon or so ago he had terrified me to the very core of my being! As ever, the big man closed his eyes and was soon asleep as if oblivious to our newfound proximity. I was left lulled by the sight of his huge bulk as it rose and fell with the rhythm of his breathing. I continued to watch him as the fire died down, noticing the long eyelashes and the unruly waves of his long, golden hair. He looked so peaceful, almost childlike. Then, fighting the warnings that came from within, I lay down by his side and felt the warmth of his breath on my hair as I lay with my back to him. Did I sleep through that night or did my nightmare grip me as usual? I do not remember waking from it, and yet I am sure I felt a hand stroking my face – a rough but gentle hand – though maybe that was a dream as well.

Next morning, he was gone again before I awoke. Had he been angry at my lying next to him like that? We rarely spoke except to exchange greetings. But from that day on, I wanted to find out more about my elusive host, and despite the awful weather, tried my best to find out where he disappeared to each day. Martha told me that his name was Elias, but I wanted to find out more about him – after all, he could still be preparing me for some further ordeal! My captor had handed me over to him, but why? At worst, he could have asked this giant - his servant - to fatten me for slaughter! At best, I had been given as some sort of gift to this community. My one consoling thought was that these people seemed to behave very differently to the group of ogres I had first encountered, so I hoped and prayed that I had just been left here. But who was this giant, for he was surely the tallest of his kinsmen, and why had I been handed to him? I was soon to discover something new about him, but not quite as I had expected.

That night there had been an even greater fall of snow, and the weight of it, coupled by the strength of the wind, had brought about a snowdrift that had crushed and buried some of the dwellings on the far side of our little valley. Fortunately, the inhabitants had not been buried alive, but there was now a distinct lack of housing at a time of real hardship. Shivering, I stared at the devastation and wondered what would be their fate? I was soon to find out that my host had the answer: our homes were to become theirs too. What struck me most about this magnanimous act was the way that Elias and his friend Birne (the man he had been with when I first arrived) organised and directed what happened next. Birne seemed to be in charge of caring for the people who were suffering from the cold – some of the worst off were to stay with him - whilst my host, Elias, was instructing those gathered on what was to happen next. So that evening, after the homes had been dug out and everyone accounted for, I assumed, we had some new companions in our dwelling. Elias and I shared the cooking and the food out and we all sat, no longer in silence, but in a warm, friendly atmosphere which I will never forget. There was no deference, no respectful distance kept from my host and the still, quiet space of our former days was gone. It was as if these people expected nothing less, and certainly as if he were a mere servant just like them. There was not much to eat but what was once ours was now theirs too. These people had lost their homes, and their food when times were hard for all, but knew they would not starve, they would be looked after and helped back on to their own feet. For once, I wondered what my Father would have made of this community, was this what he strove for? Was this the basis of our land too? Hadn't he said to me, '…your people come first. Your wishes and needs come second to theirs….' Before that fateful night, it had never been my business to care, I had simply been destined to make a good alliance. But I cared now. This new life, though hard and exhausting, was admirable and rewarding. These people cared about and for each other. They helped each other out in times of need and shared what was theirs immediately and without a second thought. What was more, I had discovered that they had a leader or perhaps leaders, in Elias and Birne.

True, it did not always appear to be as harmonious as this. Well, no, it wasn't. The snows abated, but I continued to watch Elias and Birne and I began to see that, despite their apparent youth compared to my father or others high up in our land, it was they who were called upon to resolve disputes and unrest. I now had time and confidence enough to venture out as far as their meeting place and watch the process with interest. There would often be much argument and shouting, which surprised me, as at home I had only ever heard one voice raised – that of my father. Yet here, in complete contrast, the only voices to remain calm were those of the command! Sometimes, if they spoke, the dispute would end abruptly, but not always, and I was surprised that this sort of behaviour could continue in front of the very people who seemed be in charge. But then I tried to remind myself that this must be how servants behaved, and that they were still somehow ruled from afar by the others.

The more I witnessed of these meetings, the more I remarked, how vulnerable some of these people were, living in this harsh environment. There were more men here than women, but many were old or lame in some way. However, they seemed to have overcome their various disabilities and were working as hard as the next person. This was another surprise to me, as our servants were always able bodied and picked for their strengths. If anyone became lame or sick, they would disappear, sometimes never to be seen in my household again. Here, everybody worked according to their ability – but if they did not – and disputes often arose from this – then they were summoned before the 'court'. And so, I would watch these trials, as often unconnected people did.

It was in those early days, when I couldn't understand or speak their tongue very well, that I began to notice how Elias seemed to be the centre of their world; how people came and went and flitted around him as if seeking his approval or wanting him to notice them. They were drawn to Elias like bees to a honeycomb. Where he went people would swarm around him, and what he said generally went unquestioned and was ultimately law, despite any anger or rancour displayed beforehand. I knew he was only a servant and yet I couldn't help comparing him to Father. He seemed to be some kind of leader and yet he never shouted; had no privileges whatsoever; and worked as hard as the next man; ate the same food; and lived in the same type of abode as everyone else. Moreover, he spoke to people and people spoke to him as if they were equals - so unlike Father, who had always placed such importance on status.

He made no discrimination between men and women either in the way he spoke or acted; I particularly noticed this in the way he spoke to Martha, so warmly and appreciatively, and I felt myself wishing he spoke to me in the same way too. It was foolish, of course. I hardly earned my keep as yet and we were not of the same land and did not share the same language in any case – so how could I expect him to be familiar with me? – his continued kindness and hospitality was all I could wish for….. yet I couldn't help feeling he was treating me like one of the precious items stolen from my country – a prize to be guarded and coveted but never truly belonging.

Chapter 6 'Birne'

Not all the men were old or lame. Some were most definitely not, and these, like Elias and Birne, were often the ones who ventured out into the forest for wood or game. I say ventured for the elements could still be treacherous, and often I would find myself gazing out to the woods, like the others left behind, wondering whether they would ever return, whether he would return. If it grew darker than usual or the gale howled more fiercely than before, I would be anxious. Well, now I understood that Elias and Birne were not only the masters of this community but represented much of its physical strength too, and I would feel as anxious as anyone in our fragile community. I did wonder whether Mira felt more though. Mira was the daughter of the woman who had first taken me under her wing and taught me so much. Her father was a particularly able craftsman, much admired for his beautiful pots and cooking utensils, but he had a crooked leg, which I learnt was from an accident whilst hunting in the snow many years ago. A tree had fallen on it and crushed it and he had never been properly able to walk on it again. Mira was also talented and could make the most beautiful things. I could never begin to match her speed, nor the intricacy of detail of any of the pots, cups, or beautiful clothes that she made. I could see she took most pride in making her own clothing, fitting the garments so they hugged her fine figure. Though the rough and thick material was hardly flattering, even a winter cloak looked fabulous on her. She held herself tall and straight, and her proud, blue eyes were just like Martha's but without the creases and lines of age. Her hair tumbled down to her waist, thick and wavy and a deep golden colour, darker than many of her kinsfolk. It glowed in the firelight and gleamed in the sunlight, and I wished I had such beautiful hair and such blue eyes. Her complexion glowed too, and she had little freckles around her nose and high on her cheeks. All the men admired Mira, but I could see she only had eyes for one – Elias. However, he did not appear to care for her at all. He did not particularly appear to care for anyone...... except Martha, and his friend Birne.

Then one evening, after our companions from the storm had been restored to their rebuilt homes and had left us to our silence again, Birne began the first of many visits to our home. With me he could be cool to the point of being aloof, but if I glimpsed him alone with Elias, there was a warm companionship between them which I was certainly not party to. He was not as tall as his friend but to me they could have been brothers. Huge and powerfully muscular, they towered over me and yet they both treated me with a reserved respect that left me feeling unworthy somehow. The only difference was that I always felt Elias was the more distant, whilst Birne was more direct.

The weather had at last begun to be less harsh and the birds were beginning to sing again. Buds were forming and you could hear the tinkling of the tiny streams that seemed to spring from everywhere into our valley. One evening they returned from a day's work together, but rather than leave as I expected him to do at the door, Birne came in and stayed for the evening meal. They laughed and joked together long into the evening in the firelight, mostly about the amusing antics of animals or events that had happened on hunting expeditions or in their daily work, I believed. Then they might fall silent and stare at the fire. Occasionally, Birne would look at me and I began to sense that I was unwanted, and I would glance at Elias, but he would still be staring at the fire seemingly oblivious to everything. I felt a conflict inside. Part of me knew I should leave them alone, part of me desperately wanted to stay. This troubled me – why did I want to come between these friends? Indeed, what right had I to do so? The best I could hope for was their continued respect and a roof over my head. Though I lived here, I didn't truly belong. At last I left when I felt I should otherwise fall asleep by the fire. Next morning, there was no sign of either them – the house was as deserted as usual.

And There Were Giants

It wasn't until we reached the height of spring, and my new world began to glitter in the sunlight, that Martha felt she should enlighten me. (I was picking up the language fast, thanks to her continued attention). She was gazing out at the trees, waving in the breeze, and the pale green of the new grass on the hillocks.

"Spring is here at last, and we rejoice. All that is except my daughter......"

I looked at her in surprise. "Why is that Martha?"

She in turn looked at me "Do you mean you have not seen how she loves Elias?"

I looked away, somehow, I did not feel I wanted to be reminded of this, moreover it seemed inappropriate to be talking of it behind her back. I wanted to say, "well I had wondered," but wasn't sure how to say this, so simply answered "Yes."

She searched in my eyes for a moment. Then looked away too, and I could tell there was something bothering her. Then suddenly she burst out, "You must understand this about our village, Roslin. It is time that you know....... We are not like the others." She gestured far away and then looked at me with a flash in her eyes. "We are not good enough or we are banished, unloved. We have no place with them....." again she gestured over there somewhere (she gestured a lot to clarify her words)....." Then she took both my hands and spoke to me earnestly,

"Roslin, Roslin, you must see that Elias was cast out because of his love for Birne. They are both banished. That is all our fate." She paused, looking at me to see if I understood and was satisfied that I had.

"You are a woman of high birth. Yet, I hope you are happy with us. We love you, and you are welcome here if you wish to remain with us."

I reeled with astonishment. To think I had believed we were simply servants to the others – though indeed what contact had there ever been with the other settlement? How stupid I had been! And the idea of Elias and Birne as lovers – this I found particularly hard to understand or indeed cope with, although again in my heart I had suspected there was more to this friendship for some time. Though I knew I should be happy that she had said I was loved, instead I felt suddenly fiercely angry and close to tears. Martha saw this and I could see she felt for me, but nevertheless she continued:

"That is not all, my fair one." My heart was pounding now, I did not want to hear any more, but this time the shock did not feel the same, though it left me even more incredulous. "Elias is the King's younger brother. The man who brought you here is his older brother. It is he who has banished Elias."

And then a thousand questions (and thoughts) thronged my mind, but I could not find the words to ask any of them. Instead they sprung up one by one unanswered in my brain. How could Elias be in any way related to that cruel man? Why had I been left with the banished ones? Could it be because I was unattractive? (After all I had been rejected before). Was it for my rank that I had been left with his brother then – for he was also of high birth? How could he be banished? How could a man of noble birth accept to be living like this? None of these men were on the raid – I could see some were unfit to be so, but by no means all. And why were they here?

But the most burning question of all was – could this be true, were they together, was there really love between them?

Chapter 7 'Spring'

It was now lambing season and Elias, Birne, and the menfolk took it in turns at night to help them into the world. Any struggling lambs found their way into our homes, and I found myself caring for a 'baby' for the first time. The little creature sucked and bleated so sweetly; I felt my heart melt as I took care of her. It was Birne who brought her, but Elias looked on as I now fed her and then rested her in the 'cot' he had made for her. I felt his eyes watching me and felt my skin flush as he did so, and quickly turned away. This was unusual. Elias never did this, he never looked at me or any of the womenfolk like this; it was as if he took care not to. Then he spoke: "You're a natural, it is as if she were your own," and with that he was off, ever busy, never still; leaving me wishing I was still basking in the brief sunbeam of his attention.

The lamb woke in the night, and I took her into my room so as not to disturb Elias. She was my darling and I loved her. Every moment I was not busy, I would have her on my lap, playing with her. I found great comfort in it. But Elias warned me, "Don't get too attached to her," and as he frowned, I knew what this meant: she was not my plaything, she was part of our survival. She would be taken away when the time came; that was the reality of our lives, but I couldn't bear to think about that now. I wondered how I would cope when the time came, but there was no way I could displease my new 'family', and most especially Elias, by fighting it.

Gradually, I began to learn more about the ways of my new companions and those about me. My command of their language grew quickly too for I had always been a quick learner, but I still could not bring myself to ask the questions I wanted answered so much. Instead, I would try to tell dear Martha about my homeland – about my 'privileged' life, and she would marvel at this. How she loved to caress my hands and admire my smooth skin in those early days! "How did you not die of boredom?!" she would cry, and then I told her of my brother, his untimely and sudden death from a fever, my parents' devastation, and my secret escapes from their sorrow, as best I could with my lack of words. Soon, I discovered that it had been Martha and her husband who had first come here, and that they had taken Elias and Birne into their fold when they had been cast off by their own kin. No doubt, this was why Elias and Martha were so close. But even when pressed, she would not speak any more of why they came to be there, and I felt duty-bound to respect her silence.

Of course, it was not appropriate for a woman to speak at 'Council' as they called their meetings, but I became aware that, on occasion, observations I made to Martha were passed on to them by Elias and then aired. For example, why was there no trade? How did we manage without cattle or horses? And ultimately, how would we defend ourselves against a raid? I learnt that this last subject had brought about a heated exchange with many opposing views: some recognised we were vulnerable, others felt there was no threat. In any case, little changed, and our lives went on as before – and why not? After all, my country had been so easily devastated and plundered – what was there to learn from us? And this humble community had little to lose, and few privileges compared to its neighbour's. Presumably, they agreed there would never be any danger of a raid here. So, both they and 'the Others' continued to live as if they were invincible, and perhaps they were, in this land surrounded by a natural stone fortress.

For women, there was little occasion to leave our community, for the woods and surrounding land with its beautiful river held all that we needed, and yet I still wondered at how little contact, if any, there was between the brothers. Why were their lives so separate? What could have come between them that one should live like a king and the other an exile in comparative poverty? Of course, I was glad of this distance, as I never wanted to see either of my captors again, though I remained curious about what those mighty walls contained. Once, I learnt from a hushed conversation, quickly silenced, that King Edvard's advisor and second in command, Wilfrid, was planning another raid, but the furtive glances at me were just further proof that 'the Others' were not to be spoken of in my presence. Of course, it only left me wondering more, yet I had to bite my tongue and remain patient; it was not my place to ask questions where they were not welcome, and in any case, I sensed it was to protect me – from 'them' – for which I was grateful.

Life was getting easier now and the days were getting longer. People could relax in the evenings rather than flop down exhausted, and Birne began to visit us more and more. He seemed very wary of me, and I sensed he was glad when I left to care for the lamb in my room, but Elias continued to be oblivious to my coming or going. There were silent times when I felt sure he was keeping some part of himself hidden away where nobody could touch him. I wondered if Birne thought this too. I longed to spy on them, to see what happened between them, but my sense of duty and gratitude held me back. It was not my place to do this and above all, it was disloyal to him. I would not stoop so low. So, I never did, but would still lie awake for ages straining to hear….. What?..... nothing….. I must admit I did wonder why I cared so much. After all, I had all I wanted – a home, kindness, delicious food and a more than comfortable bed. Not only that, but I sensed that I fitted into this community more than I ever had my own; despite being a stranger to these shores, despite my lack of skills and experience to be of much use, and despite the fact I could barely speak their language, I still felt accepted.

Then one evening, though I had prepared the evening meal and made the dwelling as warm and welcoming as I could, Elias did not come back from the hunt. I began to fear he had fallen and lay injured in the woods, but when I called on Martha, she gave me a warning look and simply said he might not be back that night. It was when I learnt they were indeed safely back from the forest that I first felt that empty ache inside. It would happen sometimes when the men went hunting or when Elias did not come home and even when he was there alone with Birne. There was something I was longing for – was it approval? – well I had never had that so why should I need it now? Perhaps it was the fact that he barely noticed me, that my every need was attended to, and yet I could have not been there at all. Whatever it was, it didn't go away….. and I was so glad when I found a new friend…..

I was learning more and more words and was beginning not only to understand but to speak my new language relatively fluently. It had a lovely, rhythmic quality and did not have the harsh, guttural sounds of my own. I could even begin to understand some of the gossip and managed to talk a little with the other girls – there weren't many of us, it was true – but in the main good friends, particularly Anye. Pretty and vivacious, Anye was always laughing and such fun to be with. We could spend hours together. Quick witted and savvy too, Anye was never afraid to make her observations known and could be quite mischievous at times. It was she who was forever remarking on my situation – living alone with Elias, "I don't know how he can resist you. You are so beautiful!" This would make us both laugh, and though I knew she said this in jest, I was aware that she was always well-meaning with her compliments, and I had no trouble complimenting her as she was just so delightful to be with. She was always quite critical of Mira too – pretending she was too fine to do this, or that such work would spoil her hands. It was true that Mira sometimes chose her duties according to what favoured her looks and abilities, but I could understand that. For myself, I was happy to do anything just to keep in everyone's good books and enjoyed working hard. I could sleep all the better for it and sometimes managed to avoid my nightmares altogether. Indeed, the more I worked alongside my new people, the less I was troubled by the horrors that had brought me here, and the less I worried about seeing any of 'the Others', as they were called, again.

Anye and I would always volunteer to go to the brook to get

water as it was so peaceful and pretty there. As leaves began to appear on the trees and huge bulrushes began to spring up all along the bank, I began to see that this was actually not such a bleak land after all. I recalled the muddy waters at our brook and observed that here the waters ran clear over the silt and glittered in the sun as if each grain were made of a thousand tiny jewels. Even the rocks that I had cursed on my arrival glinted and gleamed in the sunlight, as did the many streams that danced over them.

Food was beginning to be far more plentiful now and from many sources. There was even a strange green vegetable from the sea, which I had tasted on my first day in that land. But this was just one element of the wonderful fresh produce so expertly cooked by these people. For the first time in my life, I felt myself filling out slightly and gaining a little weight. This was in part due to the physical work I had never done before, though in truth I was still not required to take part in the hardest of the chores.

One day, Anye and I had gone to collect the water as usual, and were just making little flower headdresses for each other, when suddenly we heard a loud splash a little upstream. We looked over but apart from the rings working outwards from the site of entry, saw nothing at first in the water.

"It must be a branch from that tree," said Anye. There was indeed a tree there and for a moment we were satisfied with this explanation. But then I noticed something at the bottom of the brook (which was still quite deep from the recent rains). It was thrashing and struggling but not rising to the surface. Suddenly, I realised with horror that there was a human being down there at the bottom of the stream and that it was fully clothed. In a moment, I was undressed as far as I could and in the water. Down, down I went – it was not that deep, but the current was strong - and I found him. It was a young boy, his clothes obviously weighing him down, though I later learned he had been collecting stones in his pockets too. As quickly as

I could, I stripped him of his outer garments, whilst all the time he thrashed and fought to grab hold of me. He will drown us both! I thought, but then it occurred to me that if I moved to his back and pulled him up that way, he could not grab me. This worked and, still thrashing and kicking, I managed to bring him up to the surface. We both gasped as we came up. We had been down there a while and the water was still very cold. By the time I had got him out, we were both shaking with cold and shock. He had swallowed a lot of water and was violently sick. Anye, meanwhile, had screamed for help at the top of her voice and had summoned practically everyone still left in the village that day, so we were quickly wrapped up in warm fleeces and throws.

I did not recognise the boy and it wasn't until we got back to the village that we learnt the truth. By this time, Elias and Birne had appeared, and they demanded to know why a boy from the 'High Town' (which I gathered to be the name of the other settlement) was there. He was obviously distressed but, to my surprise, it was not because of his discovery or what had happened to him. He was distressed because of what had happened to me! I was amazed to hear that he had been hiding in the tree because he had been spying – on me! He had been sent by the King, no less, to see how I was being treated and to report back on my health and well-being. The irony of this news was not lost on me – why would the King still be concerned about me, having abandoned me here so long ago? Then I realised what was worrying the boy – that my health had been jeopardised – not by my custodians, but by him! This would not go down well with the King! I felt for the boy as I recognised his fear – I had felt this myself when I was at that man's mercy – and blurted out immediately that he was not to worry but that this would remain a secret and that he was to say that I was in fine health. The boy looked grateful and appeased, but I suddenly became aware of the silence all around me. Looking around at their faces, I realised that I had spoken out of place – it was not for me to give such assurances, nor to say what he should report. I glanced at Elias, what must he think? and was relieved to see that he was actually smiling at me. Then he turned to the boy and simply said, "Yes, we will say nothing about this, so go now. You know what you have to report." And with that the boy was gone, as fast as his little legs could take him.

That night, as I lay in bed, I puzzled over why the King should worry about my state of health? I had tried to ask my friends after the event, but none of them had given me a straight explanation and I hadn't dared question Elias. It made me uneasy, and I knew I would be visited by my nightmares again that night. That man had not laid eyes on me since he had handed me over to his brother all those moons ago. Reluctant to fall asleep and dream, I started wondering again why there should be enmity between the two brothers. Why was the King watching how his brother treated me? Was it to catch him out? I decided it was time to break our silence on this matter: I must question Martha further….. but by the morning I had forgotten my resolve… for I was basking in my newfound celebrity!

Chapter 8 'Early Summer'

It was supposed to be because I had caught a chill, but I could guess the real reason I had not been invited to Mira's birthday picnic: it was because he had smiled at me, and I was favoured. Since the episode with the boy, I had become quite the centre of attention in the village, everyone asking how I had learnt to swim so well and wondering at how brave I had been. Compared to the perils I had known on the sea and before this, it had seemed trivial to me, and I simply revelled in my new-found fame and favour. But I must confess the best outcome of all this was the attention I received from Elias. He boiled me broths and stoked the fire for me and gave me freshly-crushed sweet berry juice to drink – and all this when he had obviously asked Martha to look after me when I first arrived. I assumed he simply felt responsible for my recovery from my cold, but what with his attention and the warm and bright weather I was soon better. Then, on the same day as the picnic, a particularly warm day in early summer, he again took me by surprise with a question out of the blue. He asked me to show him how to swim. I gazed at him, lost for words momentarily. This must be because he feels sorry for me as I have been left out of the festivities, I thought. I was so touched that I let down my guard for a moment, smiled and replied, far too cheekily, that I didn't believe there was something I could do that he could not. Then I blushed, as I couldn't believe I had been so rude to my host! However, he just laughed – again a rare thing when alone with me – and replied that he had never been in the water and feared that he would drown if he did. Of course! I thought, he had not been across the sea like the others so had never been taught, but then I had never been taught either. When I told him this, he said something along the lines that if I could save a drowning child then my technique would be good enough for him.

No-one was working that day. My new friends were all away with Mira on the picnic and actually it was really too hot to do anything! Yes, after all those months of freeze it had now reached the other extreme and for two days now, we lazed and dozed in the heat. I felt the stare of those we passed as everyone knew that Elias never walked alone with anyone except Birne. I knew they were dying to follow us and self-consciously thought I should somehow be explaining myself to these good people. I also felt uncomfortable to be alone with him in a new place. It didn't seem right.

As we got to the water, I felt more uncomfortable still – I could not undress as I normally did, so we would be fully-clothed, and this was not conducive to learning how to swim! However, as we neared the water Elias threw off his shirt and for the first time, I saw him half-naked. It was the first time I had seen a man like this since that terrible night back in my homeland, and an involuntary shudder ran through my body as I thought of it. I felt at once that I should look away, but he was already knee-deep in the water with his back to me. I quickly hitched off my outer garment so that I was simply covered in my underclothes and ran in as quickly as I could. But I could not get the image out of my mind. That tall, lean, muscular body, surprisingly hairless compared to his bearded face and crop of long wiry hair.

Elias had stopped now, and I could see he had his own preoccupations; whereas he had had no trouble going in this far he was reluctant to go further. I cast my mind back to my very first days in the brook at home. How I had overcome my fear by standing by the water's edge and dunking my head in the water for longer and longer each time. Elias was so tall that that would be ridiculous here, so I brought him back to the water's edge and bade him kneel in the silt and dunk his head there. The idea of this made him laugh, but as he pulled his head back out of the water he gasped and had to stand up for a moment. It was still a step to overcome, but I knew that it was only once he'd managed this without gasping that it would be time to move on. Eventually, he did get used to it after several more attempts, so next, I asked him to lie on his back and do the same. "But when are you going to teach me to swim

Roslin?" The sparkling water sent shimmers dancing across his face. I stood mesmerised for a moment, then ventured as best I could,

"You cannot learn to swim until you have mastered the fear of your head going under the water." He seemed to accept this and did as he was bid but only managed to go as far as getting the back of his head wet. We would not get much further with this, and I knew exactly what step was next, yet again I hesitated. It meant that I might need to hold him. This was too much; I didn't dare do that. Then it struck me how confusing this all was, this awkwardness mixed with a desperate wish to please – why did I feel this way?....

"What is it Roslin? What do you want me to do next?" Still I hesitated. I didn't know what to say …. "What is it? Tell me."

Then I knew what to do: "I want you to go to the middle of the stream, lie on your back and I will hold your head." He thought about this. "I will try."

"You've got to trust me."

"Alright." He looked intently at me for a moment then did as he was bid and moved to the middle of the stream, in truth, he was still only waist deep where we were. It came to my shoulders, but I was used to the water and the stream moved quite languidly now it was no longer swollen by the snow and rains of the earlier months. He bent his knees and attempted to lie back, but he was still not comfortable with this. "Could I do this on my front?" he asked.

"Alright," I said, "bend forward and push your arms out like this," and I showed him my swimming stroke, "and kick your legs like this."

"And what if I go under, will you hold me?" Again, I was not sure I could do this. It was somehow not fitting, too intimate. I couldn't hold him, I just couldn't, but deep down I wanted to.

And There Were Giants

"Will you hold me if I go under?" He was gazing at me with those steady grey/blue eyes. And I remembered that first time when I had looked into them and seen pity there. There was no pity there now, but something else…..

"I'm not sure." He laughed at my uncertainty. "Look, if I go under, I'll just put my feet down if you don't catch me. It's only up to my waist anyway." And without any further hesitation, he was over and on his front in the water, thrashing away. I stood by his side ready to move in if needed but, as he said, he was only in shallow water for him, and he could put his feet down at any time.

"Now let me watch you". This was my chance to show off and I felt an overwhelming desire to do so. I dived down to the bottom and swam along the stream with the current, knowing this would look more impressive. I then curled around and returned, zig-zagging this way and that to beat the current. As I surfaced, I tried to smile modestly. And then it was all so perfect and simple – he splashed me, muttering something about my showing off, and then we were having a splashing fight in the water – all the awkwardness gone in the fun of it. We were making so much noise that they could hear us from the village and, at first fearing a calamity, this brought down onlookers to our party. Elias invited them in and soon we were all splashing and having fun in the water – laughing in the sunshine. We were playing as if we were children without a care in the world. I had never known such happiness.

Chapter 9 'The Sheep Shearing'

After all the excitement had died down and we were alone once more, Elias returned to his usual sombre, withdrawn self, and life in our household resumed as if nothing had happened. However, the village was still buzzing with the news of the day, and I could tell that Mira was by no means pleased by it. Her attitude to me was of hostile indifference, and her mother was, as ever, saddened by this. I felt sad too for it was the last thing I wanted to do to come between mother and daughter, but I knew Martha was fond of me as well, and that she was caught between the two of us in a conflict of interests, rather as I felt myself to be. There was always tension if Mira and I were together, as she resented my proximity to Elias, with everybody in the vicinity on guard, and I wondered whether this would go on forever.

I thought about that day at the brook for a long time. Most of all thinking how young Elias had seemed. In the early days I had assumed him to be of middle years, like an uncle or elderman. He was not like other young men; he was too pensive, too considered in all he did. It was as if there were a weight on his shoulders, that he must bear alone. But soon I would again see him in a very different light.

It was a day in high summer, still very hot and languid, and the due date appointed for the sheep shearing. All the men were to be involved in this task, though to be fair, there were not that many sheep, but I considered that this must be a difficult task and would therefore take a long time. I did not question that the women were not involved in this. Although many tasks were shared, hunting was an all-male province and I assumed this was similarly physical, yet I noted that the women were not allowed anywhere near the work, and this puzzled me. By dusk I was to discover why. We, the women had been tasked with setting up a feast to be shared and eaten in the main square of the village and a great fire had been constructed in the centre of it. It was to be a celebration of the bounty of summer and was to be the first festival I had experienced here. All day, the excitement grew about the feast, but I got the feeling that my friends were keeping something secret from me and giggling behind my back. Then, as the fire was lit and the food set out, I began to see what it was that was causing all the merriment. One by one, the men were reappearing to be greeted by their womenfolk. How they had been transformed! Gone were the beards and long hair. Not only the sheep but the men had been shorn as well! I was astonished as they appeared, as I barely recognised any of them, but the biggest surprise of all was the finale. I gazed at Elias and Birne – how the years had fallen away! Gone were the stoop and the heavy clothes of winter. Gone was the ragged, heavy beard and in its place smooth white skin; even their long, shaggy hair had been cut short. I felt myself impelled to gaze upon Elias, as everyone did, and saw a face so broad and handsome it took my breath away. Though still wavy, his hair appeared softer and more childlike and a warm golden colour; his soulful, grey eyes shone that night; and I had never really noticed how delightfully his mouth curved into a smile. Anye revelled in my astonishment. "See how young and good-looking they are!" she cried, "Are you not proud of your menfolk?" Anye was particularly taken with a young man who had joined the village a few years ago when he had fallen from a horse and been almost fatally injured. He had recovered all but the strength in his left arm, which now had limited movement. She had been holding back to get my reaction but now went to join him. I watched as she stroked his cheeks and chin.

I couldn't look at Elias again, there was time enough for that yet as we lived together, but I just couldn't do it now. I was annoyed at myself though, why was I so shy? Why could I not speak to nor look at the man I shared a home with? I couldn't help but wonder whether Mira was with him or whether Birne held pride of place at his side, on guard and wary as ever. Then I stopped myself and thought about the work to be done: there was mead to be poured, food to be given out. I could see Martha watching me, in that motherly, protective way of hers.

She promptly came over and took my arm, "Child, you must come and join us, come and try the mead. It is at its finest at this time of year." Gratefully, I let myself be led by her, though my thoughts were elsewhere, and soon found myself swept up by the atmosphere of conviviality.

There was laughter and singing and glorious, glorious food. Even the mead tasted good: sweet and sticky, though I was certainly not used to it, having drunk only berry juice or the pure stream water up until now. I began to feel drowsy and unsteady. Everything was beginning to blur ever so slightly, and I wondered whether I would be able to get up and walk back to the dwelling. It was only then that Elias sat down beside me.

"I think you should stop drinking that Roslin, it goes straight to your head if you're not used to it."

"Yes, I was just wondering whether I would be able to get back to the dwelling." My voice sounded slightly slurred but for once I was not stumbling over the unfamiliar words. I looked up at him then and was transfixed by a godlike vision – a haze of golden hair framed a pale face flickering with bronze in the firelight. I must have said something very strange next because he laughed out loud and said to me then,

"I'm taking you home Roslin. You definitely won't make it back alone." And after a few words to Martha and her husband, he took me in his arms and carried me back. I don't remember any more. I must have slept the minute my head touched the pillow. But the following morning I woke to the most crashing headache I had ever experienced in my life. Once again, Elias was there, awake before me as usual, having already prepared a poultice for my head and a broth for me to drink. It was the most foul-tasting liquid imaginable, but I was told to drink it as it would make me feel better. No food passed my lips that day, only cold stream water and broth, and by the time he returned in the evening I felt much better.

I was touched by his kindness and tolerance of such naivety. He had attended to me as if I were a child and the more he had, the more foolish and undeserving of such attention I felt. That day I swore to myself I would never again touch alcohol, for I knew I had made a complete fool of myself in his eyes.

Chapter 10 'Anye'

It was from Anye that I discovered the ways of love between a man and a woman. It was a full moon or so after the sheep shearing, and we had been preparing for the final feast of the summer to be held at the end of that month. I called at her house as usual to begin our daily chores and found her still in bed looking very pale. She had been feeling unwell for some days now, but this was worse than before. Her mother looked pale also and I thought that my dear friend must have some serious illness, as earlier the healer had been summoned, and I began to fear the worst. Sadly, since childhood Anye had suffered from strange fits that seemed to turn her into a wild creature and then left her drained and pale. They were few and far between but always struck at the most inopportune times; usually, at times of stress or when she was already unwell. I assumed, therefore, that she had had a particularly bad one of these, as this was how she always looked. But when at last her mother left us alone to gather more herbs, she told me some incredible news. Relief flooded through me, for she was not ill at all, though I puzzled why all were so grave: she was with child! My first thought was that surely this was great news. After all there were so few little children in our village. Then I wondered how this could have happened and indeed I didn't know. As a child myself, such questions had always been met with downcast eyes and stony glances and I had soon learnt that this knowledge did not befit a princess. It was then that she confided in me that the child had been conceived 'before betrothal' and told me how angry her parents were. The ceremony would have to take place at the next festival in two months' time. I held her hand and stayed with her that day. I knew I would not be remonstrated for staying late by Elias; he would not miss me, and he knew where I was.

On my way back to our dwelling, I pondered what she had said. The description of her intimacy with Rogen cast my mind back to the night of the raid and my mother's death. I had tried not to let myself think of it again, though there wasn't a day when

And There Were Giants

I did not think about my mother. There had been that man with the searing blue eyes, he who had crushed me with his weight and caused me such unfathomable pain before my mother had cried out….. Could Anye have experienced something like this? Surely not, for she had spoken of such happiness…. Well, in any case I had to think of my friend now. I had to ask Elias whether I might be given leave to look after her. Anye and I could still weave whilst she was in bed, and we could now be making things for the baby.

But it seemed wrong that we should enthuse about a new baby in the community when all around were bowed with shame; and Anye's sickness, which left her so weak and unable to eat properly, did worry me - why did being with child make her sick like that? It left poor Anye bed-bound and frail right up until the time of the festival. Rogan visited her every day, and whenever he arrived, I quickly left, which seemed to suit us all. Despite my excitement at the prospect of the baby, I remained troubled by the thought of what had happened to Anye. I couldn't stop thinking about the paradox of her happiness in contrast to her debilitating sickness. Also, I started thinking again about 'the Others' and my dreams returned with a vengeance.

~~~~~~

Elias awoke covered in sweat. Even early morning that summer brought an oppressive heat.

What had woken me? Ah yes, I supposed she was heading down to the river, her nightmares always woke her early, I was used to hearing her cries now. I should go too – why not – I could practise my swimming could I not? But as I followed her, I held back. I would watch a while and see how it was done again. She looked back but could not see me – I was a proficient hunter after all, I knew well how to conceal my footsteps and my bulk in the luxuriant greenery. By the time I had caught up with her, she was already in the water. Her dark hair gleamed and snaked in the water and covered her golden skin when she surfaced. She didn't know I was there – so I could watch her, look at her. Those delicate, slender limbs….. I was thinking about her hazel eyes flecked with green – those dark lashes, those full lips….. then suddenly our peace was shattered as I heard voices and laughter coming towards us – more early bathers. She heard them too and was leaving the water….. She didn't know I was there – she was so beautiful, so delicate – what clothing she had on, clung to her lithe body and I could make out the gentle curve of her waist, the outline of her breasts - I couldn't tear my gaze away. It was an image that filled my mind and intoxicated me – and I felt something stirring within me, a longing for what I could never have. Of course, she hated and despised me, and I understood why, but as the familiar feeling of rage against my brother started to build inside me again, I knew I must not let it consume me…… I must get away fast so as not to be discovered, she must not know I was there.

That evening by the fire Birne caught me off guard. I felt myself blush as he asked me what I was thinking, and I was glad of the dim glow from the fire. It was strange but Birne was quiet too, unlike him, especially when Roslin wasn't there. Actually, thinking about it, he had been quiet for some time now and it was beginning to worry me. He looked back when I asked him the same and said he was just thinking about our first time here and how he feared for the future.

"What do you mean Birne?"

"Times change but the quarrel between you and your brother doesn't go away. You still hate each other passionately and I worry that it will only take a spark to set the fire raging again."

As he said this, I knew he just wanted to protect me as he always had done, and in that moment, I felt so unworthy of his friendship, of his love. I wanted so much to make him happy, and it was in that moment that it came to me. Of course. I could do this – for him…..

~~~~~~

Roslin tried to distract herself by spending more time with her friend, but …

Just when the sickness seemed to be at its peak, it suddenly eased, and Anye could at last begin to live a normal life again. Now I had more time on my hands, I often slipped away to take a quick swim in the brook as those days it was so incredibly hot. One particularly sultry morning, I had just stepped into the water when I felt someone was watching me – I glanced up at the tree, but the boy was not there. I started to wonder again why they were watching me, was it to claim me back? I was suddenly afraid, afraid of the memory of them. I tried to push it away, but the fear kept coming back. Other early bathers were arriving now, but it was not until I was dressed and walking up the bank that I saw Birne. Strangely, he looked as agitated and wary as I had been feeling, I had never seen him look this way before and I had to find out why, though I did not really know how....

"I have not seen you by the brook before, can you swim Birne?" but he was not in the mood for such pleasantries.

"Roslin, I need to speak with you alone – that's why I followed you here. I want to tell you what was said the day that you first came to our village. I want you to know the truth." My heart froze for a moment. Was he going to tell me I must go and leave the sanctity of this place? Was my time in the village coming to an end?

"Roslin, I know you have been worrying about what has happened to you and what might yet happen. Please know that you are safe with us. That day he left you here, he gave you to Elias to keep…." He paused then added "…as his wife."

I stared at Birne – what did he mean as his wife? No-one had ever mentioned this to me before so how could it be true? Indignation flashed through me; this was impossible! No one had ever treated me like Elias' wife, least of all Elias himself! I was simply a guest in his abode. But then I looked into Birne's eyes and, with his discomfort, saw that there may well be truth written there. Then I considered the implications of this, not just for myself, but for him too. Martha had not told me this, no-one had. If this were true, then why had no-one told me? Was it a secret? How could I be his wife? Everyone knew that he was with Birne?...... Unless?..... I looked at Birne and began to see this man, who I had always considered to be aloof and hostile, in an entirely new light. It had obviously been painful to relay this last piece of information, which, if it were not common knowledge, I need never have known. But it was as nothing compared to what was to come next and it slowly dawned on me that I had completely misunderstood and underestimated Birne.

"Roslin, I must tell you a secret that only he and I share. It is not what you think you know already," he added quickly, "I have known Elias since we were children….. We were like brothers. But it is as brothers that we have remained Roslin, nothing more than that. You must tell no-one this because……" he broke off, unsure how to put what he was to say next, "because it has always been for the best that 'the Others' think – differently."

"Why are you telling me this, Birne, if it is your secret?" I breathed….

"Because at the Harvest Moon Festival Elias feels we should be betrothed – me and him – to show 'the Others' that we are indeed a couple and that we will take care of you. He thinks that is what his brother wants Roslin – that you are taken care of - and that it is what I want too….. But I know he is in love with you Roslin. You are indeed already his wife as the King's word is law, and you are the one he wants. But he can't see it. …..Neither of you can….." and with this he broke off and my heart went out to him as I knew Elias was all that he wanted too. And then he looked into my eyes and was searching for my reaction, searching to see what I would say next. To hear this latest revelation from Birne was the biggest surprise of all. To think that I could, in fact be like a wife to Elias, and to hear this from him - when he could have been betrothed to Elias himself! All at once, I wanted so much to hug him that I rushed forward and threw my arms around him, tears streaming down my face. And to my surprise and enormous relief he hugged me back. There was no rivalry there, no jealousy – just love.

Chapter 11 'Harvest Moon Festival'

My resolution of never taking alcohol again did not last longer than a couple of moons. It was the night of the festival and Anye was to be betrothed. It was so fortunate the sickness had eased in time, and she was now looking radiant and excited. Mira had been charged with making her gown and I with her headdress which was to be made of the freshest and most beautiful flowers I could find. I had already decided that once I had seen her betrothed I would drink a more moderate amount of the sweet liquor than I had before and that this would hopefully be enough to carry me through an evening where I would, no doubt, feel at my most awkward and superfluous to the proceedings. Since my meeting with Birne, we had spoken little, though his attitude to me had softened and I had nothing but admiration for him now. He had held me by the river as if I were his sister and I knew, then, that he only wanted the best for me and for Elias. How could anyone be so selfless for the sake of others? Unfortunately, as to Elias, I did not believe a word that Birne had said. How could he be interested in me? He had never shown it, and deep down inside I thought he must prefer Mira anyway. She had no trouble speaking to him, unlike me, or showing off her prowess in whatever she did. She was never awkward or shy and, more importantly, she was one of them and without doubt the most beautiful girl in the village. However, I had noted that Elias' plan to be betrothed to Birne had not been carried out. Had Birne spoken to him as well, or had he changed his mind, or was none of this true after all? I could not tell.....

It was lovely to see Anye so happy though. I was entirely taken up by her excitement and did my utmost to make her the prettiest headdress and to help her to look as beautiful as I could.

"Roslin, that's enough – now it's your turn to get ready!"

"Don't be silly Anye, this is your wedding day. You are the one that everyone will be looking at, not me."

"Um, I'm not so sure about that now Roslin. I seem to remember you were carried off by a dashing young man last time we had a festival! Have you really forgotten that?" This last was typical of Anye, she was such a tease.

She was forbidden to see Rogen before the match, but when at last they did meet for the ceremony the love in their eyes was so wonderful to see, how I envied her fulfilment.

Birne was sitting, as ever, next to Elias and appeared to look as uncomfortable as I felt. We exchanged complicit glances, and I felt that at least I too had found a friend in Birne. His eyes seemed to be urging me to come over, but I felt strangely inert. It was true that they both took looking after me seriously and I was grateful for that – it should be enough. I was offered a cup of mead and took it at once. As I did so, I felt Elias's eyes on me, and I drank and looked back defiantly. For some reason I felt quite antagonistic towards him, though actually thinking about it, I wouldn't mind being carried back to the dwelling – it would be quite fun….. He spoke a few words to Birne and started to come over. I knew why and I got up immediately, defiantly holding the cup out in front of me.

"You don't need to worry; I won't be so stupid this time. Look, I am only sipping at it – there's plenty left."

Elias smiled as he looked down on me, ignoring my words.

"That was a beautiful ceremony wasn't it. I am sure they will be very happy."

"Yes, I'm sure they will….."

This was incredibly awkward.

"Will you talk with me by the fire, when all have gone?"

"Yes….. if you wish."

"Good. Don't drink too much."

And that was it – he was gone again! I immediately wanted to drink too much. I felt incredibly nervous. People were kind and talked to me all evening and tried to get me to sing the songs that we had all been singing in preparation for so long, but I did not feel like singing. My heart was not singing. My heart was dreading what he was about to say. What if it wasn't what I wanted to hear? I wished the evening would never end. Somehow I felt safer not knowing…..

It must have been long into the night when the last drunken people left the square and we were finally alone. I had been working to keep myself awake and to stop myself from drinking the sickly, sweet drink too quickly, clearing this and that, moving this and that, ineffectually. The time had come….. But now that I sat down in the warmth of the firelight next to him I started to feel intoxicated again – or maybe it was the tumult of my feelings…..

"Roslin I'm sorry I have been so..… absent. I just wanted to say that, because I know you have been afraid and felt alone, and I haven't always been there for you."

"How do you know that? I blurted out unhelpfully.

"Birne told me that you confided in him. He said you were afraid that my brother might want you back and that he had reassured you that would never happen. I should have done that. I'm sorry."

"Elias, you have cared for me and watched over me ever since I arrived. You have nothing to be sorry for."

I am sure it was the drink that made me say the next thing, yet I couldn't help but divulge that I knew their secret.

"Birne told me something else. He told me that you two were not 'together', and yet you keep up this appearance. Don't worry, he told me this in confidence, a confidence which I will always keep, but now I know, please tell me – why do you keep this secret?"

He stared at me for a moment. This was a shock. Then another part of the mystery was revealed.

"Then you shall know. Roslin, you are not alone in being afraid. I was afraid once, not of Edvard, but of his father. And that is why I am here. I cannot be part of their world." He looked off into the distance. "You will think me a coward and maybe I am. You will think I have no ambition and maybe I haven't. All I know is that I want no part in what they do or what they stand for. This, this is what I want from life, nothing more."

"But you are of high birth as his brother. Why do you work so hard, why have you no privileges?"

"Because I want none. Don't you see Roslin? We can be happy here and have nothing. Their opulence comes from death and destruction. Here we value life – every life - and all we have we create ourselves." Then a moment later he added, "Are you not happy here Roslin? Do you want more than this?"

"In truth, I have never been happier!"

"And tell me, how has it been to lose all the privileges of your birth?"

It did not take me long to answer this either. I thought about my former narrow, confined, dictated life. Of how I had never quite fitted into the mould of refined indolence and had always wondered why I had been born to it. How my looks, my spirit, my strengths had not been good enough. I thought about the expectations, the disappointments, the denials and found it easy to answer:

"There is only one part of my old life that I miss and that is my mother. We were never close, but I feel sure she cared about me … and he cut her down….." I could not go on. I stared into the firelight. Then I felt his arm around me.

"I know how it is to lose someone. I lost my mother too but when I was very young, younger than you were….. You will never be alone here. We all love you."

He looked at me and I could see – oh what could I see? Could it be what I longed for? The only sound now was the crackling fire, which glowed in the starlight. He drew closer – was he going to sweep me up only to abandon me once more to a restless, wakeful night? He reached out and stroked my hair, so gently that I closed my eyes, mesmerised by his touch, and somehow compelled to be closer still. And then I felt his lips on mine and a thrill raced right through me so that the dull muzziness from the drink left me and I was suddenly very much alive. He had kissed me! So, he must want me after all! And not only that but it was with a desire that matched my own! I was delirious with happiness.

There were no words between us now – just a new understanding. Yet as he carried me back to the dwelling I realised that I was afraid again ….. but how could I be frightened of someone who had never shown me anything but kindness? I knew what would come and that I wanted him so much and yet I was so very afraid. I would have to trust myself to God.

Chapter 12 'Things are not always as they seem...'

I thought I knew what was to come and yet I did not. It was so strange, as we had lived together for so long and yet still knew so little of each other. As he lay me down on the bed, I closed my eyes and prayed. I sensed his presence towering over me and realised that I was trembling as my mind transported me back to the last time a man had done that. Elias frowned for a moment, and I hoped I hadn't displeased him with my anxiety. I tried closing my eyes again to calm myself, but this just intensified my fear, until suddenly I felt some covers being gently laid over me. This was unexpected and I opened my eyes. Then he lay down next to me and held me close to him. I began to tremble again. It was so stupid of me, but I couldn't help it.

"Roslin, you don't need to be afraid of me."

"I know, I'm sorry. I don't know why."

"Listen, I know what you have been through. I have been through it too."

I looked at him in disbelief, but his eyes spoke the truth. Suddenly, I recalled the time we lay side by side next to the fire and that harmless intimacy again. I wanted to listen, though I questioned how a man of his stature could ever have been afraid of another.

"Have you not wondered how my friendship with Birne was turned into a relationship? Well, it was my half-brother Edvard who believed that it was, and he had reason to believe it too. I am going to tell you a story that will surprise you and then you will know everything and perhaps then you will trust me."

It was then that he told me the story of how our community first came about.

"I was 5 or 6 when I first came to his attention. He was King of all and High Lord of this land. The most powerful man in the region. My mother and I lived in the next township with my father, a farmer, and we were very happy, but King Hadred was not. He already had a son by his previous wife but that was not enough for him – he wanted more. He wanted something unnatural – me. I looked like my mother – fair and tall for my age – and he forced my parents apart and adopted her as his new wife and me as an adopted son. He was careful to show that he raised me and his own as equals. Everything Edvard had, I had, and my mother also wanted for nothing though we were both forbidden to see my father again, which broke my mother's heart. As the moons passed, there was something about him that made me grow wary, and then one day, when I was about 6 or 7, it began. The terror, the abuse. It was also shortly after the time that my mother, who had been pregnant when she was betrothed to him died in childbirth dragging her poor unfortunate baby into the other world with her. He cared not, for he had two sons and all he needed and never married again. I used to long for the times when he would be away on a raid, his other passion – usually for many moons at a time – and would wish that he never came back. One day, when I was about your age, our secret was forced into the open – by Edvard. He discovered us together and immediately jumped to the conclusion that it was me that had 'led him astray'. It had, after all, been decreed by his father that men of that persuasion should leave our township as they could not lead the life of a true warrior, the one of rape and pillage that has been our tradition since time immemorial. I suddenly became an evil spirit who was trying to ruin his father. To save face and preserve this lie, the King was forced to banish me, and following this was his last raid. He was killed in action, and Edvard immediately assumed his rightful place as leader. And as you know, he has continued in the line of 'great warriors who bring great bounty' from their rampages.

So now you know the whole story Roslin. I am used to living a lie here with my dear friend Birne, to protect this community of 'the banished' and you must understand I know what it is like to live in fear."

I was astonished, for yet again, all had not been as it seemed. I had had no idea that this huge, strong, powerful man could have been so vulnerable and helpless and could have suffered so much as a child. I was shocked, but also sorry that I had assumed things about him that had been so wrong. He could truly understand what I had been through, and I could feel his pain and loss too. We had both been sullied by our pasts. Both of us were victims of the same line of men. Now, all I wanted to do was hold him in my arms, as I had done when Birne had surprised me with his story. And when all I did was take his hand and lie a little closer, he seemed happy enough and asked me for my story. I told him what I could, though I could not bring myself to talk much of the raid; only that it had been Edvard's companion who had captured me and Edvard who had killed my mother after she had cried out some kind of curse on him. On hearing this Elias nodded his head knowingly, and a cool smile spread over his face.

"What is it? What do you think she said?" I demanded, wondering if he could possibly know.

"I believe your mother was protecting you with a curse on him if he ever harmed you – and that is why he so graciously handed you over to me instead of taking you for himself. He knew I would look after you. Exactly what she said I have no idea, but one thing is for sure: she paid for that curse with her life. She must have loved you Roslyn."

The bitter-sweet of this was too much and hot tears of grief silently ran down my face. How I wished I had known that love before, how I wished I had done something to deserve it. Elias kissed them gently away, lay down his head, in that endearing way of his and immediately fell asleep. Watching him now, all my previous apprehension quite gone and replaced with gratitude and love, I lay my head next to his, and slept. No dreams broke my slumber that night.

Chapter 13 'An end to silence'

The next day, however, felt like a dream. I was basically treading water until that evening when we could be alone together again. First, there was the great tidy-up from the night before, but then there was Council meeting upon meeting upon meeting, as we were now entering the 'winter down' period when there was much to be prepared and achieved before the bad weather returned. It occurred to me that it was during this winter down period, this time of hard work, that I had arrived, a shadow of my current self, a naïve, useless girl, an outsider. The discussions were endless: where, what and how to store. Where and how to repair and strengthen against the winter. What new bedding/clothing/fleeces were needed etc, etc. and there must also be provision for a new baby: Anye's child.

At last evening came, so Elias and I could sit together in the firelight and talk, not only of our past but also about our future, though one subject – the bitter end of my old life - was not broached again. Despite the busy day, we talked well into the night – I suppose we were making up for lost time – and there was an ease about us now that had not existed before; it was as if we had become different people overnight.

As the embers crackled gently in the dying fire, I thought how this man had waited almost a year now for his rights as a husband. It was surely time to repay his kindness and patience with me. It was the least I could do. I stood and made my way to the doorway of my bedchamber. I looked back but he was still sitting there watching me. I smiled briefly then turned back again silently and this time he followed. The room was in shadow, but I could see his dark silhouette framed against the last glimmer from the fire as he made his way towards me. All of a sudden, my old fear gripped me like a vice – as before, I was powerless to suppress it, though I tried desperately to push it away, I simply had to know.

He was stripped to his waist and approaching me – just as my 'liberator' had done, bathed in the firelight that had destroyed all I had ever known – but then I felt him move me aside as he sat on the bed and started to undress me. For a moment I remained frozen to the spot, still trembling, then it slowly dawned on me that there was something different about this to what I had been anticipating, for he was no longer bearing down on me, but I was now looking down on him. This was somehow reassuring: it was here and now, not what had happened before and something inside me started to relax and begin to feel. Before tonight, I had been ashamed for him to ever see part of me uncovered but now, in the darkness, as I felt him caress and kiss me, it was as if I were the most beautiful creature imaginable and I could feel myself beginning to respond. He was still below me. Every touch of his lips sent a thrill through me, and a crazy feeling of desire started to well up inside me. Perhaps I could do this after all? Perhaps, though I was still trembling ….. and then he lay on the bed and said gently:

"Roslin I want you to love me…"

"I already love you…."

"No that is not what I mean, I want you to <u>make</u> love – to me…."

And then I understood – it was I who would be in control – he had handed all his power and dominance over to me so that I could feel safe – and suddenly I felt the crazy feeling intensify and envelope me; he knew me, he understood me, and above all he cared about me. As I lowered myself onto him, pushing him deep inside me, it was the most incredible moment of my life. The fear was gone, and there was no pain; I was whole again and riding, riding him. The desire grew and grew and became more and more overpowering, almost unbearable and yet I kept going. Hearing him moan with pleasure too just intensified it more. And then finally I felt wave upon wave of fire and pleasure envelope us both and I lay myself down upon him and held him close to me, our bodies drenched in sweat.

As we lay there, Elias by now asleep in my arms, I thought to myself how the stories had never told of the <u>gentle</u> giants from this land; oh, how I wished I could tell <u>that</u> story.

It did not take the townsfolk long to suspect that something had changed about us. Of course, those closest to us, Martha and Birne, were the first to notice but said nothing. However, when the rumours and gossip began, we knew it was time that the truth be told. Birne's stoicism was remarkable. He never flinched at all but stood by his friend throughout. It was indeed he who bore the brunt of the bitterness and resentment of some of the men as they realised that they had been misled about Elias' and Birne's relationship for they could never bring themselves to rail against their ultimate hero, a man who had understood and treated them so well. It was then that I deemed I must speak out and tell the people the truth about us – that we had not known that we had feelings for one another for a long time, that Elias and Birne did indeed love each other – and 'who were any of us to judge another for their feelings anyway?'. I felt all eyes upon me as I spoke, and again I felt that I had spoken out of hand. But Jelem, one of the oldest men in the village, came over to me and took my hand. He then turned and spoke to the rest of them.

"This girl of high birth has come to our village and embraced our humble way of life and learnt our language. She has saved one life and brought the greatest of all happiness to our leader. She is wise beyond her years – indeed who are we to judge, when they have both accepted us for who we are! I, for one, am proud that she is one of our community, and I wish Roslin and Elias a long and happy life together."

There was a pause, and I was taken aback by the emotion and kindness in the man's words. Then there was a great cheer and slowly but surely all began to join in chanting our names. We had won their respect. We had been accepted once again into our own village.

Chapter 14 'The Curse'

It was no surprise to me that I had missed my monthly; after all we spent every night together and it had only taken one or two illicit encounters for Anye to fall pregnant. And now I waited for the terrible sickness to begin; but I waited in vain, and so our passion continued unabated – it was like an obsession – and when I was not with him I would daydream, and Anye would tease me constantly. Birne, too would comment on us as 'lovesick' and smiled, but I knew inside that he did not. It was so sad; I did so wish that he could find love too. A moon later and still no bleed, and the healer confirmed my pregnancy. This time the people were delighted when we announced our news and there was great celebration for there were indeed so few children amongst us. Most newcomers were in their teens or older – cast off for one reason or another – and were immediately taken into the heart of our community and taught our ways. Anye blossomed and developed quite a belly but, as usual, I hardly changed shape, though I felt my hair had lost its lustre and my complexion had become more sallow.

By the time of the first snow, when I had just begun to show a little, we had a fateful visit which was to change our lives. One evening, I heard a shout and rushed out of the dwelling to see great spirals of smoke billowing up into the sky far away. It was a sign – that he was back – fresh from another raid. I shuddered at a sight that brought back such vivid memories, and immediately went in search of Elias – desperate for reassurance – but instead he frowned,

"Soon there will be trouble. He will come and he will learn what has become of you."

"But what harm could come of that? I am well and safe and that is all he wants to hear, is it not?"

"I am not so sure this news will please him. As far as I know, he is still without a true heir. A son of his own."

I had not thought of this and fell silent. We rarely spoke of the king now, but I knew that the King cared for two things only: to better his stores of loot and to father a son and heir. The old, familiar worries began to creep back into my mind, and Elias sensed this and added, "Roslin, you mustn't fear. He will not come between us. I will not allow it."

"And what could you do to stop him Elias? You have no power over him. He can do as he wants with any of us, you know that."

"He would have to kill me first!" he spat out grimly and turned away and strode back to our homestead. His anger took me by surprise, for Elias was never rattled by anything, though I was to discover that this was a shadow of what was to come.

My maid once told me that fire can come from the least expected source, and she was right. I took her words literally at the time, as the stories of the giants who burnt down whole communities were still reeling in our minds. But I saw their meaning in another light that day when Edvard came. As before, he was surrounded by his fine men on their fine horses and remained seated there looking down on us lesser mortals from that great height as if we were dirt.

By his side, was the man I recognised as my captor and 'liberator' from my hiding place. A shiver went down my spine, and I could not bear to look at him as I was brought forward to be inspected, though in my mind's eye I could sense his searing blue eyes were staring at me. Then I noticed how Edvard was glaring at Elias.

"I think there is something you have omitted to tell me brother," he glowered. "Why keep it from me? You know you cannot keep a secret from me, don't you?"

Elias said nothing, just stared back blankly and steadily.

And There Were Giants

"Well, is it yours? This child? Well? Is it or not?"

"What concern is that of yours?" Elias retorted and there was a short intake of breath from all around us.

"That wretched witch warned me that if I ever harmed her child then I would remain childless. So, not only did I ensure her safety but, in my charity, I gave her to you in full knowledge that you would look after her. And indeed, you have – and now you will be giving me that child in return for my charity."

The twisted logic of this shocked me to the core. Once more, I felt a pang of loss as I finally understood what my mother had done for me – Elias had guessed correctly that it had been a curse, and in their tongue too – how could she have known their language?! Or perhaps he had twisted this as well? There was no knowing. And now he meant to take our child from us!

"You may have taken everything from me in the past, Edvard, but you will never lay your hands on our child."

Edvard looked taken aback for a moment, as if he hadn't anticipated such resistance to his command. Then dismounted from his horse and strode up to Elias until they were facing each other in the centre of the square. We all stood rooted to the spot; eyes fixed on the two opposing giants. Elias was taller, but Edvard was huge too – and broader - built like a rock. For one more excruciating moment, the two faced up to one another, then, through gritted teeth, Edvard spoke; the sarcasm was obvious.

"Younger brother, I think you have forgotten who you are, indeed, what you are. I am King here and you – why, you are nothing – not even my full brother. Of course, you will do as I say. But, if it makes you feel better," he turned and began to walk back to the horses, "you can give her back to me. I would be happy to take care of her now that I know she is fert....." But he never finished his sentence. Elias had rushed over to him and grabbed him by the shoulder and swung him round with such force that he overbalanced and fell to the floor. Everyone gasped, some couldn't even bear to look, now we truly had reached a point of no return.

"Get up!" Elias spat.

Edvard slowly got to his feet, and they stood staring at each other, fuming. Surely, surely, he wasn't going to fight – the king? Elias, the level-headed, serious, calm, gentle Elias? No, this wasn't the man I knew.

"I see, so you want to fight me for the child, do you?" Well it is not negotiable, Elias, my mind is made up. I want a son."

"And what if it is a girl?" it was my voice, sounding high and tremulous.

Everyone looked around and stared, in turn, at me, "what use would you have for a girl? I will never forget who you are. You are a tyrant and a bully who thinks nothing of laying to waste peoples' lives for your own gain. We owe you nothing and your people should know that."

The people were looking at me as if I were mad, and he began to laugh mockingly again, though I felt sure there was now something in his eyes, a glint of unease maybe. However, he did not acknowledge that I had spoken and turned back to Elias.

"Alright, I will fight you for the child. That will settle it once and for all."

I closed my eyes and prayed. I had hoped that my intervention would prevent this, but it had failed. Edvard's mind was fixed, and nothing would steer it off course. Moreover, Edvard knew he would get his way without losing face, as all knew he always did.

And so, it was to be. There was not a sound from anyone. None of our people dared move. My captor, Wilfrid, handed his own sword and shield to Elias – and I wondered desperately how they could deem this to be fair as he owned no weapons and never used them – but Elias took them without comment. The face I knew so well was back now, the face that gave nothing away, utterly composed again. I couldn't bear it and was about to throw myself between them when I felt Birne holding me back. "Don't be afraid Roslin. This is the only way now." I turned to look at him, incredulous – how could he bear to see the man he loved hacked down in front of everyone? But Birne's eyes were shining and there was something about his face that stilled me, gave me hope.

Then, at a signal from one of Edvard's men, they sprang into action, Elias doing his best to defend himself from the ferocious attack of his opponent. Edvard fought with a competence that seemed invincible. Elias, in contrast, seemed only just able to defend himself from each attack; it was all that I could do to watch. But, suddenly, out of the blue, Elias swung his sword and caught Edvard across the chest. He swooned and staggered backwards; a line of blood clearly visible through his torn clothes. Nobody had expected that, and there was a gasp of surprise, but the moment did not last long for almost immediately they were fighting once again, this time at loggerheads, weapon against weapon. Now, it was Elias' turn to falter and be thrown to the ground. To be sure, we all thought that was it and he was down and lost, and I prayed for him to be spared, but suddenly and totally against all expectation, he sprung up and was fighting again as if nothing had happened.

From that point on, it began to dawn on me that they had done this before, probably many times before. Not only that, but it was as if the balance of power were shifting now, and that Elias was growing in vigour and expertise. It was not the uneven match I had expected at all but a prepared and rehearsed battle, which they both expected to win, even if one side were a little out of practise. How could this be, if Elias had not known the life of the raids? How could he be such a proficient fighter? Was this really the same peaceful, unassuming man I loved? He was now moving with a grace and agility that belied his great size and we all looked on in wonder. Could it be that he was actually gaining the upper hand?

And then he caught him. It happened as quick as a lightning flash, and I could see that this was indeed Elias' strength – he somehow had the advantage of strategic thought, the power of surprise, and he had caught Edvard out. It was as if he had missed a beat, struck out of rhythm; and now Edvard was lying on his back winded by the blow and – dared I believe it – defeated!

Elation swept over me, only to be crushed just as quickly as I watched Elias rest his sword on Edvard's chest. Still no-one moved, no-one made a sound, no-one could take their eyes off that sword. With all my body and soul, I willed him not to do it, not to have his brother's blood on his hands; then I started, as the menace in his booming voice rang out. Once more, it was the voice of a giant I did not know, "No son of mine will ever follow in your footsteps! No, I have not forgotten what happened to me, nor who I am – I was your father's plaything! Your family destroyed mine just as you still delight in destroying the lives of those around you."

I half expected him to plunge the sword into that heaving wreck there and then, I think we all did, but to my relief, he instead thrust it at the feet of the unsuspecting Wilfrid, then turned and addressed us all, "My wife is right: he is using and abusing you all and those he burns for his own gain! And if you are not fit for purpose, or if you die in the process? Then you are forgotten, wasted." And finally, to Edvard's men, who were staring at their master unsure of what to do next, he growled, "Take him back to where he belongs... and <u>never</u> accompany him here again...."

And with those last words he stormed off.

And There Were Giants

We were left united with one thought, though the irony of the situation had not escaped any of us. There was now no doubt who was the greater warrior.

Chapter 15 'Born to be a warrior?'

There was no immediate end to Elias' fury, and he refused to talk to anyone. Birne was the only one who seemed to understand this, and I recognised that again it had fallen to him to help me through this latest crisis. As Elias continued to glower at the fire in silence, Birne led me back to his own dwelling and sat me down, just as Elias had done a year earlier. It was not until I was calm and had taken some drink, that he told me of how he had first come to know Elias ... and the king.

Don't worry, Roslin, he will be fine. He just needs time. We must leave him be for a while."

"This is all my fault." I blurted out. "If I hadn't come here, none of this would have happened."

"No, Roslin that is not true, and you must not blame yourself. You have given Elias untold happiness, a happiness he might never have known, and believe me I am glad of that. Elias has always been my greatest friend and I know he adores you. He just needs time to calm himself. In truth, I have always believed that this would happen again. Yes, they have fought before, but they were children then. You see, Elias loved, probably still loves his brother. They just could never see eye to eye – Hadred saw to that. Strange though it may seem, Elias always wished for his brother's approval – he has told me so.

But you must realise that this confrontation has finally revealed the truth: that Elias could be a great warrior – he has defeated the King himself, supposedly the best warrior in the land. Not only that, but all now know that he can father a child, whilst the King cannot. This means that there is no longer a reason for him to remain here. He could return to the High Town and champion the life for so long revered by our people. He has potentially taken the place of the King, Roslin. Yet Elias has always abhorred the life of the warrior and wanted nothing to do with it. He has even been happy to pretend he was something he was not to avoid it.

Roslin, let me tell you our story; forgive me if you know some of this already but I believe you do not know all. Years ago, when Elias and I were boys, we joined the firstborn sons who were taken from their families to be trained, by the sea, as the next generation of warriors. Everyone aspired to join the privileged elite – those handpicked to front the battle with the king when they came of age - and it was obvious from the start that Edvard would be beside his father one day. There was, however, one other who stood out from the crowd – I am sure you can guess who I am talking about now, though he would never have mentioned this himself. It was the King's other son, though everyone knew that he was not 'of the line'. Well, Elias could outwit any opponent and the King soon spotted this and became ever 'fonder' of his adopted son. This did not escape the notice of his true son who had always resented the attention his father showed Elias. However, he did not yet know the extent of his father's affection and before he made that terrible discovery, he goaded and teased Elias until at last he found a weak point – his mother. Elias had adored his mother and still remembered her though she had died when he was only very young. When he heard the disparaging and crude remarks about her he flew into a rage and practically beat his brother to a pulp – he had to be dragged off him. Unfortunately for Edvard this seemed to make Hadred favour Elias even more and instead of punishing Elias, he turned against his own son, and the jealousy grew and grew until the day Edvard discovered what had been happening in secret. Elias may have already spoken of this abuse, but you may not be aware that he found his father with me. I was also his victim. Elias need never have said a word, but when he found that I was to be banished he confessed that he, too was his father's prey and then there was no question that Elias must be banished as well to save his father's reputation. So, we were both cast out, forbidden to return and came to live here some ten years ago. Although the truth about Hadred was quickly covered up by both father and son, it broke Hadred and I am convinced to this day that he gave himself up to grief and despair at having lost Elias, on that last raid."

I thought about all this for a while, and then said, "So what will become of us now? We cannot leave this enmity between them to fester on and on. Something must be done to bring peace between them. I feel it should be me that does this."

Birne looked at me, horrified, "whatever do you mean? There is nothing you can do. They will never see eye to eye."

"Let me go there. I will speak to him. I will tell him that he has fulfilled my mother's dying wish. I will say that if he leaves me and Elias alone, we will never threaten his authority."

Still he stared at me, as if lost for words. Then, he smiled gently and replied, "Your courage never fails to amaze me Roslin, but Elias would never hear of it, and you must think of the safety of your child. Your words of peace and conciliation are admirable and perhaps, just perhaps, we could convey them to the High Town someday, but if we do send this message, you should not be the one to bear it. We must trust in the gods that this present truce is kept."

Chapter 16 'New Life'

Birne woke to the news that Anye had given birth….

A new life, a boy! It was early morning and only Anye's family and the healer were allowed in the dwelling, but the news was spreading through us like wildfire. There was great celebration and cheer – for this was, after all, our first baby for some time. But then, as the crowds began to disperse, a problem was reported from the house: all was not right with Anye. The baby was well, but there was a complication – there had been no afterbirth – and then a further blow was dealt us as we stood out there helplessly – she was developing a fever, and neither the women nor the healer knew what to do for her.

We conferred and there was only one answer – we must go there and fetch their doctor. It was her only hope; we did not have the expertise. I wanted to go myself and at once, though I knew this wasn't wise given our latest altercation with the King, so it was Rogen who ran all the way, in spite of the recent snow. However, on his return – the two of them on horseback – I immediately regretted not going myself, for there before us was a man no older than myself, indeed probably much younger. Surely this was yet another insult from our great ruler, for how could a man so young be their best doctor!

"My name is Janmat, and I have been sent to help your friend." He gazed at me and Elias for a moment, smiled briefly, then asked to be shown the patient as quickly as possible. By now, poor Anye had become dangerously feverish, and we just stood there side by side with her family in the dwelling and prayed for a miracle.

The young man knelt beside her, felt her brow, and gently dabbed her forehead with a damp cloth. He then proceeded to give Anye's mother strict instructions – to prepare this potion and that poultice – and as he worked, I noticed his white, slender hands and the adept sensitivity of his touch. Not once did he hesitate, or falter and I had to admit that everything about him spelt confidence and demonstrated a wisdom beyond his years. His manner was calm and deliberate whilst all around him was panic and fear.

By midnight, Anye had begun to bleed a little, and the fever had begun to subside and finally, after what felt like one of the longest nights of our lives, there came from her body the evil that had been destroying her. Pale and exhausted, yet lucid again, she begged to be given her child – a child who had mercifully slept through most of this nightmare – and as he was laid to her breast, we realised that she was saved, and that we owed her life to him.

It was a truly wonderful moment. A birth in our village was a rare and much anticipated event, but the peace and joy after such a night of fear was truly miraculous. We would not hear of him leaving straightaway after working all through the night, and I at once offered him my dwelling in which to rest. It was the least I could do after my initial misgivings about him. And strangely he seemed in no hurry to leave. It was remarkable, but despite his provenance, he did not seem to look down on us, nor did he appear to hold us in any contempt, but calmly and diligently continued to attend to his charge, and Anye continued to recover her strength over the next few days.

He was so young and yet so skilled and accomplished. Others came to him and were helped or healed too. Despite myself, I couldn't help but admire how he worked and those gentle, thoughtful eyes – could this modest, diligent, unassuming man really come from the High Town? And sometimes I would catch him looking at me, too, and we would smile. Each night by the fireside, we would talk and laugh with ease, as if we had known each other all our lives. I was to discover that he was the King's doctor no less – I had not expected him to boast of such a thing – but was nevertheless impressed. Strange, then, that he should be spared by 'the Others', I thought, but his next words were stranger still, and he spoke them in a lowered voice, as if he did not want anyone to hear. He had been glad to be spared the warrior training so that he could follow in his father's footsteps. To hear one from the High Town say such a thing was confirmation to me that he was not a typical 'Other'. He was proud that his whole life had been dedicated to caring for the sick and infirm; he did not want the warrior life. As the days went past, I began to dread the day he announced his work with us was done, or he was called back to the High Town. Indeed, why had he not been summoned already? I could only think that Edvard was afraid to do so now, and that Elias had at last succeeded in taming his jealous brother.

Then one evening, as I prepared us a meal and he stared into the fire, Janmat began to speak of a time that I had tried to erase from my memory.

"I remember you Birne, and Elias." And when I looked at him enquiringly, he added, "Oh, I don't expect you to remember me. I joined a few years after you, and not for my ability, nor for being first born – I told you, I was simply there to follow in the steps of my father the doctor; but you, you were the best." I then waited for him to recall Elias' and Edvard's ability and strength.

"We had to watch you, the elite, as you would soon be warriors yourselves and of course everyone admired the King's sons. Elias stood out – but I am surprised he has grown so tall, for he was not then.... but you, I remember you also. You were always there, waiting your turn. They would be summoned first and Elias' hatred for his brother would often get the better of his gentle nature but you, you held back and rarely showed your strength. But you were obviously a very gifted warrior Birne, and Hadred certainly seemed to favour you." He paused. Then looked me straight in the eyes, "So, it wasn't true, then, why you were banished? You and Elias I mean."

I looked back at him and replied carefully, "What does it matter now? Elias and I have always been happy here and we would never go back."

He considered this, then looked away. "Birne, I have a secret that I want to share with you."

"Are you sure that's wise? We are not from the same worlds you and I," was all I could manage, though I could see that his values were not so very different to our own.

"Well, that's just it Birne. I believe I am of your world. If the King knew about me, he would gladly be rid of me."

My mind was in turmoil now. I was not prepared for this. I didn't know what to do or say, but ever calm, ever steady he approached me and said, "You have been so kind to me in offering me your bed, but it would be the ultimate honour if you would offer to share it with me."

And when he kissed me, I knew the passion we felt for each other was mutual. Now it was my turn to find the happiness that my dear friend Elias had already discovered.

However, the cold light of day brought home to our troubled land a new truth and a new realisation. Janmat's horse was missing – and so was Mira. She had escaped under cover of night to 'the other world', whilst Janmat had begged me to let him stay with me in ours.

Mira was beautiful and no doubt wasted on us, but surely the loss of their finest doctor would be a great blow to the High Town. This was not an exchange the King would tolerate lightly, and it would bring new strife to an already strained relationship. I realised that I had, unwittingly, added yet more to the burden of my dearest friend.

Chapter 17 'Mira'

Roslin pondered the consequences of Janmat's and Mira's decisions….

Mira did not return, and we all thought that the end of the snow would herald the King's reaction to Janmat's defection. Fortunately, it did not. Instead, Martha and her husband were granted leave to visit Mira and came back proud that she had been taken into the King's own household and satisfied that she was well cared for. However, none of us could have been prepared for what was to become of her. Spring followed the snows early, and my time for delivering my own baby drew near. Now that our fears over Anye and her baby were thankfully long gone, I spent as much time as I could with them both, and soon I found myself involved in his daily care, whilst Anye napped. As I looked at that child, I began to feel such a bond with him as if he were my own, and it started me reminiscing again about my own lonely childhood and how my mother had never been involved in my own care but had been like a visitor, an onlooker in my life. I wondered if she had ever longed for me. Or had it suited her that way? What must it have been like to be separated from her child at birth and kept at arms' length?

I was so lucky, pregnancy agreed with me – unlike Anye, I had hardly suffered any sickness at all – and I had now filled out to what was probably, for any other girl, a normal weight! I noticed people looking at me and remarking on 'how well' I looked. It was so strange to think that I was actually being admired!

It was late morning one fine spring day, and everyone was making the most of the good weather to complete their outdoor chores, when I heard the familiar sound of horses' hooves in the distance. Surely these were the unwelcome visitors we had been expecting, and I hurried to fetch Elias in dismay, but when we returned, it was not the King who headed the party but Mira sitting alongside my old arch enemy. She did not look out of place at all as she sat perched high above us, as if she had ridden a horse all her life. I could see she was wearing a face to match her new position and clothing too! How he stared at me that man; it gave me the shivers as before and I again felt his eyes boring into me. Mira noticed this too and a familiar look of annoyance and petulance crossed her face.

"And so, you are back again Wilfrid, and how is your master?"

"He is well and bids you good health. We are here on a matter that concerns the King and to give you important news. First of all, he has decreed that Janmat may remain here as he is not fit for our cause. However, he should return immediately on duty if ever required to do so."

This was great news, yet we waited with bated breath as he had said this was but the first decree. True to form, it was Mira who spoke next. She said simply, directing her words at Elias:

"And he bids you know that I am now carrying the King's son."

We were taken aback by this news, for it was common knowledge that the King had had his concubines heavily guarded for years now to protect his line, but that none of them had ever fallen with child. No-one uttered a sound, except Elias who warily replied:

"Then you must accept and take my heartfelt congratulations to the King."

She looked at him then with an almost hurt look in her eyes, and I wondered whether she could still be in love with him. But how could this be so, if she had voluntarily taken herself away to be with 'the Others' and had won the ultimate prize? No, Mira had ambition for greater things. She surely now expected to be treated like a true queen, and she was certainly acting like one.

And There Were Giants

Suddenly she was down from her horse – as if she had ridden all her life – and was making straight for me. Instinctively, I moved back a few steps – as if she were about to slap me – but she took me by the arm and, as if it were an afterthought, called back to Wilfrid and his men that she wanted a few moments alone with me. And so, we left them standing there; Elias with no desire to welcome his new guests, and neither Birne nor Janmat anywhere to be seen.

She led me to a quiet, open spot, sat me down on a mossy bank, looked at me with an intensity that only she could muster, and whispered urgently under her breath:

"And so, you see, Roslin, it has fallen to me to take care of him. Only I know how. You never understood him as I do. But you will have to play your part if it comes to it. If you don't, then he will surely die at Edvard's hands, whether it be in battle - or not. Now, if it is a boy and mine is a girl then you must give him up – do you understand?"

I looked at her incredulously; how could she speak of our unborn children as if they were cattle to be traded? But something inside me was trying to understand: it was true there had been no retribution from the High Town following the King's humiliation and Janmat's departure; so could it be possible that Mira had cleverly found a way to calm the feud between the 'brothers'?

"Mira, I don't fully understand what you are saying, but hear this. Whatever child you are given will be precious and a future king or queen. Whatever that child might be, you are giving your people a great gift, Mira. And the hope that one day we might live in harmony alongside one another."

Mira was furious now as she could see from this that I was not going to play according to her plan. "Why do you not understand? They are plotting to destroy him by whatever means. Having the longed-for son would remove the need. Of course, you must never breathe a word of this to anyone."

Strangely, I felt not so much a fear of Edvard, but the chill of Wilfrid's cold blue eyes, as if he were in front of me again.

"I have known he is capable of that for some time, and we are all afraid. But thank you for this warning Mira. We will have to be ready when the time comes."

On hearing that, she turned to leave, dissatisfied. But then I called for her to stay.

"Mira, Elias said himself that he stakes no claim on this land, and neither would any son of his. Edvard would do well to remember that. But Edvard should know this too. Elias and he are divided not over which child should be heir, but what he or she would be heir to. Elias would have an end to the raids and all that entails. If Edvard could only consent to this and live peaceably, then perhaps we could learn to live together as one people."

Mira looked at me pitiably and then snarled under her breath, "well this child would hold no claim either and yet he will be King! That is the one thing I always despised in Elias – his neglect of his own power, his total lack of ambition. He could have had the entire realm eating out of the palm of his hand after that fight and yet all he aspires to is this….. and you – you are no better – you who have royal blood! Well you deserve him!" and with that she was off, back to exert her power and ambition.

Afterwards, I wondered what she had meant by her child not holding any claim to the kingdom. This puzzled me, as any child of Edvard was automatically his heir, but I knew that her words, however spiteful and derogatory, had been spoken to me in confidence and that I would do well to keep them that way. I really did believe she wanted to protect Elias. And so, I did not divulge what she had said to anyone.

Chapter 18 'Marte'

We soon agreed to call her 'Marte' after the friend and neighbour who had first cared for and welcomed me, and her father before me, into the village. Martha was delighted, though she was still saddened by the loss of her daughter to the High Town, and the rift between Mira and me, and hoped this would not provoke her further. I had been so convinced that I was to have a boy that would bring untold strife to our community, that I was too surprised at first to feel joy that it was a girl. Then, no sooner had that fully registered, then I feared that Elias would be disappointed! Surely, he too wanted an heir. But I should have known he was never one to follow convention. He had stayed with me through the entire birth, despite the disapproval of the healers, and surprise of our people, and was the first to hold her, finally handing her over to lay her on my breast with tears in his eyes. And now the village would have to share him with yet another female! It made me smile to think of it. Then I wondered what Mira would say. What if she too had a girl, what then? But of course, she wouldn't for she would somehow contrive it otherwise. I had every faith in her!

Well, now I could relax in the belief that Marte would be safely left with us as she was only a girl! She would be our child to keep, we could love and nurture her without fear or recrimination, and at last a blanket of love and happiness suppressed all the pain and anguish that had preceded her birth. I could now marvel at this tiny, dark-haired creature: she was certainly not pretty, but there was something so adorable and vulnerable about her that I felt overwhelmed with gratitude and love. Over the following months, Marte grew healthy and vigorous and gave us such joy. Though those first few moons were exhausting, we both loved to spend time with her and she, in turn was such a good, even-tempered baby, though her physical strength and energy surprised everyone.

As predicted, there was never any word from Mira, Edvard, or any of the 'Others', about our child and I took it that we had not, as usual, played our part in the grand scheme of things and that therefore there had been no need to make contact. The summer came, and for once Edvard had not departed on a raid. He doubtless wanted to be present for the birth of his own son and heir. Life continued as if it were a beautiful dream. It was simply perfect, perhaps too perfect...

And then came the greatest irony of all, just when our two communities were living side by side in relative harmony for the first time in living memory - it happened.

Chapter 19 'The beginning – of another end?'

It is pitch black and yet I can feel the walls of my prison closing in on me, suffocating me. And if the walls do not crush me, then the flames outside will slowly lick me to death. I can hear the people screaming: not because the fires are destroying all they own, but because there are giants as big as trees squashing them one by one like flies, and I can do nothing to stop their agony. I feel so helpless, a tiny, puny thing slowly being crushed to death, and I am powerless to stop it, but what is this? I can hear a voice….. it is Mother calling for me….. wanting me….. I must save her; we must get away from the giants…..She has me by the hand – she will release me, and we will escape together into the blanket of darkness …..

Suddenly there is a blinding light, and a hideous face appears grinning at me like a demon. There is no sign of Mother now – she has abandoned me. Light floods in as the walls recede, and I am free momentarily, only then to fall helplessly into the claws of the giant. The face draws nearer and nearer, the vicious grin gets wider and wider, and those eyes bore holes into me with their searing glare; he will surely snuff me out like all the others. But no, mine is not a merciful, quick death. Oh no, there is first torture, unspeakable pain as I have never known before, deep searing pain cutting through my body, splitting me in two…..

I was coming up now, fighting to get away, fighting to breathe, and as I emerged from my recurrent nightmare, I recognised that smell. It was a long time ago, when I was young, green and in a different land…… Suddenly I was properly awake and shaking from the realisation – this was <u>not</u> a dream. It was reality. There was burning somewhere near – and – yes, yes, this was a raid! My eyes burst open, and my attention was drawn at once to a flickering light - that light I'd seen before. I came to my senses then; how could this be a raid? I wasn't in my homeland anymore. I was amongst them – in the land of the raiders. Yet still there was something about that unsteady glow – it seemed to be coming from the direction of the High Town. Couldn't that just be the dawn? I scrambled to my feet and made my way unsteadily to the doorway, and there on the horizon was the glow, but there was smoke too – great plumes of it rising into the sky and blotting out the stars. This was not the dawn; it was still night and there was burning…… I was suddenly gripped by a learnt fear and foreboding. I must wake Elias. We must act fast!

One glance at the horizon and Elias sounded the alarm and all gathered in the main square, staring at the smoke and flames. Soon everyone was shouting at once, voices raised in shock and confusion. What could this mean? Was it an accidental fire or could I somehow be right: that it was a raid, with an enemy in tow? Then Elias held up his hand and quiet was briefly restored. He trusted me – they trusted me – in believing it was a raid. He began to gather some of the able-bodied men and was about to turn to me when we heard horses, and there before us were desperate faces.

"We are sent for Elias! and Birne! They have surprised us as we sleep. You must help us, or they will destroy everything! The King is in mortal danger!"

So, this was confirmation! For a moment time stood still. Would he go? He looked at me, and I knew at once.

"Roslin, we must leave. You must get those that stay to safety. In case they come here."

And with that they were gone, thundering off towards the smoke….. You could just make out faint cries now and the glow was growing ominously brighter. He had chosen me! With a pounding heart, I summoned everyone round. There was no time to think. There was no time to gather belongings. We had to hurry together in strength so that any stragglers could get support if needed, and then disperse once we reached the woods. The trees grew close together, so it would be difficult for horseback riders to follow us there. But there was barely any moonlight – they had struck under cover of darkness – so it would be difficult for us to see our way too. Yet we could not risk torches.

I feared they would question me and look to a man for direction, to those elders who spoke at Council, but I suppose the urgency in my voice, and my experience of such horrors, carried me. They rallied around and listened to me, and to my surprise, the voice that left my mouth rang out clearly and authoritatively. I put Mira's father, Halvor, at the lead, ensuring there were strong with any weak, and placed myself at the back – I must make sure everyone reached the woods and also, I thought, if we were pursued, then I would be the first to see.

As we began our escape, I recalled my first thoughts on seeing that grand township: no surrounding wall, no defences, no strategic viewpoint. It was incredible that this had not happened before. But who were these attackers? Surely, they were not from over the water, as how could they have surprised us? I remembered the guard as we arrived and had learnt since that the few other landing places on this rocky fortress of an island were also heavily guarded as the warrior training camps were situated there. So, could this be a rebellion from within? But strangely, as these speculations struck me one after the other, there was not one moment that I doubted that this was a raid.

I held our sleeping child in my arms, wondering if she would ever see her father again. It was a chilling thought. I tried not to think about what could be happening now – had they been slain already? Or was there hope? As we hurried along, I prayed as loudly and as fervently as the next person.

Of course, I had suffered before - I alone knew what it was like to endure a raid – but though my mother's untimely death had always haunted me, I had not known such love as I now had. How I suffered that night not knowing, not knowing if he was safe.

Once we reached the forest, we split up into our groups and forced our way through the closely packed trees, scratching ourselves against branches, not able to see where we were going, but intent on moving on and on, desperate to hide as far as we could from our aggressors. But there was no sign of any pursuit. The only sounds and sight of flames came from afar. Eventually, our group of the lame, the old and the very young, came upon a little clearing in the trees and we wordlessly made our way into this and buried ourselves in the undergrowth. This would be our resting place until our time came – whatever the outcome might be.

We must have slept, because it wasn't until daylight that I felt the baby fumbling for my breast. The acrid smell of smoke still filled the air, but there was sunlight peering through the trees. I strained my ears to listen - everywhere was silent but for the gentle sounds of insects and birdsong. The others had awoken too and were murmuring softly amongst themselves. Suddenly, the sound of breaking twigs startled us to attention, and we exchanged alarmed glances - had we been pursued after all? But the sight of a deer and her fawn appeased us, and we fell to watching them, as they in turn eyed us warily. We stayed there all that day and only dared move to forage for berries and search for water. But the following morning, the not-knowing was too much:

"What should we do now Roslin?" whispered Anye. Dare we go back? You told us a day and a night's wait should be enough."

I thought for a moment, then looked to the sky again. If they were still there, then there would still be smoke and burning. Convinced that they must have gone as quickly as they had attacked, I realised that I was desperate to find out what had happened to our loved ones and our village. Return we should, but as carefully and watchfully as possible.

It was almost dusk by the time we returned in dribs and drabs to a ghostly village, which was entirely as we had left it. They had not even bothered with our community at all! Either they had not known or cared about us. But our men had not returned! Halvor and Martha were by now sick with worry about Mira, and Anye feared for her Rogen. We looked mournfully at each other, wondering what we should do – stay, or go there to the High Town? We were longing for news of course, but what if danger were still at large? What if we were greeted with a sight worse than death?

Many consulted us as they came back from the forest, yet still we dithered and it was only as dusk fell again on the village, and I had all but decided we could still not risk the journey, that we heard the gallop of horses. We had no idea whether these were friends or foe. Frozen with fear we had nowhere to turn and nowhere to hide – had I made the wrong choice to return?

~~~~~

After the call for help, Elias' mind started to race….

Yes, there was no question, this was an act of revenge and I had to get there before they hacked him down. He was ever the foolhardy one, too headstrong and proud, believing he was invincible. This had been a long time coming. But he was not without weakness, and I didn't trust Wilfrid to save him. Quickly, I glanced at Roslin and knew at once that I could count on her to lead our people to safety. It was she and she alone who had remarked on our lack of defence but for our rocky shoreline, and it was she who had spoken, so wisely, of what we should do in the event of such a disaster.

As I picked my way through the flames, I headed, not for the main building, but straight for the courtyard. That was where they would fight. There would be glory for one but not the other and I believed that fury would have its way if I did not get their first.

And indeed there he was. Cowering before his judgement. Petrified. Wilfrid was nowhere to be seen – no doubt looking to his own survival. And where was Birne? For a moment I wondered whether Mira were safe, but I would have to trust that to providence for now. This was where I was needed. Moving in, they were suddenly aware of my presence and that I was not as defenceless as the others who had obviously been caught unawares – probably fast asleep on watch. Edvard, at least, was brandishing his sword before him, but they did not fight like us, there were three, no, four of them all closing in on him, we were hardly even. Then suddenly, Birne burst into the square and now we had a chance. Yet Edvard just stared at us, still rooted to the spot. I wondered at his discomposure – what had befallen him? Where was the warrior in him? Quickly, I glanced at Birne, was he up to this? Well, to his eternal credit he had already launched himself into the fight like the magnificent warrior he could have been, and I could see the fear in his opponent's eyes. And I too could do this, I could defend him – there was no choice. I judged which was the leader and his second and lunged towards them. And so, we fought, two on one, struggling, but somehow surviving….. until…. just as I was beginning to gain ground, just when I thought I might be able at last to do something of worth in his eyes, a great fireball from nowhere fell amongst us and suddenly everything about us was ablaze. The enemy scattered in search of safety, and in the confusion, I wondered whether this might just clinch a victory for us, but then I saw what had happened: Edvard had fallen, crushed under the weight of the mighty brand. I could do nothing. I hoped, then, that the blow had killed him instantly and that he felt nothing for I will never forget the horror of watching him burn before my very eyes. We just stood there – the battle already won. They had not come here to plunder, this was no raid; they had come here to claim back what was already theirs, and to wreak revenge. And with that end now met they turned and were gone, as quickly as they had come.....

It did not take long for him to resurface again, out of the shadows as always, had he known all along? Could he have divined all this? The look of horror – was it for my benefit or did he truly mourn his master of so many years? I cast my mind back to the days when we fought; Birne always ready to stand for me, and Wilfrid? Wilfrid, too, could always sense when the time had come: to step forward if it were to bask in his master's glory, or make himself scarce when all was lost. Well, he had not been there tonight...... Then as he stood there looking at me with Mira by his side, the realisation slowly dawned on me. He had been protecting his own! The King was not his first priority anymore, now that she was with child – of course, it must be his child, not the King's at all!.... It was time we talked. Time he confessed..... but he spoke first – ever pragmatic, ever resourceful.

"I know what you are thinking. That I abandoned my lord at his time of greatest need and that this must be my doing. How you are wrong! It was he who bid me protect his wife and heir, and wouldn't you if he'd asked you? In any case, I loved him. I wouldn't have stooped so low as to summon your help otherwise. Oh yes, we quarrelled, but you know as well as I do, he was a fool sometimes – and you quarrelled with him too, didn't you? Well, we both did what we could for him Elias. What harm was there in that? After all, we both know our place now, don't we? Neither of us was born to rule and yet one of us must now. And it is you who are the peoples' choice Elias. Not I. It is you who has won their hearts, not I. However you judge me in all of this, believe me in one thing – I did not bring about his fall!"

I considered this for a moment and knew in my heart he spoke the truth. Roslin could never trust him and yet I believed him somehow. Certainly, if Edvard really had bid him to go, he would have been a fool not to. It had ensured his and Mira's survival and that of his child at the very least. Moreover, there could now be a path that he might take – one that he would surely take given half the chance – for his future and for his son's. The more I thought about it, though, the riskier it became, could I trust him? I knew Roslin would question it, yet it could work. It could be the answer, the answer that would bring stability back to our communities and restore the status quo. It was time to test the water….

~~~~~~

As the men returned to the village Roslin's relief was overwhelming….

They were covered with burns and cuts, but it was summer and there were thankfully still healing plants to be gathered. I knew our dwelling would become a healing centre and that we would be temporarily homeless, but I didn't care. I still had all I wanted. We quickly learnt that all could have been lost if our men had not arrived when they did, as they had been taken completely by surprise, but there was something about the men that told us this that that was not all.

As I clung to Elias, he held me tight, and I could feel the grief. I wondered then who we had lost, as miraculously all our party had survived. Why was he so sad? I waited, we all waited for him to be ready to tell, and eventually he gathered everyone and said,

"The stone is still standing, and homes can be rebuilt. In fact, they only came for what was rightfully theirs. It could have been a massacre, but we managed to get as many people away from the fire as possible, and they soon left…. But not before taking the King." There was a gasp from those who did not know this already. He looked grave now, and I couldn't help wondering why he should feel such sorrow for one he had apparently not wanted to see again.

"Last time he plundered too close to home. They found him and now he is dead. I couldn't save him….."

There was a pause as we reflected on this momentous information, then Jelem asked for one and all: "So who will rule us now?"

"Wilfrid becomes guardian of the throne until Edvard's son is of age." At this he looked furtively at me, he knew how I feared him, "but he takes it on condition: that there is an end to the raids, and we live side by side in harmony. We will help them rebuild and restore, but they must respect us – he has sworn this in front of his people, and they have all sworn allegiance to us."

I looked at Elias and despite my renewed fears, couldn't help smiling at what he had done. Of course, this was what he would want: peace and harmony at the expense of a kingdom that could have been his. But Mira's words still echoed in my head. Elias may still not be safe whilst Wilfrid was alive. He may have been granted much of the power and rule of his predecessor, but the people were aware that Wilfrid was nothing more than Edvard's second. What if he sought to destroy Elias who had more right to the role than he? Not only that, but there was also the possibility that he may not agree to the constraints of the allegiance – he did not owe Elias anything. Or did he?

When we were alone at last Elias held me close.

"For all the hate I felt for him, now that he is gone I have so many regrets!"

"Jealousy ruined your relationship with your brother, Elias. Your stepfather's wrongs were endured by both of you."

"He could have been so different. If only I had tried harder to relate to him instead of always being his rival for our father's affections, if only our lives had not been overshadowed by the false glory of the raids. Sadly, instead of trying to understand him, I always let my feelings get the better of me."

"You told me he knew your weaknesses and took advantage of this. That was why you reacted the way you did; you cannot blame yourself."

Then he looked at me and fell to his knees.

"I do not deserve you Roslin. You were so brave when you took charge of the weakest and most vulnerable in our village. You must think me weak not to take my brother's place. Please forgive me Roslin, but I have always known my birthplace and I have never aspired to rule this land."

Kissing the top of his head I knelt down before him and spoke from the heart, "Elias, we all know you are not weak. You are more worthy than any in this land and the people know that. We all look to you now to ensure that the power you have handed to Wilfrid is used wisely. The responsibility is great and the consequences of a disagreement, or worse, are dire. It is not the easiest road you have taken but the noblest one, my love. My only concern now is for your safety in case your trust in Wilfrid is misplaced."

Elias held me tight, and we stayed there for a long time just holding each other and thinking about the future. For what would the future hold now? Would Wilfrid keep the truce? Would we be able to live in harmony alongside the Others? Only time would tell.

Chapter 20 '… over time…'

Whilst our expertise was useful to the High Town, they accepted us, and respect did begin to form between our two communities. Our dwellings had never been on a grand scale, but we nevertheless had some fine builders and roofers amongst us, most of whom had had to learn more about survival than just how to fight battles. And whilst we were useful, at last we could trade our skills and work with commodities such as livestock and even horses. Thus, our village grew stronger with more provisions to survive the cruel winters, and the High Town buildings were restored to their former glory once again. The snows were not so deep that year, and that winter brought another new life and an heir to the throne at last. Despite the freezing conditions, Janmat was able to return to the High Town to attend to Mira and delivered her safely of the boy Edvard had wanted so much! Not only the High Town celebrated that day; both of our communities hoped this would now bring a lasting stability to our region.

Spring appeared once more, and all stayed quiet and peaceful, but at the back of our minds Elias and I were always questioning whether Wilfrid could remain content. Though on the outside the High Town was as impressive as before, much of the riches it contained had been lost or burnt in the raid and the kingdom's coffers consequently much reduced. Moreover, the Others had been used to a certain standard of living as well as fine possessions….. I thought of the craftsmanship of my people – the jewellery and tapestries and what they had captured from us alone.

One day, I was surprised to receive an invitation from Mira – to see the baby. This puzzled me greatly. Why would she want to see me, I wondered? – we had never been close. And then I considered whether this might be a pretext to deliver another message – but there was no need surely? After all, there was no question now that she had the boy they all wanted. So why the invitation? Perhaps it was simply to crow over her success and my failure in delivering a potential heir? Well, that wouldn't bother me, and I was interested to see the High Town again in any case. Would there be any improvements in its defences? And furthermore, I had never been inside those walls – in the end, my curiosity overruled any doubts I had at going.

As I entered, I braced myself for a frosty reception, but Mira always had the capacity to surprise me…..

"So, what do you think? He looks just like his father wouldn't you say?" she said rather too brightly.

"He's beautiful Mira, you must be so happy!"

"Edvard would have been so proud, but fate decreed that he would never see his son. That was a cruel blow that cut him down in his prime."

I simply replied again that he was a beautiful, healthy child, and that she must be proud, but inwardly I couldn't help casting my mind back to her words to me when she had announced her pregnancy … about her son not being an heir….. A thought had crossed my mind before – what if this wasn't Edvard's child at all, but Wilfrid's? She was always by his side these days. If this were the case, then little Njall would not be a true heir at all.

"Yes, he is, isn't he….. And now we have an heir to the throne – Edvard's son – we can be strong once more. A true kingdom."

"Yes, indeed Mira – we are all delighted. It is great news for everyone. And maybe we can now all live in peace and prosperity."

She looked at me and I could see from her face that I was not giving her the reaction she had hoped for, once again…..

"Well I'm not surprised you did not come before, after all, you haven't given Elias an heir yet….." I had been expecting this reproach sooner. "No heir for your community….. but don't worry Roslin….. perhaps the next one will be a boy….."

"Mira what do you mean? We are one community now with Wilfrid as our leader. There is only one heir.

She looked at me keenly, and I wished I could read her thoughts. What did she want me to say? Then it came to me – perhaps she was afraid of what she had let slip to me back then on the bank – she wanted me to confirm to her that he was indeed sole heir.

"Mira, I have not told anyone what you said to me back then – not even Elias. I do not question that your child is sole heir. You must not worry that I or Elias ever would. All we ask is that we live in peace and harmony now and forthwith, and that there are no more raids. And Mira – what of Wilfrid – are you to be betrothed to him? For if you are, then his sons would also follow in the heirdom – would they not – so long as the truce be kept?"

This had the desired effect! This was what she/they wanted to be sure.

"Roslin, I'm sorry I haven't always been as kind to you as I should have been. I suppose I didn't want to be in your shadow – but you must understand I only did what I thought would be best for everyone – not just me. I was never as pretty and clever as you, I never spoke my mind before the people, and you won him, yet I have become the desire of not one but two leaders, and that will have to be enough for me."

Again, this outburst astonished me. Did she really believe that I was prettier and cleverer than her, for she seemed to speak from the heart? For once, I was lost for words. We just looked at each other for a moment and then I held out my hands to her and she was in my arms at once. I could have cried as I held her….. to have lost an enemy such as this was wonderful, but to have made a friend where once an enemy stood was infinitely better! Perhaps now our children could grow up in peace and prosperity and possibly even alongside each other! Oh, how Martha would rejoice in the news that we were united!

But it was at that very moment that Wilfrid chose to enter the room, and all hopes I had of a lasting friendship with Mira were shattered. He stopped short, looking confused at first and no doubt wondering why I was there. Then, as he had done before, he devoured me with his eyes, and I shivered under his gaze. Those narrow, blue eyes cut through me like a knife. I could sense that Mira was burning with curiosity and rage to know why he still looked at me like that, and I must confess I wondered also. Had he not found all a man could desire in Mira? Or was this his unfathomable contempt I was feeling? As quickly as I could, I made my excuses and left; I didn't want to stay a moment longer in his presence. And so, no sooner had I been reconciled with Mira then we were driven apart once again.

~~~~

As Wilfrid entered the room, he was surprised to see the very person who dominated his thoughts yet had always remained so distant. He could not tear his gaze away from her....

She has certainly transformed from that pale, sniveling wretch I first set eyes on all those moons ago, and now each time I see her, my desire becomes more and more difficult to hide. She is without doubt the most beautiful creature I have ever seen and with such gravitas and dignity it takes my breath away to look upon her. I still don't understand why that fool gave her to his brother. He might have known it would turn against him in the end and why did he do it when she was mine first in any case? He owed me that much at least after all the times I saved his skin. Still, she was so insignificant then; it is true we only brought her back because of the curse. He would do anything to have a son.

But now at last I have a plan, a plan so fool proof that no-one will ever suspect it, to claim back what is rightfully mine! And maybe soon, in spite of every hindrance I have had to endure so far, I will be able to have my heart's desire….. after all.

~~~~

Roslin tried to accept that all would be well, but she still had doubts…

Not long after that strange meeting, we heard that Mira and Wilfrid were to be betrothed and a festival held in their honour, a festival for not only the High Town to enjoy but our community also. For the first time ever, the two communities were to be brought together in celebration. It should have been a great and momentous occasion – the pinnacle of all that had happened – to bring us together, but I felt uneasy still. There was something about Wilfrid that made me so. Something I just couldn't fathom, that I alone feared. But I couldn't share my feelings with anyone – it was like a huge burden of shame and inexplicable guilt prevented me from doing so. I decided I needed to know more about Wilfrid; maybe this would help me to understand why I feared him still. The betrothal ceremony was an excellent pretext to ask questions about him, and so I casually brought up the subject with Elias and this is what he told me…..

"He was always there, for as long as I can remember. A strange one that Wilfrid – difficult to gage. He rarely spoke his mind and usually only when he vehemently disagreed with Edvard, which was more often than you'd think. He was more prudent than Edvard, you see, more able to foresee danger and problems, and was always ready to point them out. Otherwise he would just stay somewhere in the background. Never part of the action, but waiting, to pick up the pieces I suppose, in case Edvard overstepped the mark – which he often did. I never liked him. Too smarmy and flattering – always looking for an opportunity to better himself, and I suppose by sticking to Edvard he managed that very well." Elias paused for a moment,

"Are you still afraid of him Roslin? For surely this act of betrothal must be allaying your fears somewhat."

I didn't answer, just questioned him further,

"And was he part of the elite? How did he fight?"

"Oh, he was part of the elite alright but rarely called on to fight at all. On the contrary, he was Edvard's second, advising him on strategy and waiting and watching in the side lines...... I seem to remember him fighting with Birne once though..... Oh yes, that was quite some fight..... at first, we thought Wilfrid's strategies would win him the contest, but after a long struggle, Birne just outwitted him, and he came off second best. Still, Wilfrid was never one to be down and he quickly pointed out how his second had missed Birne cheating and blamed his defeat on malpractice. Though no one could say for sure they had witnessed this, no one could question it either as it was history now and one word against another, so Wilfrid's defeat was blurred, and its memory clouded in controversy. Where he really excelled was in planning, and I believe Edvard used this skill of Wilfrid's to his advantage in the raids – Wilfrid always knew where and when to strike and when to leave too. Moreover, his mastery of navigation was apparently second to none, probably passed on from his father who was a great seafarer and warrior. In any case, there was no-one better to guide the ship back safely to land than Wilfrid. Edvard owed a lot, if not all, of his success to him. But don't worry Roslin, Wilfrid could always adapt his skills to suit his situation, as I feel sure he will now. With the people behind us he will look at our partnership and see strengths there, where before Edvard saw none. Also, I believe him to be a man of his word."

"I hope so, and you are right, we have the people's backing in this, but I feel so defenceless here Elias. We must plan for if things go wrong. What if he plots to destroy us - as we curb his ultimate power - and he succeeds – what then?"

"Indeed, that is always possible. I suppose I suffer as my brother did from over-confidence in our strengths, perhaps it is a flaw in our people too. I will call a meeting of Council, and this time I promise we will act and plan for all eventualities."

"They will question it Elias. And if they do, we can point to the High Town raid and blame that….. You are all skilled at fighting - by the rules - you have all had the training in attack, but now you must demonstrate you have learnt lessons in defence, even at the hands of your own. We must make it a priority now to protect our community."

As my giant looked down on me, I could see a man who truly wanted to do what was best for his community. He towered there, seemingly invincible, but he could listen too, and he could understand. To me he was a great, yet humble man and I couldn't bear to think that anything might happen to destroy him.

Chapter 21 'Within the wall'

The proposal to build greater defences won at the first joint Council between the Low and High Town and, shortly after that, work began on the Great Wall. A wall surrounding the High Town was to be built first – our wall would come later – after all, the ruler lived there and had been the one real target of the raid. The task should have been much easier as there was stone in abundance in this land; wood to make carts; and horses to carry it, but nobody anticipated the effort and dangers involved in such a scheme. There were injuries, one fatal, and questions began to be asked again whether they needed it at all, especially amongst those in our community who would not benefit from its protection, until ours was built. It began to divide us again both within and between our two communities, and I even began to question myself. Why had I instigated such an ambitious project? But then I only had to look back at recent history and the history of my own people to answer that.

I recalled how Father had ordered the building of our wall on first hearing of the raids along our shores. There had been terrible stories of whole townships burnt to the ground and all possessions and livelihoods lost. But some of the story tellers, mainly monks who had lost everything but their lives, were not content with telling us these bare facts. Now I realised that in their telling, the raiders had taken on superhuman traits: they were not of this Earth but were giants sent to strike us down with the wrath and power of the Devil himself. Their skin was white and blue and their hair like burning straw. They could uproot trees and squash women and children in their vice like grip and some stood as tall as trees. When my father heard all this, he decreed that his wall would be built taller than even the keep at the top of our hill. But that never happened, for our raid came when it was still under construction and indeed the wooden gate was its greatest weakness. I remembered vividly seeing it smashed and in pieces as I was dragged away – it had not been strong enough. Now it was I who could look on these mistakes from my past and guide those in the present. I had to protect these, my new people, ironically the giants themselves, from <u>their</u> foes……

And what had I learnt of my new companions? Well, it was true they were far taller and broader than any I had grown up with, yet they ate, drank, celebrated, and felt anger and loss just the same as we always had. There were some differences in their behaviour and attitudes, of course, but then there had been stark differences between those of the High Town and the Low Town, and these, I believed, were simply due to upbringing and learned values. Just as there had been the high and the low born in my land, there was a similar hierarchy in the High Town. Yet here, in The Low Town, people did not live in that way. Could this present climate of unity between us change all that? If the time of the raids and all they stood for was finally over, then we could perhaps start to think and behave more like each other. Sadly, the Great Wall now stood for many as a symbol of the High Town's continuing dominance and superiority over us. But one fact rang true throughout my experience of the 'giants': these were no creatures of myth but living, breathing human beings, just as we had been.

A year passed and though we had progressed far in building our defences, our trade and food supplies had suffered. It was time to specialise and specialise we did. Again, I found myself involved in the planning and again I found myself heard – for we had now embarked on the road of change, and I had the backing of Elias, the centre of everyone's universe. But I knew my popularity waned the more we changed our way of life. Nobody liked the changes at first, but slowly people began to see that we might, indeed, be able to prosper without the income of the raids. We became a centre of excellence for stone masonry and woodcraft and our cloth and weaving also became worthy of trade with the small communities we neighboured in this land ….. Another year passed and the wall was finished. Mira was delivered of her second child – another boy – and Wilfrid's heirdom grew stronger once more. Trade was not restricted to our two townships now but reached out to more far-flung places such as Elias' father's community, where before there had been little contact. I wondered what had become of his father after the cruel treatment he had received from Edvard's father. Elias never spoke of him….. I thought I would ask Martha as she had known Elias for so long, and sure enough, she had a truly horrific tale to tell:

"Oh Roslin, you have no idea how cruel and how intent on his prize King Hadred really was. Once he had an eye on something or someone there was no stopping him and he wanted Elias more than anything. Of course, it had to be under the pretence that he desired his mother for his wife rather than the boy, and so he took them both and forbade Elias' father (I believe his name was Haiden) ever to try to see them again. However, he was not content to stop there. Haiden's farmstead was very successful, and he had amassed fine stocks, which Hadred wanted for himself. Under the guise of a raid, Hadred seized and burned the farm, and mysteriously Haiden burned as well. None of the local people dared to believe that Hadred could have turned upon their kinsman, moreover they were not of the mighty High Town and so there was no redress. Of course, he kept this knowledge from Elias' mother and Elias did not learn the awful truth until he tried to be reunited with his father after he was banished. Poor Elias was devastated when he reached us and has never spoken of his father or mother since."

I shivered at the cruelty of the man. He had destroyed Elias' family for his own desires and without a thought for any of them. And what if Wilfrid were as cruel as him, what then? Given his new-found powers, what was he capable of?

But Wilfrid continued to reign as a conscientious and pragmatic leader with no rulings or actions to make us concerned. To our relief, he seemed to welcome change, as long as it brought prosperity, and so our village continued to build and to grow both in strength and reputation. In fact, there was enough respect now for people to move freely between the two communities and live where they chose. However, the most reassuring fact was that the desire for the raiding way of life appeared to have diminished under his rule.

Janmat's cures were so highly prized that he began to take on apprentices to help him in his work, and they would travel across the land on his reputation alone. Still mindful of my concerns about defence, Elias and Birne set up a warrior skills foundation – entirely built on peacekeeping. This was to become the first joint enterprise between the High Town and ourselves, as young men were to be trained in weaponry skills or their production. Under their guidance, I had every faith that the foundation would be used for defence and not for war, and Wilfrid seemed quite content with this. Yet, there was one stalemate, amongst all the achievements, which was that the ships lay idle, and I knew that this troubled not only Wilfrid but many in the High Town also.

I had been reluctant to stop feeding Marte as it had drawn us so close, but she grew up and that period in our lives was over. Soon, I began to long for another child, but the moons passed, and I did not conceive again. There was talk that I worked too hard during this time of rapid innovation, neglected my home life and that this was why I did not conceive. It was hurtful to think that I might be following in my parents' footsteps in putting my 'kingdom' first rather than my family and I tried even harder to be a good mother to Marte, who in truth seemed to be a happy and independent little child.

The wall was all but finished and a great gate was being drawn together with the finest wood from the forest. This gate was reinforced with iron struts, another of my suggestions that had been heeded by Council. Where trees had been cleared for timber, we planted a nursery of saplings near to the river so that we could always have a plentiful and close-by source of wood to work with. And so, we developed our forestry skills too, for after all, trees grew so well in our land – it seemed a waste not to harvest and manage them as well….. I believe it was this last idea of mine, proposed by me to our Council, which finally gave me the credence to be heard at the Great Council of the High Town.

It was as I was planting new trees in the nursery that the first seed of an idea took hold in my mind. I had just crossed the river in the new boat, and it reminded me of those great vessels that had carried me and all the stolen riches from my land across the sea. Suddenly, I had a thought: did we not have commodities of our own now to trade with other lands? And then another: did we not have mighty ships that could carry us over the sea and give us the opportunity to sell our wares and our skills far and wide? Ideas turned over and over in my mind and slowly began to grow into a plan for a new and prosperous future, built on our existing strengths but founded on peace. How I longed to share this vision! But I deliberated over it for days, for surely it had to be well considered, before finally deciding that it was time to talk to Elias. He listened to me without comment or interruption, and finally when I had finished said simply: "Roslin, your ideas are worthy of the Great Council, and you must be the one to present them." I couldn't believe it! – I had only meant to share them with him and our village, and now my voice could be heard by the highest in the land. There was one stumbling block however: a woman had never been heard there before. But I had Elias' backing, and Elias paved my way…..

As I entered the chamber, the silence was oppressive. All eyes were upon me and their hostility plain to see, but it was the undivided attention of Wilfrid that spurred me on. Many looked to him to turn me out, yet he stood firm, and for once I was grateful for his approbation. Moreover, this gave me newfound confidence, for I knew how to appeal to him and win his approval. Was he not the great navigator? Did he not long to use his countrymen's prowess on the waves again? Would he not excel in forming new trade routes with the knowledge he had gained of foreign lands? His quiet attention did not falter, but my speech was greeted throughout by the protest and questioning of others, and I had to stand my ground:

"How do you expect us to trade when before we seized and destroyed – how would we be greeted now?"

"It is true there may be suspicion and hostility at first, but we would have to signal our new way – with envoys bearing samples and gifts, and by day rather than by cover of night. Our ships should not instil fear either but be proud ambassadors of our intentions."

"And what of our warriors at the training camp – will they become nothing more than peasants and market tradesmen?"

I had anticipated this too; it was nostalgia still felt by many from the High Town for the old ways.

"No, like Elias and Birne, I do not believe we should lose our ability to defend our realm. I have not forgotten the night our High Town was raided. Never again. We will make peace with our neighbours, but we will not be without a trained army, willing and able to fight should the situation arise. There will be a wall and an army here to rival any other in existence, and we have a natural stone fortress of an island. Rest assured, there is a place for everyone in this new way – all skills and interests are considered, and no-one will lose out."

There wasn't a single problem or drawback I had not agonised over myself many times before, and by the end of the hearing I could tell from the discussions that followed that the mood was turning. Elias backed me in all I said, but when at last Wilfrid gave his studied yet unreserved approval to the plans, I knew that I had won them over. His eyes had never left me as I spoke, and I could tell, from his final speech, that my vision for reinstating our seafaring way of life under a new guise particularly appealed to him. Elias smiled at me as we left for our village.

"You have not only given our people a new direction but have changed the course of our history once and for all. No longer will we see ourselves as masters of domination and destruction, but will look to form new friendships and alliances, learn from our neighbouring lands, and share our skills with them. You have given us a reason for peace now Roslin. Not only that but you have given your sex a new status in our community too. From now on women may be invited to be heard at Council, and not before time! I have often thought it should be so."

As he said these words I thought of Mother once again – how would she judge me now? I had never done anything to make her proud whilst she was alive. Might I finally have won her respect, as I had my husband's, perhaps even Father's too….. or would they still disapprove of my rising above the aspirations of my sex? If only they could see me now, if only I could have had one more chance to make them proud of me.

~~~~~~

It was about the time of Mira's birthday and there was to be a grand picnic to celebrate both this and the coming of her second son. I was invited, as were all the women from our village, and I hoped that she would receive me as kindly as she had before. We had not seen as much of each other as I had hoped, following our reconciliation of two years ago, and I felt that she still did not entirely feel comfortable in my presence. We had barely spoken at the betrothal festival, but this was in part because he did not leave her side and I had no wish to be anywhere near him. I still felt that I held a peculiar fascination for him – as if he were drawn to watch me yet was careful not to. These days, however, whenever I glimpsed him, I felt I must study him also.

Without doubt, the most unsettling thing about him was the way he could stare with those searing blue eyes; it was as if nothing could escape his notice. And if his gaze met mine, I felt as if he were looking into my very soul as if he owned it. A thick crop of unruly hair often fell across his face and the skin that was not covered by his great beard was lined and weather beaten by the sea so that he looked old beyond his years. His thin lips curled slightly but rarely hastened to smile. He was not particularly tall for his race, but he had a commanding presence and only spoke or moved with carefully chosen words and gestures. I had to admit I admired his strengths as a leader and did not doubt his capability, but I supposed I could never forget that first experience of him and this was no doubt what clouded my judgement of him. Sometimes, I wondered how he treated Mira, indeed whether he showed her any of the love and respect Elias did to me, but I never had the opportunity to find out and I rarely had much opportunity to observe them together. As to her feelings for him, I couldn't help but think that his sole attraction in her eyes had been his status, and that all along that was what she had craved more than anything.

Mira always enjoyed fine weather for her picnics as if she held some power over the elements. The previous year's event had been bathed in glorious warm sunshine and it looked set to be so again. We had spent the day before gathering berries and preparing all manner of tasty morsels for the occasion and early that morning we set off to the High Town in great anticipation. As ever, it was an entirely female affair, though of course the children came too, and so we made very slow progress towards the town and were consequently very hot and bothered when we arrived. The women there brought us wonderfully refreshing drinks, though in truth mine had a strange aftertaste – too many under-ripe berries I supposed – and we rested a while before setting out again to the place where Mira and Wilfrid had been betrothed. I was just gathering my bags and about to pick up Marte once more, when I started to feel rather dizzy and nauseous – just as I had done the first time I had tasted mead. Anye noticed at once and came to my aid, taking Marte and looking at me with concern.

"What is it Roslin? You don't look at all well!"

"I'm not sure….. perhaps it is just the heat and having to carry Marte so far – she is so heavy now…"

"Sit awhile with me and we'll catch them up later."

And so, we sat and waited, but I felt gradually worse and worse until I had to lie down. Mira and Anye took me up to her chamber and laid me down. And we considered what to do.

"Don't worry about me Mira, just go with the others and I'll stay here until I feel better. I'm sure your maidservants will take good care of me."

"I will stay too."

"No Anye, if you don't mind, take Marte with you and enjoy the sunshine. I would hate to think of you missing all the fun because of me. I don't feel so bad now I'm lying down….. I'll be fine….."

The two exchanged glances but as I was so adamant, decided to go, for a while at least.

~~~~~~

As I lie here, I wonder what could have come over me so suddenly. I am so rarely ill, and I had no warning of this. Perhaps I am with child again? This thought rallies me for a moment, but I became more and more lethargic, until I can barely keep my eyes open. Suddenly, I hear a door open in the room as someone enters. Everything is a blur and I struggle to make out who it is and fail….. My head feels so heavy, and I am slowly losing consciousness. It isn't until I feel myself being picked up that I recognise that this is a man, not a maidservant, and that there is something not quite right about this……

I force myself to open my eyes again and see myself moving slowly and steadily - towards a dark hole – in the wall? – is that possible? My bearer and I are closing in upon this hole nearer and nearer – could this be Death? Has Death come to swallow me up? NO! I mustn't give myself up to Death; I must live for my child and Elias! Desperately I try to call out, but no words come, and I feel so leaden I can barely move to free myself. Then a familiar voice whispers in my ear and I feel a chill cutting through me. It is indeed Death - but in human form.

"Are you still with me Roslin? Can you see where we are going? This is where I found you – I thought you might enjoy this – we will be safe in here – no-one can see us in here and no-one can hear us…..Now you can be mine once more."

Desperately fighting now to keep conscious and escape, I now see where we are going – it is my greatest nightmare coming back to haunt me once again – the worst way I could imagine to die – enclosed in a tomb – and I will never see my beloved Elias and Marte again. A thousand images flash before my eyes: the brook with Elias, the lamb and Martha, Mira glaring at me, Anye laughing, the god-like image of Elias, Birne's kind face, little Marte….. but as they fly past, a grainy curtain gradually drapes itself over my eyes and I feel that my life must be draining away from me into darkness.

Chapter 22 'Am I still alive?'

There is a humming then a babbling like giant insects – I cannot make out anything clearly. Ah no, those are human voices but what are they saying? I strain to listen. Then I am suddenly conscious of how enormously heavy I feel – like I am sinking down, down through the bed or floor or wherever I am – sinking down into the earth. And there is a light coming from somewhere – it is hazy and opaque, but I can see a silhouette of something through it. Is it man or beast? Am I with God or below the earth? Then slowly I begin to see it is the outline of a human – it is someone I know, but I can't yet make out who it is – how strange, my brain just can't work it out. But slowly I am rising now, my limbs are becoming freer and lighter, and I am beginning to see – it is Elias, and there is Anye, and Martha and Janmat and Birne and they are all here looking down on me, and I am lying in my own bed.

I try to sit up, but my body is not ready to do this yet so I flop down again.

"Don't try to move Roslin, you've been taken ill and it's probably best you stay still and rest. Just take a little of this to drink."

He gives me some water and I feel suddenly insatiably thirsty as if I want to flush an evil spirit from my body.

Now Janmat is before me; he is looking serious. "Roslin, try to remember – did you eat or drink anything before you were taken ill?"

I try to think but can't – I can't even remember what has happened. Why I am feeling so terrible…..

"It's too early to question her. She needs to recover her strength." At this, he and the others leave me and I am alone with Elias. Suddenly, I burst into tears without knowing why. It is as if something has sapped all my strength and scrambled my brain. I just can't think straight, and I can't remember anything, and yet I know deep down inside that something awful has happened to me. He holds me tight……

A day and a night pass and I begin slowly to return to my old self, but I sleep fitfully. I keep seeing the same vision over and over again – a giant is carrying me into a deep dark hole and there is no way out again. I begin to dread going to sleep for fear of living this nightmare again. But although I am used to having nightmares, I realise that this is different to any dreams I have had before. There is no fire, no screaming, just a complete and stifling silence. It is no longer Father but the giant who confines me, and I can't understand why this has changed. It is as if Father, Mother and my people have disappeared, and I am alone with this one giant. This is now my destiny and my undoing.

~~~~~~

My friends went over and over with me the events that led to my strange illness. Anye recalled the drinks served to us as we arrived and the possibility that I may have been poisoned in some way. But for what motive? Why should anyone from the High Town wish to poison me? Could it be that someone disapproved of my newfound power that much? Could it be that I was still blamed for the loss of the old ways? Yet, both communities thrived as never before. Though no-one could answer this question, it was eventually decided that I should not go to the High Town again in case of foul play. This finally spelt the end of any kind of reconciliation I may have had with Mira. She came to visit me shortly after, full of what seemed to me genuine concern. But thereafter all contact I had with her ceased as suspicions lay unproven and I was bid not to return her visit. It also meant that I could not speak at Council again – at least for now…..

I never could remember anything about that terrible experience beyond arriving at the High Town for Mira's picnic.

It was as if none of it had ever happened, as if my mind slept for the duration of my illness…….. Then one morning I was sick again, and we feared that my strange affliction had now returned. Did this prove I had not been poisoned after all? We all dreaded what he might say, but, when Janmat examined me, he looked greatly relieved. It was no illness at all, on the contrary, I was with child again as I had first suspected! Then suddenly, in my mind, everything seemed to fall into place: so, I had been sick just as Anye had been with her first pregnancy (albeit more acutely). Strange, how this did not affect me the first time, and this didn't explain my new nightmare either, but as I arrived at this new conclusion, so my dream troubled me less and less and I felt as if an enormous weight had been taken off my mind. I was determined to work less, rest, and take care of myself for once and for the sake of my family ….. and so I waited, in excited anticipation, for the arrival of my longed for second child.

Chapter 23 'An Unexpected Visitor'

After three months exactly, the worst of my sickness left, and I felt well again. But this time I was not taking my health for granted. Despite the fact that my old energy had returned, and I felt able to take on everything as before, I was careful not to and instead spent as much time as I could with little Marte. That summer was glorious; Marte and I flourished, and we gathered an abundant harvest of food and materials for the coming winter. And by the time winter did arrive we were amply prepared for whatever the weather threw at us. Then, in the depths of the snows, my time came. I had looked forward to the birth so much, expecting it to be as miraculously happy as before. However, I was to be bitterly disappointed. Unlike my first birth experience with tiny Marte, which had been mercifully quick, this was a drawn-out and tortuous ordeal. Finally, and after one of the longest nights of my life, I gave birth to a boy. Of course, he was already a giant! A huge baby and ravenous with it. He was twice the size that Marte had been and grew bigger by the day. I spent all my time feeding him or feeding myself. Indeed, it was as if he was draining me of all my strength and taking over my life - it was relentless, and although I had my friends and family around me, so should not have felt so isolated, somehow this was not as rewarding an experience as my first time with Marte. I put it down to the cold and dark and the fact that I could not spend so much time with my husband and lively little daughter.

It was during one of those endless feeds, when all about me were at work or play, that the door of the dwelling swung open and who should stride in but Wilfrid! The sight of him unannounced and unaccompanied took me back for a moment. He towered there in the doorway, and I felt so small and vulnerable and exposed. He should not see me like this, it wasn't right and yet here he was gazing at me in that unsettling way of his. There was a prolonged silence, neither of us wishing to speak first, and then he came a little closer and stared down at the child examining him carefully.

"So, you have given Elias a son. A fine, strapping boy by all accounts."

"Yes, he is strong and healthy – all we could wish for. I am sorry but I am not sure that Elias will be home for a while yet – you had best go to the Round House where they are….."

"I have not come to see Elias; I have come to see you – and the child. I wish to bring my….. our congratulations…."

He paused then started to move away until he was nearly in the doorway again. I thought he was going to leave, but then he turned,

"Roslin, I would like to see you and the child again. I know that you have despised me from that first night long ago, but you must understand that I am different now, I want things to be….. different between us."

"What do you want from me Wilfrid?..... Does Mira know you are here?" He chose only to answer the first question,

"I wish to see you and the child and that is all….. Roslin, I have never harmed you and I never harmed your mother – if I had, I would not have sons to my name."

So he still believed my mother's prophecy – I was surprised as he had no proof that she had had such power, yet even as I thought this, I remembered that Edvard had never had a son and yet Wilfrid had, and maybe that was proof enough. Maybe he thought by asserting this, it would in some way win my approval but why would he want that? How could he delude himself into thinking he had not harmed me that night of the raid, the legacy of which had been my fear of men, until Elias had shown me a different way. Moreover, his and Edvard's actions were undoubtedly the cause of my continuing nightmares. My eyes narrowed as I thought this, and I considered rebuking him and telling him how wounded I still was, yet as I saw him there almost cowering by the door I paused; I wanted him to be different, I wanted not to fear him anymore, and above all I wanted to forgive this arrogant man. But something deep inside bubbled to the surface and I burst out:

"You have no idea how much harm you have done to me! Though it may not be visible, I will always carry the pain in my heart. To this day I still have nightmares about that terrible night and what you did to me ….. But I am willing to forgive you, Wilfrid, if you promise, on your life, never to inflict pain on me or my family again."

He winced visibly as I spoke, then replied earnestly,

"Indeed, I swear upon my life that I will never harm you or your family Roslin. Please forgive me and let me do for your son what I will do for….. my own. He will follow in my line.

I believed he genuinely thought this would please me, but I was immediately worried again. I had heard words like these before. "Whatever do you mean Wilfrid?"

"That he will follow in my line….. That is all….." And with that he quickly bade me farewell and left.

As soon as Elias returned, I relayed all that had been said and saw him frown at the last of it.

"He is not going to try to take the child away as Edvard threatened. He could never do that now,"

"I don't think he intends to, Elias, there was no mention of such a thing, but his reasons for coming here at all do puzzle me. He is a strange one."

"Yes, I cannot believe there is any reason to fear – he has two sons already. I believe this is an attempt at reconciliation Roslin, he wishes to make peace by recognising our son."

Wilfrid continued to visit me about once every moon, always

unannounced and always alone. Mira must have learnt of this, but although she visited her family occasionally and even me once or twice, they never came together. He assured me that his recognition of our son was part of our alliance, which pleased Elias though he never acknowledged it, but I was not so easily reassured. There was something not quite right about it, but I could never fathom what it was. I never encouraged Wilfrid's visits; on the contrary I was as cool and offhand as possible with him. But they continued nevertheless and over time I got used to them, assuming he simply wanted to honour his agreement with Elias and show how he held the truce; yet this did not explain why his visits to me were always private. I never lost my mistrust of him either, though he never gave me reason to fear him again either and so I dreaded him coming less and less. In fact, I began to feel strangely flattered by his unwavering attention – he was always so willing to listen to me and actively encouraged me to speak my mind. He appeared to grow fond of little Eddval too, which might have concerned me more if it hadn't been for the fact that he had two sons of his own, and later a little girl, and never threatened to take him away from us. As for Mira, she remained distant and I sensed she was keeping something from me, though I never felt able to question her about it. Could I detect a hint of jealousy – over her husband's visits to me perhaps? It was difficult to tell with Mira - she was always so proud and regal, and lived so sumptuously - how could she be jealous of me when I had so little in comparison?

As he grew, Eddval continued to be big and strong with a healthy, fair complexion but I couldn't believe how my two children could be so different! Little Marte, with her dark hair and eyes, was so lively and talkative whilst he was so quiet and brooding..... and sometimes, sometimes I would catch him just sitting there, silently watching me and Marte with those brilliant blue eyes.

PART II

THE GIANTS' CAUSE

Introduction

Wilfrid is now protector to the throne until Njall comes of age. This power was invested in him by Elias, stepbrother to Edvard, the former King. Elias presides over the Low Town now called Lowton. Wilfrid is supposedly only Njall's guardian, but Njall is in fact his and Mira's son.

Edvard, the former King, gave Roslin to his stepbrother Elias, having abducted her from her homeland during a raid. Wilfrid has secretly longed for her for some time and has in fact fathered one of her children, Eddval, though no-one knows this.

Anye is Roslin's best friend.

Family Tree

Mira and Wilfrid have 2 sons and 1 daughter: **Njall** is in fact Wilfrid's son, though Mira and Wilfrid have always pretended he was the son of Edvard the former King. **Valdis** is their second son and **Larna** is their only daughter.

Roslin and Elias have 1 daughter and 2 sons: **Marte, Eddval** and **Haiden.** Eddval is actually Wilfrid's son, though only Wilfrid knows this.

Anye and Rogen have 1 son and 1 daughter: **Per** is the oldest of all the children whilst **Patrisia** is the youngest.

Chapter 24 'A step too far'

Feeling as awkward and uncomfortable as ever, Per glanced furtively from friend to friend to gage their reaction:

This was going too far now. It was dangerous! I gazed across the river and then back again at my friends. Why did they always do this? Why did <u>she</u> always do this? Why couldn't we just laugh and chat, or do normal things; why were we always testing each other? Well, from the way they were looking at her, with heads held high, I could tell no-one would back out of this one. Only I was left questioning my ability – as usual – and balking at the risk involved.

"Don't you want to then?" Marte's eyes were flashing with excitement. She was so sure of herself, so strong and agile. And yet I doubted anyone could do it, let alone Marte. She was the smallest girl I knew – that slight frame and indomitable spirit no doubt inherited from her mother; the beautiful, dark-haired woman who had been brought here from another land far away. Now as I looked at her, I wished she wasn't so daring, so challenging. Was she testing me, us, or was she simply pushing herself to the limit? It was impossible to tell, and how could I stop her now when the others were so desperate to join in? Then, as if to call my bluff, Eddval removed himself from the proceedings, brushing it off as if it were the most trivial thing in the world. Strange though, I'd have thought he'd be the first to want to impress his sister. They were so close.

"Do you know what, I'm not sure I could be bothered to break my neck today. Ask me when I've got less work to do. Plus, I'm supposed to be at training by sunrise tomorrow and it will be dark soon. You go ahead and I'll watch, if you're quick – I'll beat anything you do, tomorrow…." And with that he was off, rather too quickly I have to say, to sit further up the bank as a bystander…..

That just left me, Njall, Valdis and little Haiden – Marte as always would be the only girl involved. Larna, wide-eyed, had already blurted out she would get into trouble for spoiling her clothes, though in truth she looked petrified at the mere thought of climbing so high, and Patrisia, my sister, was definitely too young – I wouldn't hear of her trying it.

"So, who wants to go first – or shall I, as I suggested it?" cried Marte.

There was a pause as everyone thought how to work this to their advantage. Then Njall piped up:

"Of course, it should be me as I will be ruler one day so I should lead the way."

Strangely, Marte glanced at me next, not Valdis, who should after all be next, being Njall's younger brother. But I remained tongue-tied.

"Alright Njall, you can be first, but I will need to demonstrate and then we will see if you can do it better..."

All the time she said this she was darting looks at me, daring me to say something. Patrisia nudged me, obviously keen that I should not lose face in this latest competition. Eventually, all I could think of to say was,

"I'm not sure I can do it. Actually Marte, I'm not sure anyone should do it. It's too dangerous and I don't want you to try. How about we …."

"No! You've no need to worry about me Per, I know what I'm capable of and I can assure you I can do it. Just watch!"

She pushed past me as she said this, obviously disappointed that I was not fool enough to join her in this, her most ill-advised dare yet. I tried to grab her arm, but she squirmed away and stared at me defiantly, "and don't try to stop me."

Marte made up for her lack of height by being supremely

confident and impulsive. The exact opposite of me. She was also every bit as beautiful as her mother and everyone adored her, especially Eddval and Njall, who were forever vying for her attention when they were together, though Eddval obviously had the advantage of proximity as he was her brother and lived with her. Oh, and I was supposed to be her best friend; well, our mothers were best friends, so we had grown up together, but I often thought she only said this for the sake of our mothers. Sometimes I wished I were more like her so she might like me more. I was 14 now and the oldest of our 'clan' and quite possibly the most boring and unadventurous too. Marte was less than a year younger than me, but she was such a free spirit, and so intent on having adventures. In a way she was like Valdis, independent and strong willed; and yet she could be so kind and thoughtful too, like a sister, I thought ruefully.

As she climbed, the others watched awe-struck, she was so agile, swinging herself up from branch to branch far quicker than any of us could have done. We could see, now, that she had the advantage with her size. When she reached the top of the tree, she beamed down at us and laughed at my concerned face.

"See how easy it is! Now watch this..." and she carefully edged herself across the branch that overhung the river far above. It was at this point that I closed my eyes and prayed that the branch would not give. Had she done this before? Did she know it would take her weight? And if it took her slight frame, would it take ours?

"You're not watching!" again this was directed at me.

I gazed up at her and tried not to cringe as I saw her gather herself like a beast about to pounce, and then leap across the divide to the tree on the other side! Unbelievable that she could expect any of us to do that! She just about caught hold of the branch and it dipped perilously down as she tried to gain a better hold on it. After a breath-taking moment, I couldn't help but admire the audacity of the girl; whatever was it that made her even think she could do this in the first place? Then she was scrabbling along the branch hand on hand – I could scarcely bear to look – but somehow, she managed to get to the trunk. She had indeed crossed the river 'without swimming, rowing, or walking over the bridge!'. It was incredible! As she set her feet down on the branch below, how she smiled as she waved down at us. Quite an achievement!

I thought the danger was over, I thought she had managed to do it after all, despite my misgivings, but she was still high up. All of a sudden, there was a cry, and she was tumbling down, followed by another cry as she crashed into a branch on her descent, and then a splash as she landed half in the water, half on the bank in a crumpled heap.

I was the first to wade through the water and reach her. It wasn't particularly deep, now we were in full summer, and had not really broken her fall, so I hoped against hope that the branch had. At first, she was silent and still and there was a terrible moment when I thought she might be dead, though in truth she had not fallen so very far. Then she stirred and opened her eyes and my heart leapt – she was still alive! Something instinctive told me not to move her, though I longed to put my arms around her. She stirred again and I dreaded that she might be paralysed or worse, but then she managed to sit up unaided and rubbed her shoulder and arm. It was bleeding from where the branch had caught her. The others rushed up and now Njall and Eddval were on their knees beside her. Patrisia was sobbing uncontrollably, and Larna had her arm around her trying to console her. Valdis stood back from the others and looked at a loss as to what to do or say. Eddval and Njall were now vying to be the closer to her, as usual.

Oblivious to all this Marte moaned, "What a fool I've been!"

"Come now, we must get you back to the village. Can you stand up or shall I carry you?" Njall asked, taking charge as always. Eddval glared at him and practically shouted, "She is my sister so I shall take her back thank you very much." And since he stood as tall as Njall, though he was two years younger, he was certainly big enough to carry her.

Whilst they were arguing, I tore off my sleeve and bound the cloth around her arm, stemming the bleeding. She looked up at me gratefully and whispered, "I should have listened to you Per, you were right." And then to all of us, "Please don't tell my parents, let me talk to them first."

"You did cross the river as you said," I replied, before Njall or Eddval could lift her up. I did so regret not holding her whilst I had the chance – now I knew they wouldn't let me. Njall looked at me, surprised that I should be so supportive after my earlier chastisement, before adding, "Yes she did, but enough is enough. Let this put a stop to these challenges now Marte; you've got nothing to prove to us. You know we could never have done what you did just then." And with that he scooped her up (fortunately she had not broken anything but was just badly bruised) and carried her off without a backward glance, Eddval scurrying along beside them, leaving me with Valdis and the girls trailing behind.

Later that evening, as I called in on Marte to see how she was, Roslin was smiling and had her arm around her daughter by the fireside. I was certainly not expecting to see her forgiven so easily, but they beckoned me in to sit by them and Roslin explained:

"I was just the same when I was her age. I could never be still but longed for adventure and was often in scrapes like this myself. But in those days I acted alone whilst you, Marte, have your friends to think of – no more dares like this again, do you hear me? …. Marte is unfortunately just as I was – I only hope she survives long enough to become a mother – then she might settle a little!"

They were both laughing now, and I was soothed by the atmosphere of relief and the strong bond of affection between them. Roslin was a wonderful person, so gentle and dignified always and I couldn't imagine her ever having been as excitable as Marte. Still, she had the responsibility of her family and her friend's illness to bear now, not to mention her occasional appearances at Council to prepare for. There was no time left for adventure!

Chapter 25 'Moving on…'

I was 18, and my apprenticeship was finally complete. I could now go forth as a fully-fledged doctor and set up my own travelling practice. As I stood ready to leave, Janmat came over and patted me on the back. He had been such a conscientious and thorough teacher, impossible to rattle and a great inspiration to me. How I wanted to be like him, calm and proficient in all he did. Everybody revered and trusted him; though he could not cure all, there was no doubt he did everything in his power to do so. Apparently, my own mother owed him her life following my difficult birth; she had lost several babies since and had developed a chronic illness after having Patrisia, which he had tried everything he knew to allay. There had been times when we had thought she may be finally cured – long spells of good health as in her youth - only for her to relapse once again for seemingly no reason whatsoever. In fact, it had been the desire to find a cure for my mother that had encouraged me to start my training in the first place.

"Well, Per, I will miss you, you have undoubtedly been my finest student, but the time has come for you to go forth and broaden your experience. Remember, you will always be a student of life and sometimes you will make mistakes, but never lose faith in your abilities. Sometimes, as you know, fate has other plans for our patients, but you are armed with all that I know. Go forth now and learn more, never close your mind to study."

Unlike most of my fellow students, I had decided not to travel away on one of the ships searching for business on foreign shores but to begin my journeying closer to home in case I were needed here. Mother was frail, and I could not leave all the caring to Father, Patrisia and her friend Roslin. This way I knew I could come back at regular intervals. And this way I could still see Marte too. These days she had taken to listening to the debates of the Great Council and was no doubt there now. She probably didn't want to say goodbye any more than

I did.

I was wrong about that though. Just as I was about to set off up the path leading to the High Town, she appeared, running to catch up with me....

"Per, I'm so glad I caught you before you left. I thought you might try and sneak off without saying goodbye. Good luck and don't forget to come back soon. We will miss you." And she hugged me so tight I thought she would take my breath away. I wished I had an excuse to be held like this every day, but this would be the last occasion for quite some time.

"I'll be back soon, don't worry. But send for me if you need me - for anything at all."

"I will, Per." She looked deep into my eyes and for a moment I thought she might be about to kiss me, but I tore myself away, I couldn't prolong the goodbyes any further, and was off up the path again as quickly as I could and without a backward glance.

~~~~~~

Marte remained surrounded by her kinsfolk and yet she felt strangely alone:

When I returned home, Eddval looked up and read my gloomy look at once.

"You're not going to mope all day long because he's gone now are you? I doubt we'll see him back here for a long time, so you'd better get over it quickly. In any case, we need to concentrate on our own calling and study as much as we can in preparation."

Eddval was convinced that he and I would one day rule over Lowton. Our township was smaller and the buildings less imposing, by far, than Highton; nevertheless, it had a boundary wall with a sturdy iron-girded gate too. But I feared he was wrong: Father would never let Eddval and I rule here when he had always wanted the two townships to be united under one ruler. In any case Wilfrid was in power until next year when Njall came of age and then it would be largely up to him, though I knew there was a decree of old that bound the both of them to allegiance with my father in whatever they did. I had never quite understood why Father should have that power, when he seemed to want none, and I had asked Mother to explain it to me long ago.

"Your father was the adopted brother of Njall's father, Edvard, and on his death could, by rights, have claimed the throne. He was so popular with the people that he could even have laid claim before that, but as you can see your father had no desire for power. He was happy living humbly here with us. However, his past experiences taught him that a ruler's power could be misused unchecked, and so he decided to set up a Council which could question what the ruler decreed and could even make suggestions that he would have to hear. And that is how we live now Marte, as one, though we are geographically divided."

This all made sense but for the geographical divide, which to me and Eddval made governing the two separate townships difficult, especially as Lowton had a Council of its own over which my father still presided.

"You and I – we could rule this place together one day Marte. That way Njall could still be ruler of his own domain and have Valdis as his second."

Inwardly, I was delighted that Eddval wanted so much to rule jointly with me, as our land had never before had a female ruler. Indeed, our Mother had been the first woman ever to speak at the Great Council and I was determined that I, too, could change the course of our history. Eddval's faith in me was pivotal to this confidence I had; I couldn't have wanted a better brother. Not only that but he was so considerate and aware of my every need unlike all the other boys I knew – well, with one exception – Per.

Time passed and Eddval grew more and more restless living at home. He did not see eye to eye with Father these days and they quarrelled about the silliest of things, though mostly about Eddval's ideas for Lowton one day. Father tried to involve Eddval more at his and Birne's 'Warrior' Training Foundation, but though he showed promise there, he had set his eyes on a higher role than taking over the Foundation and would not budge in his mindset. Then one day, Eddval decided that he had had enough of arguing. He started to spend all his spare time gathering wood and stone and then without asking for permission, started to build his own dwelling. Fortunately, for once, Father approved of the idea and the location, so they ended up building it together and move he did. The bickering stopped immediately, and harmony was restored to our home once more. For a while, this arrangement seemed to suit our family very well, but I missed Eddval and began to spend more and more time away from home myself with him, talking excitedly about our future and of Lowton. Without the caution and interjections from Father, Eddval was free to create his new vision unchecked, and I became more and more enthralled in his ideas for our future. Admittedly, the thought that Father was not there to dampen our spirits fuelled the excitement and added an element of risk that I had always craved. Sadly, in those days I could not see how well Eddval knew me; how intricately he knew my strengths, weaknesses, and desires, and thus tailored his vision to flatter my ambitions and confidence.

But one evening, when I was about to leave for Eddval's dwelling, Father took me by surprise with his words. I had not anticipated his continued concern.

"Marte, I am happy for you and Eddval to take your places at Council, but I do not feel it is right that you should be planning to undermine the rule of Njall, who I have every faith will make a very good King. If you visit your brother, you must be back by dusk and there will be no talk of ruling this township, do you understand?"

It wasn't only Father's disapproval of my allegiance with Eddval that made me start to feel guilty whenever I visited him now. I began to realise that others were not happy about our relationship either. This was probably something to do with a conversation I overheard between my mother and Haiden, who always seemed to be on Father's side in every argument.

"I just don't like the way he is with her these days – it's as if he has her on the end of a string to pull along as he wishes, and she will follow him wherever he goes. But Marte is the eldest! She should know better than to always take his side no matter what, even when she can see he's wrong. But no, he can't put a foot wrong in her eyes. He is so marvellous and only because she thinks he would share power with her. I don't believe he ever would."

"Haiden, as you know, Eddval is third in line to the throne and that is all. He will have his place at Council and may well act as Njall's second or take on the management of the Warrior Training Foundation one day, but it is very unlikely he will do otherwise. As to Marte, well she is just taking a keen interest in the running of our community, and will no doubt speak at Council one day as I do. Don't worry, they are young and have their ideals – I was like that once and every bit as headstrong as Marte."

"But that's just it, Mother, she isn't headstrong at all when she's with <u>him</u>. She is under his control and there is no way she isn't. I just don't think it's right."

"Haiden, they're close, that's all. Are you maybe a little jealous of their closeness perhaps?" she added with a twinkle in her eye.

"No, I'm most certainly not. I just hate the way they look at each other. I would never treat my sister like that!"

And with that he stormed out, no doubt angered by mother saying he might be jealous, though at the time, I couldn't help thinking he might be. It left me feeling a little uncomfortable though. Was he right about Eddval's hold over me? It was true I felt a duty to him as he was so kind to me, and he was only my younger brother. Nevertheless, I began to feel uneasy when we were alone together after that. I couldn't exactly see what was wrong with it, after all we were just a brother and sister who had great plans for the future together. However, my visits became less and less frequent….. and I saw that Eddval noticed and was displeased.

Chapter 26 'An Unprecedented Event'

Eddval and I were not the only ones who felt at odds with our lives from time to time. There was no-one more disaffected or more seemingly out of place than Valdis. When we were children he had often tried to think of bigger and better adventures than me, though his older brother or I usually stole the limelight. Sometimes when we were young, I used to look at him – he was about my age, only a little younger – and wonder whether he and I might be betrothed one day as we appeared to strive for the same things. And yet we did not – for he was a cold one – never keen to talk or laugh with anyone else and he usually kept himself to himself. This I couldn't understand for though I loved adventure I couldn't bear to be alone and craved attention. He was certainly the more handsome of the two brothers, but he had none of his brother's charm or wit. Indeed, Njall always knew what to do and say in a situation, whilst his brother would just look on uncomfortably as if he wished he could melt away. I liked Njall and felt these days that he liked me too, but he was nothing like me either. Still it was flattering to think that a future King might one day take an interest in me. It might work well in our favour if Eddval and I were to rule Lowton.

It was the beginning of summer and time for the ships to set off in search of trade with lands far away. I was glad Per had chosen not to go with them as there were times when the voyagers did not return. Sometimes, they chose to stay wherever they landed and set up home there. I didn't like the thought that Per might never come back. I hated the thought that I might lose my dear friend altogether; separation was bad enough.

Now, Valdis had always shown great promise with his seafaring training and wished, like his father and grandfather before him, to go on such a journey. But no-one was prepared for the fact that, at such a young age, he would take himself off as a stowaway on one of the boats! Everyone was horrified that he should have done such a thing – an heir to the kingdom as well – his father would never have allowed it (but this would not have concerned Valdis at all as he was always caught up in his own world, without a care for anyone else). Sure enough, when Wilfrid learned of this, he was furious, and a search party was immediately sent out. Records of each boat's voyage were kept assiduously, so his passage could be traced fairly easily, or so they thought. However, Valdis had planned for this and had escaped the ship as soon as it had reached its first port of call, knowing that this would make him more difficult to find as he would have longer to get away before his absence was detected. It was an age before they eventually traced and brought him back home, and they definitely should have punished him more than they did, for I am sure it only made him more determined than ever to leave again….. if he were not restless enough before this journey, the events that followed surely pushed him away.

Unfortunately, Valdis was not all the search party brought back with them. His attempted journey had tragic consequences for Highton. Unbeknownst to him he had taken refuge in a place where a strange and sudden sickness was slowly making its sinister way through the local population. On hearing of this, his rescue party had wanted to leave as quickly as possible, but they were charged with finding Valdis first so leave they could not. Now as I mentioned before, Valdis had no desire to return home to face the wrath of his father, so their task was long and drawn out. By the time they found him, the disease had managed to secretly catch hold of one of them. He carried it across the seas without a single sign or symptom – indeed it was as cunning a stowaway on the return journey as Valdis himself had been on the outward one. It was not until they had been back for some days that the first case manifested itself and then there was no stopping its fury. No one was safe, not only the old and frail or indeed the very young were its victims. It would suddenly appear where before the sufferer had been completely fit and well, and seemed to follow no particular course. Mercifully for some, the invalid might be taken in the night with barely any symptoms at all; unluckily for others, they would suffer a raging fever with convulsions then fall into a stupor, never to recover again, and only occasionally would anyone escape without consequence. No-one knew how it spread or what caused it – only that it was unerring in its path of destruction. Never before in living memory, had our people suffered such a terrible outbreak of such a devastating disease. I supposed we owed it to the purity of our water, or the severity of our winters, or simply our isolation on this rocky isle.

The disease had no respect for status either; it even had the audacity to afflict the most important family in the land. Though, ironically, Valdis, the source of the plague, was one of the lucky ones and hardly suffered at all, the rest of his family fell gravely ill. Soon there was barely anyone left in the royal household to care for them as their servants and seconds fell sick too. A desperate plea for help was sent from Highton, and an emergency meeting held in Lowton as to what to do. This was a raging epidemic and a serious threat to the heirs of the kingdom. Yet we at Lowton had not been touched by the sickness! Should we go to help them or stay here where the disease had yet to take a hold? As we met at Council, Father appointed Janmat to speak, and all eyes were fixed on him as no-one doubted he was the highest authority in such matters.

"Until now, I had never before encountered this terrible disease, but I have since carefully observed it, and it is my firm belief that it is passed on through proximity. This is why no-one but I has been to Highton recently and I believe that is why we are clear of the disease. Now, what I have to say may seem like heresy and cruelty, but I believe there is nothing to be gained by us going to them in any number – there is no antidote and no plan of care that we know for sure will help. Therefore, I say that I will go, but that our people should stay here, within these walls, and wait for the disease to take its course. We can of course supply goods and medicines but leave them at the gates. I alone will go to the royal household and to those well enough to care for those that are not. I will try to ensure that they work to my instructions. That is all we can do for now."

All stared at Janmat – all knew he was intending to risk his own life for ours and those of any survivors in Highton. His judgement may indeed seem harsh on our neighbours, but what use would we be if we too became ill and died? His logic had spoken, and yet the Council struggled to agree to his proposal. He was praised for his courage, but there was obvious concern that we could lose a great man and our best doctor to the disease. However, Janmat stood firm and assured them that he would take every precaution he could not to become ill. He also suggested that communication be maintained throughout, though from a distance, via those who would bring provisions. Birne at once volunteered to head them, standing firm by his partner's decision. And so, it was finally agreed that Janmat should make the ultimate sacrifice by returning, alone, to Highton. It was a bitter and tragic parting as we all knew he may never come back alive. We were all reluctant to see him go but none more than Birne, his greatest friend and partner of many years. Then, to add to my consternation, someone suggested that Janmat's apprentices should be called back to help him. I felt my heart grow cold at the thought that Per might be the first to be summoned back as he had deliberately not travelled far. I had not reckoned on this and hoped against hope that this would not be agreed! Janmat considered this for a moment, and I held my breath, praying that he be spared. Eventually, he replied that he wouldn't hear of it whilst he remained alive, he did not want to waste any young lives unnecessarily, especially as they might be able to take his place should he fall to the disease. With this he was gone without further ado, and we were left waiting…..

We waited, practically walled into our township, for three whole moons. Every day we dreaded that news would come of Janmat's death, and yet we resisted the temptation to follow him into danger. We were largely self-sufficient and were donating as much as could be carried by messenger, in food and medicine, yet we felt we should be doing more for them. There was practically no contact now between the two communities except for the occasional much anticipated messages sent by Janmat, who remained alive despite all our forebodings. Any messengers, headed by Birne, would ride up to the gate, beat on it and we would all be hailed to the open square. It was soon decided that this should happen at the same time each day, so that both communities could be ready for news, or provisions. At these times, my heart would be in my mouth lest the worst should have happened to Janmat, and his two remaining apprentices might need to be summoned.

Every now and then great palls of smoke rose into the air, and we wondered at this – did it spell further disaster? But the daily messengers said this was all part of Janmat's 'cure' and that we were bid to stay where we were and to keep sending provisions.

At first they talked of progress, with fewer new cases, and that Janmat's policy of minimal contact was working, but we were finally shocked to learn of two pivotal casualties of the disease: first Mira, Wilfrid's wife and Njall's mother, and then Wilfrid, the guardian of the throne himself. There was a hushed silence as all heard this terrible news – and what of Njall – the heir apparent? We were told he seemed to be recovering, though it was not yet certain he would survive. Valdis had never really succumbed and his sister, also seemed to be better though still very weak. Then everyone wanted to hear of Janmat, and we were greeted with the assurance that he was still alive and well and thinking to return; as long as there were no more fresh cases and only when he was sure he did not carry the disease himself, undetected as it had arrived on our shores.

As ever, I was relieved that Janmat lived another day. Mother too was moved, and I noticed that she was very quiet and thoughtful that night. She was, of course, close to Martha,

Mira's mother who lived alone now, and was old and frail. She had practically become part of our family and I knew she still missed her daughter, who had long ago left our community for Highton and a better life. Poor Martha would no doubt be devastated by this news. Moreover, I knew Mira and mother had been distant friends, but I had always wondered why her husband Wilfrid had visited mother here so frequently as we were growing up, and never accompanied by his wife. (Indeed, despite her mother living here, Mira had hardly come at all and had always found an excuse to leave again as soon as possible). He rarely wished to speak to anyone else, though he was always tolerant of Eddval's aspirations, and never attended our Council unless specifically invited, or if Mother was speaking. I wondered that Father never seemed to be bothered by this – or perhaps he was – and tolerated it for some reason. The bond between him and Mother was so strong, I supposed nothing could break it. In any case, Mother remained deeply troubled by Mira's death and maybe Wilfrid's as well. I couldn't tell.

~~~~~~

It took a while for Roslin to come to terms with her feelings. There was somehow no logic to them….

I was free of him at last, but why did I feel so bereft – as if a part of me was missing? I had never really understood why he visited me so continually. Was it that I was the one conquest he never made? Did that bother him? Well if it did, he never showed it, if anything he seemed happy just to see me…. And Eddval.

Elias never knew what I meant to Wilfrid but then I never understood either. So humble and contrite to the end yet so dominant and cruel at the beginning – did I ever care for him? I am not sure I was ever able to forgive him that first encounter, and yet he became such a prominent feature in my life. Had he truly transformed from that sadistic giant into a conscientious and principled human being as guardian to the throne? He certainly never gave us cause to think otherwise. Did he feel he had a duty to protect me as well, following Mother's curse? And would he really have handed over his power to Njall, as he had been due to do, or had fate conveniently determined this for him? He was certainly a caring father to the end; not only that, but he treated Eddval better than his own father did sometimes – strangely Wilfrid always seemed to identify with him, even when we could not. Well we will never know now whether or how his guardianship would have ended….

….. Elias knew that nothing happened between us of course, and I would never lie to him – but what did Mira believe all those years I wonder? She must have rejoiced, like I did, that there was no enmity between the two men, and that Wilfrid made no attempt to strike Elias down. Did she suspect there was something between me and Wilfrid though? No, she would surely have accompanied him on his visits to me if she had suspected anything. None of us was ever the wiser as to his feelings for me. But yes, I suppose I will miss him, or perhaps it will be the attention he vested in me and his kindness to Eddval that I will miss? I simply don't know…

Chapter 27 'In Sickness and in Health'

Marte and her family rose to the occasion:

There was so much to discuss and consider now. How much more aid would Highton require and how could we provide this? What would become now of Njall and his brother and sister? Would Njall be fit enough to take his rightful place without his stepfather's guidance? He was almost of age now - but would he fully recover his health? We would have to wait and see. And see we did the following month when Janmat returned once more, bringing with him the bereaved children of Wilfrid and Mira. The crisis was over, and the disease appeared to have been beaten, but they were weak and heartbroken – and so they came to regain their strength with us.

The death toll had been high and almost everyone had lost someone. Janmat was given a special award for bravery and a ceremony was held in his honour. Not all from Highton had accepted his policy to protect Lowton and keep us from attending to the sick, but all recognised what he had achieved. The disease had been practically eradicated now and had never taken hold in Lowton. Certainly, whatever Janmat had done seemed to have worked. He spoke of how he had built a temporary camp outside the wall for survivors and the unafflicted. He told us of the horror of having to divide families who desperately wanted to tend to their sick relatives. He stood firm by his decree that we were right to stay away, only leave provisions, and pray for a miracle.

Njall was still weak, and Valdis deemed too young, so Elias, Birne and Janmat took charge of setting the community back on its feet. A few other children were brought by Janmat to stay in Lowton, and our numbers temporarily swelled, and our previous absence was in the main forgiven. There was some concern, at first, that we might now be bringing the disease into our community, but Janmat was certain we would be safe, as he had been careful only to bring survivors of the disease – like our young visitors. It was his belief that the evil had been expelled from their bodies and could not return. He confessed that he, too, had had a mild form of the illness, but that he had recovered quickly, and had not ever been incapacitated. As the weeks and moons progressed, free of the pestilence, our minds were further reassured. I had thought there would be more resentment from the survivors, but we had Janmat to thank for their attitude, as he had spoken to them as well and told them how we had been instructed to play our part. We could only help from a position of strength and isolation. In any case they were grateful for their lives.

And so Eddval could no longer enjoy his homestead alone. Njall and Valdis moved in with him whilst Larna stayed with us. Gone were our quiet times together when we would plan our future and instead, we were tasked with looking after our friends. Eddval resented this lack of privacy, but the fact that our 'guests' were deemed higher in status than us riled Eddval no end. When of old there had been a physical distance between us, Eddval had coped with his situation in life well enough, but now that they lived amongst us and he was expected to care for an invalid who mattered more than he did, he found it extremely difficult to bear. Not only did he find caring for Njall onerous, but he hated it even more if I showed Njall any kindness. Njall preferred my company and actively sought my attention at every opportunity. It was at times like this, when Eddval and Njall were at loggerheads over who was to care for him, that Valdis and I would be caught in their battle of wills where neither of us wished to be! Although they took pains to speak civilly to one another, I felt sure that somebody's temper would snap soon, and that this atmosphere was really not conducive to Njall's recovery at all. I also felt sorry for Valdis; after all, he must be fully aware that if he hadn't tried to run away, none of this would have happened. He was even more solitary and brooding than before, and I had to do something to make things better between us for all our sakes.

But before I had a chance to act, Valdis effectively removed himself from the conflict altogether by moving back to his empty home in Highton. He had no need for company, his health was intact and as it happened there was still one servant, who had managed to survive the epidemic, who could attend to him. Still, I hoped that he would be strong enough to bear his guilt and grief alone as there was no persuading him to come back. So now it was down to me to try to resolve the differences between Eddval and Njall. At supper one evening, when we were all gathered around the fire and Eddval and Njall were staring daggers at each other following yet another altercation, I spoke up,

"I have been wondering, Father, as Eddval struggles on his own to look after Njall, whether it might not be a good idea if Eddval and I lived together and Njall stayed here with you. We would be happy to come over every day to do our part in looking after him and Larna and I feel it would be better if the brothers and sisters could be together."

I noticed that Haiden objected to this idea, no doubt because it left him out, but I felt his feelings would have to be sacrificed on this occasion to restore the peace.

Father looked at us all and considered this for a moment before he replied.

"It may not be long before Njall is strong enough to take up his position as leader, but I cannot send him back until I am sure he has a good and loyal second. Eddval, I cannot help but feel that Marte is trying to keep you apart because you cannot get on with one another and that does not herald a good partnership. How can I consider you for Njall's second if you are continually at his throat?"

Eddval looked taken aback for a moment. What was this? Why was Father suggesting such a thing when Valdis was the obvious candidate for such a position as he had been all along? Eddval had no wish to be anyone's second – his sights were on higher things as Father was very well aware – the governance of the Lowton, with me....

"You cannot possibly still be considering me for such a position after all that I have said? You know what I aspire to, Father, and you have completely disregarded Marte in saying this too! How could you suggest such a thing?"

"Because I am sure that Valdis would be better suited to another role in our kingdom – he is a fine seafarer and could manage our affairs in trade so well, but I cannot see him as ruler of this kingdom, nor even as second in command. And I do not feel he wishes to have such a role either."

There was a silence – we all knew that Valdis did not have the leadership qualities that either his brother or Eddval or indeed I had shown for that matter. Moreover, he rarely spoke and never engaged in conversation, even less so since he had lost his parents. However, if Father were prepared to consider things from Valdis' point of view, why could he not see Eddval's? This was just leading to another impasse between Father and Eddval, and it had been my intervention that had brought it to the fore! But just as I was regretting having said anything at all, Mother who was ever the peacemaker, suddenly interjected,

"That is a good idea of yours Marte – for you and Eddval to stay together and Njall to move in with us. It would give your father the opportunity to talk with him and prepare him for his role, and you two get on so well. It would indeed be a better arrangement."

Father always listened to Mother and so my idea was accepted after all, though I could tell that Haiden was not happy about it. But at the time, he was on his own there.

Slowly, Njall and his sister recovered their health, and though he never fully recovered the strength he had had before the illness, mentally, Njall was more than ready to take up his new position. Time had healed, to some extent, the loss of his stepfather, but Njall wanted desperately to honour his memory. And he began by celebrating his late stepfather's achievements on the occasion of his investiture. Everyone was impressed by his selflessness, not least Father, who was very pleased with Njall and seemed to have great faith in him. A beautiful new sword was commissioned for the occasion by Elias himself, engraved with the finest carvings that symbolised strength, honesty and integrity, all the values that Father admired more than anything. I have to confess to feeling a little jealous when I saw it. We had never received such a gift, though I knew Father loved us more than his life and had always showered us with affection. And though I scolded Eddval for saying this showed where Father's favour really lay, I privately felt this too.

Larna recovered even better than her brother and was back to her usual self, preening and beautifying herself at every opportunity. She really was an expert in doing nothing in particular. While at first I believed she was simply not capable of anything due to her illness, I soon discovered that she was actually quite used to letting others do things for her. I recalled Mother's tales of how she had lived in a royal household in her former land and how she had been expected to do nothing for herself. Mother couldn't abide laziness in us and chided us constantly if she thought any of us were not doing our part. Yet Larna seemed to have been brought up that way and, to add to my annoyance, could get away with murder sometimes as our guest. I had thought how lovely it would be to share my home with a 'sister' at last, but Larna's love of clothes and jewellery meant nothing to me, whilst my talk of the High Council and work to be done or adventures to be had bored her to tears! So, when Larna followed her brothers home, I did not mourn her departure; but neither did I move back home. Frankly, I was enjoying a bit of attention myself, and not from my busy and responsible parents either. No-one questioned that I should remain in Eddval's dwelling. Not for now anyway…..

Chapter 28 'The Root of Evil'

It was bitterly cold that winter. So cold that we feared we might fall prey to the terrible illness once more, or simply succumb to the elements. But we were as well prepared as ever for the great snows. Winter provisions had been stored despite the great illness – just later into the autumn – the animals were housed in barns and our homes were thoroughly insulated. Winter clothing had been made afresh for the season and we were shod against the cold in fleece-lined boots. Yet nothing felt better than to be huddled around the fire for warmth and this would happen earlier and earlier as the nights drew in. Sometimes when we were side by side like this, I would notice that Eddval's hand would stroke me gently and I derived great comfort from it. He was so kind and so loving, and in those days, I had great respect for him and no-one else mattered. I neglected my friends, the rest of my family, and devoted more and more of my spare time to my brother Eddval.

On occasion, he would kiss me on the cheek before we stretched out by the fire together. It seemed so innocent at first – we were surviving this great winter adventure together, helping each other to gather firewood, gathering snow for water and attending meetings whenever we could. Mother and Father were always at hand to help us and were never far away. There was no cause for concern. But they were not there at night, and slowly things began to change between us. Eddval started to kiss me on the lips rather than on the cheek, and when I shrank back in surprise, he would laugh and query my response. Then that kiss would become more and more insistent, until one day I felt his hand on my breast, and I knew that what was happening between us was wrong. I gasped and tried to move away, but Eddval was too strong for me, and he went further and further. Despite myself, I felt myself responding to his advances – this actually felt welcome and strangely exciting and daring – and then it was all too late. We could not go back; we had gone too far….. The following morning, I could scarcely bare to look at him, but he held my chin and forced me to look him in the eyes.

"Marte, what happened last night was only the beginning of what we are to become. We will rule here one day, and we will help this township to become an even greater stronghold than it is already. We are as one, you and I, it is the only way, and we are the stronger for it! You must see that!"

I nodded, for what else could I do? He was so certain, so sure that all was well and right. And yet I feared it was not.

That night the snow fell even deeper, and I knew that we would be cut off from Lowton and possibly snowed into our dwelling. If this were the case there would be no escape, no reprieve, I would be lost to this new way.....

It was wrong, it was evil, but it was also incredibly pleasurable, and I had to admit I was caught between my conscience and my own desires! It was like living at the peak of a very high mountain and at any moment you could fall to your death and be smashed to pieces in the valley below. I knew we could be discovered, and so did he, but even that did not stop us.

The following morning, Father dug us out of the snow with his bare hands. They were blue with cold, but he was smiling, and the sight of his great reassuring bulk immediately reduced me to tears. It was all my fault! I had allowed this to happen and now I was too weak to do anything about it. Not only that but I believed I owed Eddval my silence and complicity and this, above all, weighed upon my conscience. Naturally, Father assumed that I was crying because I had been frightened to be cut off like that, however briefly, and Eddval was certainly not going to enlighten him. Instead, he put his arm around me in front of Father, as if it were the most natural thing to do in the circumstances. I couldn't ask to move back to my parents' dwelling, Eddval would never allow it. He would hate me for it, and I couldn't bear that. But my predicament did not last long, for there came a new crisis, which broke our cycle of sin once and for all.

Chapter 29 'The Secret'

Before the illness that devastated so many from Highton, I had no idea what it was like to care for an invalid on a daily basis. But Patrisia had grown up having to look after her mother and was mature beyond her years because of that responsibility. Per, too, had taken his turn in looking after Anye and it was to find a cure for her recurring illness that he had trained to be a doctor. Anye's husband and Roslin completed the circle of carers, as she could never be left alone. It was a mysterious condition, which seemed to have come to the fore since giving birth. There were times when she appeared to be perfectly fit and well, but there would also be times when, without warning, she would suddenly fall to the ground in a terrible writhing fit which, more often than not, would be followed by a thoroughly debilitating illness. To be perfectly honest, I was rather scared of her – well not her, but what possessed her in this way - and I was so proud of Per and Patrisia for their acceptance of and ability to cope with this terrible affliction.

Patrisia and Per were very alike in many ways, but Patrisia was definitely the more confident of the two. Although Per was very practical and level-headed, Patrisia was the more daring and always keen to rise to a challenge. Her attitude to her mother's illness was an example of this: she was able to cope in what I would have deemed to be the scariest of situations. As children she had always wanted to accept my challenges despite being the youngest amongst us, though Per had never let her. Anye had sadly lost several children since having Per, yet somehow when little Patrisia was born, she had hung on to life and fought her healthy and robust way to where she was now. Even though she was younger than me, I felt we were friends she and I, and I was always willing to help wherever I could. Our mothers had always been best friends and I could see why: Patrisia shared her mother's easy going, witty personality, which made it easy to want to help her, but I did hope that she did not have the same troubles when she had children of her own.

And There Were Giants

It was cold and moonless the night when Patrisia came seeking my help for her mother. Eddval and I were locked in an embrace as she burst into our dwelling with her torch blazing. Like a thunderbolt had struck us, we sprung apart and blinked guiltily into the light. Patrisia's face, pale and drawn from lack of sleep, grew puzzled as she frowned to understand what she had seen. "What is going on Marte?" she asked slowly….

"Nothing, nothing, we're just trying to keep warm Patrisia, It's such a cold night." I blurted out….

"Oh, yes of course…." then there was a pause as if she was trying to recollect her thoughts, then, "Marte, please come quickly, Mother is ill again, Janmat is away at a birth, and we need your help!"

My mother had called for me in Per's and Janmat's absence. I could help prepare the herbs. For once, I couldn't have been more glad of an excuse to leave and rushed off with her as quickly as I could after throwing on some outer garments. I mustn't let her see how little I had on when I had complained of the cold!

As I followed her, my mind was in a whirl of panic. If I said any more about this, it might draw attention to my concern, and she might suspect us more – but what and who would she tell of what she'd seen? How could I explain it? What would happen now? And all through the present crisis, mine seemed to eclipse theirs and I hardly noticed the time or effort of that night at all. It took a while for Anye to calm and take her draft, but at last she was comfortable and apparently sleeping, so I fell once more to worrying about Patrisia again. Would she confide in someone? What if Per came back, what then? Would she tell him? I suddenly felt so terribly ashamed and mortified. What had I done?

As dawn broke, sending shimmers over an icy landscape, we were ordered back to our dwellings to get some sleep. But instead of returning to Eddval's, I followed Mother home and slept fitfully for a while by the spent fire. When I finally made my way back to his abode, it wasn't to sleep – it was to take my few things back to my proper home. I knew he wouldn't be there now, so this was the best time to do it. I would just have to think how I was going to explain this to everyone.

Mother was surprised to still see me there when she awoke later that morning but didn't say anything. This worried me still further: had Patrisia already said something? But I soon realised that she had done nothing of the sort and that Mother was simply waiting for me to speak first. She could tell something was wrong, she was so thoughtful like that. I was just beginning on my rehearsed speech when Eddval burst into the dwelling… it occurred to me then that I should perhaps have spoken to him first and agreed what we should say together, but I had already begun – and I could feel my face starting to flush – this was becoming more and more of a nightmare! Eddval strode up to me and demanded why I had removed my things from his dwelling. Mother was taken aback – she rarely saw us at odds – then recognised that this was between him and me, made her excuses and left us alone together. I trembled as I spoke,

"Eddval, this cannot go on. I can't stand it any longer….."

"Can't stand me any longer? Is that it? and since when have you been feeling like this?"

"No Eddval, I didn't say that. You are taking this the wrong way. I just think that it is time we had some space from one another…. That's all…."

He glared at me then barked,

"What has Patrisia said? No doubt she is spinning a web of lies about last night. Well, I can assure you there is nothing wrong with us living together and keeping ourselves warm on a cold night."

And There Were Giants

I stared back at him unbelievingly – was he beginning to believe in a spur of the moment story?! Surely, he should understand my point of view in this. I swallowed, then tried to say, as calmly and as steadily as I could,

"Eddval…. since last night…..I have been thinking about…..what has been happening……and I can't live like that anymore. My mind is made up. I am staying here from now on…."

"So, it's true, you have turned against me!"

I was near tears now; he was wearing me down.

"No! Please Eddval, try to understand. We can't go on like this. It will break me. Please, leave me now and try to understand!"

For a moment he stood there fuming and I thought he was going to strike me but then he turned and stormed out without looking back. I stood there shocked to the core. So now he hated me too! It was more than I could bear, and a storm of tears surged up inside me. Then Mother was back, holding me, rocking me back and forth in that comforting way of hers, not asking me to stop but simply rocking me whilst I wept uncontrollably.

It was a long time before I was calm enough to speak again. Mother made me one of her herbal drinks to sip, and slowly the sobs that wracked my body began to subside and I began to feel the effect of the potion. I felt lulled but strangely dead, as if my feelings were no longer mine. It was no use, I couldn't tell Mother – my wonderful, kind, thoughtful, brave, and noble mother. She would despise me too. And what would Father think? No, it was a lie or nothing. I couldn't tell the truth. So, I spoke of a rift – I no longer wanted to be part of Eddval's plans and he hated me for it – well I suppose there was some truth in that. I couldn't be part of Eddval's plan for the two of us at least. I had never wanted it to be this way and now I was ashamed – not of him but of myself. I had been so weak, so unprincipled. Haiden was right about me, I was pathetic and despicable, and would never be able to hold my own like Mother did.

This feeling did not leave me in the days that were to come. Mother and Father were very worried about me and pleaded with Eddval to speak to me, but he refused, and they despaired. When I look back on those times, I knew my family was behind me, I knew they loved and supported me and yet I knew they were not armed with the truth, and therefore I did not believe I deserved any of it. And so, it continued – my grief and isolation. There were days when I felt so bad that I could scarcely dare show my face outside, and so I took to staying in bed later and later. No one could understand it: how could I be so weak and listless where before I had had such energy and drive? Why wouldn't Eddval back down from his argument with me and why had I taken it so badly? And then I had a visit from Patrisia.

Her eyes were wide and concerned as she entered the dwelling. I knew she felt uncomfortable, and yet strangely I didn't have the strength to make her feel any easier. These days I had little strength for anything.

"Marte, I heard you were ill. I've come to see if there is anything I can do to make you feel better."

"Oh, I'm fine really. Thank you for helping me out with work, I should be back soon…."

"Marte, there is a meeting at Council tomorrow. We are all wondering whether you will be there?"

"Oh, for sure…." I trailed off. In truth, I didn't much care if I did go to the meeting. Eddval was sure to be there, and I couldn't face seeing him again.

"Marte, wouldn't it be a good idea to talk through your differences with Eddval? Surely it can't be so bad that this argument must go on forever?"

I looked at her then and I wondered – had she actually discounted what she had seen that night after all? Did she believe it was just an argument? Dare I mention it now? It was true she was the youngest of us all – had she not understood? This thought lifted my spirits a little and I sat up. I had to find out!

"Patrisia, it was that night when your mother was taken ill, that Eddval and I ...'quarrelled'. I suppose you noticed it?"

Patrisia looked at me askance. "But you two were together when I saw you in an embrace! Were you trying to make up?"

Patrisia really could be hoodwinked! "Yes, that's right we were. But the following morning I decided that our differences were too much, and I had to move out, but Eddval has been furious with me ever since."

"Oh, I see. Marte that is really sad. You should really try to make it up with him. Maybe you should go back to living with him again?"

I smiled when actually I wanted to scream. "Well, I am sure he wouldn't have me back now. No, I'm fine here and will get better soon – just you wait and see."

But Patrisia was still not convinced she had helped me enough. Her next idea plunged my mood yet further into the depths.

"Marte, I am not sure you can get better on your own. How about we send for Per to come back to see you? Would you like that?"

I hoped Patrisia did not see the horror I felt inside!

"No, he is fine where he is. I have no need of any more treatments; I am just really tired. Please don't worry him – he doesn't need to know about any of this. I will tell him all about it when he returns one day and sees me when I am well again."

"But he might cheer you up. You were such good friends!"

"Thank you but no. And now Patrisia I hope you don't think I'm being rude, but I really do feel very tired again. I could really do with some more sleep."

Patrisia left very sorrowfully indeed, for I believe she had really thought she could help. This could not have been further from the truth though. As it happened, her visit was a catalyst for my falling deeper and deeper into a melancholy that left me unable to leave my bed at all. Everything became such an enormous effort that there were days when I felt I could barely open my eyes or look upon my dear parents anymore. I loved them so much and yet I felt I was becoming more and more of a burden to them. And then I started feeling that I was a disgrace to the family – I could do nothing for myself anymore – I was nothing but trouble. It was a spiral of despair, for the less I could do, the more guilty I felt, until I barely had the strength to continue. And then I began to feel that perhaps it would be better if I were not there at all....

Chapter 30 'Self-destruct'

Roslin grieved for the child who was slowly and explicably slipping away from her….

It was spring – the birds were singing, and the sun had melted all the snows away and yet my lovely, vivacious daughter remained in winter, her spirits drowned in apathy. Indeed, I feared she would not last 'til summer. Janmat could do nothing for her. He gathered herbs and tried to make her drink, but these days she scarcely had the will to eat or drink. We tried everything we could think of to lift her from her terrible lethargy. Even Eddval at last swallowed his horrible pride and deigned to visit her, but that had not helped either. Nothing seemed to help until one day, news reached us that Valdis had taken the opportunity of the annual departure of the ships to leave for foreign shores once again. He had not really fulfilled his role as second at Council, as we had feared, and I doubted we would ever see him again. Now it was not so much this news that surprised us but why this should interest Marte so much. Then the thought crossed my mind that perhaps she had secretly been in love with him all along and that Eddval had discovered this and disapproved in some way? He had always been so protective of Marte, which was why his recent anger at her seemed so uncharacteristic. But I couldn't really believe this, as she had never seemed in any way close to Valdis when he had been with us and did not seem distressed that he had now left, if anything she seemed quite pleased. So perhaps she simply took some relief in his leaving – maybe this would heal the rift between her and Eddval?

And slowly Marte did begin to recover and regain a little strength, though she was still painfully thin. She seemed to have purpose now where before she languished hopelessly. I wished she could tell me what troubled her but, instinctively, I knew she was keeping something from me, from us all. I had tried to find out, Eddval too, but to no avail. These days he was more and more taciturn and at odds with us all. It was as if he held a grudge against us, particularly his father, who deserved none of his anger. If anything, Eddval deserved our reproach after what had happened to Marte and how long it had taken him to do anything about it. I took heart in Marte's recovery, though, and decided that she probably wasn't strong enough to tell me yet but might unburden herself to me when she was fully well again.

Then, one day, and without any warning, she was gone. Somehow, she had managed to get herself up and out of the house without telling a soul where she was going and had simply disappeared. My first worry was that she had so little strength, she may have fallen somewhere. A frantic search was begun for her, we hunted high and low, in all the places we thought she might be: the Council Chamber, by the brook, at Eddval's dwelling, anywhere and everywhere, but she was nowhere to be found. And then we heard she had left by the gate - this was astonishing! We hadn't thought she had the strength to leave our dwelling let alone the township! It was only when we discovered she had taken a neighbour's horse that we realised she could have gone quite far by now. So, we hurried to Highton – where else would she be? But there was no news nor sight of her there either! Panic was setting in by now as we racked our brains, wondering where she could have gone, and then it came to me. She had gone for the last ship! She was thinking to leave us, as Valdis had done! I realised now that that was why her spirits had lifted when she had heard of his escape. We must hurry before it left!

Why did Marte want to leave us? I never did understand. When we finally arrived at the jetty where the boat was due to leave, we found that it had already departed, and our hearts sank for we thought we were too late. How long was she gone? Would we ever see her again? Yet we were to discover that Marte had not left on that boat after all. For there, at the jetty, was another ship we had not seen before – though one not dissimilar to ours in size and shape. And there she was, looking up at a man over twice her size! This unexpected sight threw me back to my arrival on this isle and my very first encounter with Elias. It was a wonder that this frail and demoralised version of my daughter should appear so self-assured and at ease as he towered over her. Yet I could see she was speaking to him. That man could have been even taller than Elias, I thought. He was huge and of the same colouring as our people, yet his clothing and whole demeanour were alien to me. Despite the intimidating presence of this stranger, the relief I felt in seeing her again was overwhelming and I felt tears brimming in my eyes as I watched her so bravely standing her ground. Elias put his arm around me as always and we made our way towards them together. And so, began a new chapter in our lives….

Chapter 31 'A Change of Fortune?'

To our astonishment the huge man knew our tongue though he spoke it in a faltering, foreign accent. After Elias had introduced us, we learned that his name was Logan, and he was the envoy from a not so distant land come on a peaceful mission to form an alliance with ourselves. He did not have many men, and I was surprised that he should come in such a bold and unprotected manner. Such visits from foreign shores to our land were rare but one on such a mission even rarer. Back in my homeland, I remembered, long ago, it had been me that had been escorted by my Father's men to form an alliance with neighbouring realms by marriage. King Hageland obviously felt he had nothing to lose by sending these men and this ship on such a mission, as they had heard that our raiding past was long gone. But why should they wish to form an alliance with us? We were separated by the greatest of divides – the sea?

When we arrived back at Highton, a hurried meeting was called at the Great Council Chamber. Though Marte was obviously exhausted by now, her eyes were shining, and I certainly wasn't going to stop her from being present whilst she was enthused like this. By the time Njall arrived, the hall was full to brimming. Such a visit was unprecedented in our lifetime, and everyone wanted to hear why they were here. At last their chief in command – the man named Logan - relayed the full reason for their mission. Their king was in search of a wife and had heard tell of a beautiful princess in these lands. He had been sent to convey his tidings and to request the hand of the princess. In return, our land would be given a great gift of gold and the promise of an alliance through increased trade or armed resources in times of battle. All eyes were on Njall – what would he think of this? Indeed, what would Larna think of this? for she was the prize to be traded here. I shuddered as I thought this. It was certainly my old life come back to haunt me again. I remembered the way I had been sent out to prospective suitors like goods to be traded. Growing up, I had been groomed and prepared for a kind of domesticity that was always alien to me, and I had been very afraid of the complete strangers I had been presented to. Was this to be Larna's fate too? Was she to be bartered for an alliance where we needed none? We had all we needed and had bolstered our army defences, so what real benefit would such an alliance bring?

In truth, Njall looked quite taken aback by the whole situation and I could see he was out of his depth here. It was also obvious from her reaction that his beloved sister Larna had no wish to be traded in this way, yet he did not want to displease his visitors with an outright refusal. We could see at once that he must be given time to consult with us, and Larna of course, and think over the proposals; then (to my mind) he would have to let them down gently with a refusal which would not offend them. At least I hoped that would be the outcome.

The envoys seemed quite content with the request for time to think over the proposal and they were shown to Njall's homestead where they were offered the finest food and mead we could provide. Certainly, they appeared in no hurry to leave with Njall's decision; on the contrary, they seemed happy just to take in their surroundings for a while, admired all they saw and were delighted to accept our hospitality.

During the time our visitors were guests at Highton, we never had cause to suspect them or question their motives for being there. Why should we? They were obviously of high birth, given their vessel and the way they conducted themselves. In fact, I was most impressed with their diplomacy and tact. They were so flattering of all they surveyed and so respectful in all they did and said.

However, it was Marte's reaction to this that horrified me the most, and I believe she was the most taken in by them. Despite all I had told her of my past and despite her own upbringing and all her aspirations with Eddval, she had nothing but praise for their words and proposals, and the bitter disappointment I felt at her words to us the night before their departure will never leave me.

"Father, Mother, I have a proposal for you – one that I want you to take very seriously! I am sure that Njall would never wish to send his sister across the seas, furthermore I could see from her face that she is fearful of such a proposal. As you know, I have been very ill and have been close to leaving this world. Now I feel that I must indeed leave this land, not in death, but for a new life. I want to offer myself up as wife to this foreign king. Then we would still be able to form the alliance that is hoped for on both sides! I am daughter of the Leader of Lowton, Father – I know you do not see yourself as such but such it is! I am now prepared to leave as ambassador for this land and to do my duty."

Elias was speechless, and so was I for a moment. Then the grief poured out of me again, I couldn't stop myself,

"Marte, you cannot do this! For one they will never accept you as you are not of the line!" (I dared not speak of poor Marte's frail figure and drawn looks following her illness) "and for another, you cannot do this. We love you and we need you here with us. How do we know you will be safe there? We know nothing of these people!"

Now Elias interjected, his eyes full of sorrow too,

"What you are suggesting is honourable, my dearest child, but I am afraid I am with your mother on this. You cannot possibly go. We have no true knowledge of these people and their ways – only words and a semblance of finery. How do we know we could trust them with you our precious daughter? No, if Njall is not prepared to let Larna go, then I am certainly not prepared to let you go in her place."

I thought Marte might still fight our verdict, but she simply turned away. She had never disagreed with her father – not even to take Eddval's side – and this was not going to be the first time. However, Marte's chance meeting with the envoy and his men did seem to distract her from her sadness for a while, and though she did not regain her spirits of old she did begin to recover a little.

Njall's final decision was as we all expected. There was no way he could ever let his sister go. However, he took all our advice and sent gifts and even invited their King himself over the seas to be received by us in honour and for trade talks to be undertaken. Everything was discussed amicably enough and there were smiles and handshakes all round. So, when they left us there was every hope that we would indeed be on the brink of some new partnership. As it happened, the King did accept the invitation to visit, but not in a way that we had ever imagined.

Chapter 32 'Watching and Waiting'

Months passed and we heard nothing from our new 'allies'. It was autumn now and we assumed that the King may have delayed his response to the following spring, as preparations for the oncoming winter were no doubt more pressing. We thought nothing more of it. In any case, other matters had taken precedence for us as my dearest friend, Anye, had fallen ill once more. After all these years, I could detect the warning signs that something might be amiss with her. There would be times when her eyes would glaze over and she would look at me blankly, and I wondered whether she might be dreaming. Other times, she might complain of a headache that would then disappear as suddenly as it had come. One day, as we were sitting weaving as usual, she stopped and looked up, and I could see that blank and fixed expression take over her face. At once, I went over to her and led her away to the bed, as I usually did just in case, and she frowned at me – as ever completely oblivious to what had just happened. As I predicted, it wasn't long before she had one of her terrible fits – one after another, which you would have thought would take all the life from her – and indeed seemed to do this time. She just wouldn't wake up, and we began to fear the worst. None of Janmat's herbs seemed to have any effect either and she remained like this without taking food, and barely any drink, for days – there was no way she could last more than a week like this. Finally, a volunteer was called to search for Per. We believed he had travelled away to a village at the far reaches of the island and we hoped that he would return in time.

Three days passed and Anye's condition remained the same. It was as if she had fallen into a deep and irrepressible sleep from which there was no return, and yet there was still hope whilst there was breath in her body. At last we heard the signal from the gate and there he was – heavily bearded now and taller, a more mature version of his former self. As a child, he had been the image of Anye but had taken the quiet, reflective nature of his father. Now as he stood there by his mother, I saw the tears falling on to her seemingly lifeless body and knew that it was time to leave them alone. I must tell Marte of his arrival in any case; perhaps he could work a miracle on both his mother and my daughter! He had always been so close to both of them.

The days passed and there was still no change. To my surprise and disappointment, Marte avoided being alone with Per and only came over when she knew I or someone else would be there too. To his great credit, Per's shock at first seeing her was cleverly disguised. He simply asked her if she had been ill as she looked 'pale' and did not mention that she had lost so much weight at all. Of course, we told him about the great sickness that had afflicted Highton, and he had been angry that he had not been called back. But this was nothing compared to his anger at not being present whilst Marte was ill. Well, when I say angry, Per was nothing like Eddval, his was not anger directed at any one of us, it was more like anguish that he had not been there to help; after all, he and Marte had grown up together. He sensed not to question the cause or onset of Marte's illness – and Marte studiously avoided all mention of it as far as she could. To me, it was as if her pride had been wounded by the fact that she had been so ill, and she didn't want him to dwell on it. She had always revelled in her own strength before. I watched her closely in the hope that she would start to improve, but though she seemed to be able to eat and drink again, she still did not revive her original spirits. Per watched her too, but from a distance, he could hardly leave his mother at such a time ….

And what of Eddval through all this? Well, he had continued to keep himself to himself – largely forgotten in the other problems and events which bombarded us. I am ashamed to admit I had not felt I could talk to him these days. Deep down, I believed he had been the cause of Marte's melancholy leading to her illness and that he had never done enough to help her recover. Moreover, I had felt my hostility towards him reflected back at me and yet I felt unable to heal the rift between us. There were too many other distractions and too much else on my mind to worry about him as well. It was strange, though, for it was as if someone else were taking care of him, for he seemed to be surviving very well alone and away from all his family. He had not been ill, nor lost any weight – all he suffered from was an unprovoked anger towards us, no doubt stemming from Elias' plans for him not agreeing with his own. There was something wrong about resenting the behaviour of your own child, but I couldn't help it and neither, I believed, could Elias. Though he had always striven to hide it, I could tell Elias trusted and respected Njall more than he did his own son. They had never got on, never seen eye to eye and Marte's problems had just made this ten times worse. So, the silent feud continued between us. Eddval and Marte doing their duties but keeping as separate from each other as possible, and Per wondering quietly at all the changes that had taken place during his absence.

It was the fifth day of Anye's illness and there was still no change for better or worse. Per sat by her bedside as usual, wetting her lips with water as she had still not taken food or been able to drink properly, and we were worried she would just waste away. Then softly he began to hum the old songs we used to sing together when he and Marte were children. That he could remember the songs at all was surprising in itself, but that they could finally stimulate a reaction in Anye was astonishing. Suddenly, the most fleeting of smiles crossed her lips and her eyes fluttered open briefly only to promptly shut again. We both stopped what we were doing and rushed closer to see if it would happen again. Nothing.

"Keep singing!" I cried and joined in myself.

After a while, there was the smile again and then, to our enormous relief and joy, Anye opened her eyes fully and looked around her curiously.

"I'm so thirsty," she said quietly, "could you give me a drink please?" I had hoped he could deliver this miracle by coming back to us, and he had! As Per gently lifted his mother to a seated position and gave her a drink, I quickly ran to spread the news.

Anye was very weak for several days but continued to make a good recovery, and we wondered whether Per would leave again for his posting. But when I broached the question with him he was decided.

"No, I won't be leaving again. I am needed here, and it is not just Mother I am worried about, Roslin. You have of course told me all there is to know about Marte's illness and yet I feel there is more to it than we think. I cannot leave when there is the possibility she might regress again, and I want to see if I can find out anymore. The key to the mystery is somewhere here yet it is well hidden, and I intend to find it and cure it if I can. Until I have done so, I will not be leaving."

I knew he was right about Marte. I had suspected this myself but had not found any clues, and now I had an ally in this quest, I felt greatly encouraged. Surely together we would find the true cause of Marte's unhappiness.

Chapter 33 'Our Friends from across the Sea'

Marte's life was in the balance once again:

They came at dusk – our new 'friends' and so-called 'allies' from across the sea. The guard should have suspected something suspicious earlier. Why were they here so late in the day? Their excuse was a storm at sea with strong winds that blew them off course. Why did the guard not doubt their story? Well, these were our new friends and allies were they not? So the guard had let them land as before, and though night was fast approaching, Logan, that great giant of a man who we had met not so many moons before, and his second were escorted to the High Town, whilst the others stayed behind – to slaughter our guard. There were more of them this time and they had cleverly concealed their weapons. Then, under cover of the fast-approaching night – the rest arrived – and waited. They had done their research well – or so they thought. Logan and his man had been within our walls and secretly noted every strength and weakness, and here they were within those walls again. They could easily overcome those who guarded the gates. It wouldn't be easy to fight our men who were so well trained, but they had the advantage of night, surprise, and a strong, though small, army themselves. Every one of the guards at the jetty had been killed so there was no warning, and by the half-light of a crescent moon, the rest of them proceeded to Highton – in force.

Mother was shouting, shaking us to wake us up. Father was still half asleep and telling Mother, "It is just one of your nightmares again!" until the smell of burning quickly told him it was not. Beyond, in the distance, we could see the smoke rising and covering the sky in great plumes as it had done many years before the wall was built. Was this a raid? If so, how could they have managed to breach the guard and the defences of Highton? It was walled and guarded, as was our township…. And then it was a mad, frantic rush to be armed and prepared for battle. Every man and boy had a weapon, and they were all summoned now to the main square. At first, all was confusion and panic, but then Father spoke, and I admired his calm authority. It was as if he were king, and all fell silent as they listened and obeyed.

He spoke of the time long ago when there had been just such an attack on Highton – at dead of night and without warning. They didn't have a moment to lose! They must be prepared and ready to fight as they had been trained to do, and as they left, the gate closed again to protect our vulnerable. Of old, we had listened wide-eyed by the fire as we heard this battle tale. I had been a baby then, carried away to safety by Mother, who had been left in charge of those left behind, whilst Father had gone to fight. Now Father was speaking in the present – and he spoke of hope. Back then, as now, they had only targeted Highton and here lay their mistake. It was one flaw in their battle tactic. One bit of knowledge they did not have. They did not know the significance or location of our township and who resided there! It was true, that when our so-called allies had been welcomed into the bosom of the High Town, they had met Father and Birne and knew they headed the warrior training camp, but they believed us to be one undivided kingdom. They were not aware we remained separated as two townships and why should they? And so as before, all those years ago, Father was to head our men towards Highton for our own surprise attack. But a surprise in turn awaited us: the identity of our enemies!

Mother and I stood shivering as we returned the gaze of those who stayed behind. We were now prisoners of our own wall and there was nothing more we could do than prepare ourselves should the worse happen. We were in a fight for survival now, but my mind was preoccupied with something else, something that had happened before the men had left. It had been so brief, over before I could register its significance, and yet it had since given me such strength. It was an embrace and a whisper and then he was gone – gone to fight and maybe never to come back again. But it meant I had to stay strong – for him alone. He still cared for me. He did not know my secret, but then he never needed to….

~~~~~~

Per knew what he had to do:

I don't know what possessed me that night. Where I got the presence of mind, let alone the strength, to fight as I did. It was as if I became someone else entirely. Maybe it was from Marte that I gained the courage and conviction. Elias had led us to the main gate, and we had found it open, and all ablaze within, and so we flooded in and dispersed to our stations as we had been told to do. I was behind him all the way – but as we approached, something drew me to the front, whilst I sensed Eddval holding off and dropping further back. Were they still alive? Surely all was not lost. At last we found Njall, well defended by his men, but already wounded. Larna and her women were mercifully nowhere to be seen. Elias led a charge, and we were upon them, fighting not only our opponents but to avoid being burnt alive by the fires, which raged around us. Why should they have set fire to everything like this – surely there would be nothing left worth stealing? And then, suddenly, I was alongside the king himself with Elias on the other flank – his second was down, his guard was lost, and we were all he had left.

It was all I could do to hold them back with my sword as Elias and now Birne led the attack. I had taken up the position of second now – there was no other and I understood that role – no one was going to get near Njall whilst I was still alive – it was as simple as that. And so, we fought – like mad men. And every time I saw a new threat, I would let out a roar which signalled a fresh charge, a fresh attack on our enemies. At last, when I thought I could go on no more I saw the great giant himself was upon Elias. It was the very giant who had come to our land as an ally and friend before! A new rage and vigour awoke within me, as I realised what had happened, but now I was torn – go to Elias' aid and leave my post, or stay with the king? And it was only at that moment that I wondered at Eddval's absence – where was he? Had he been slain? In any case there was no sign of him, just when we needed him most. Fortunately, events made up my mind for me. Birne had somehow got the better of his opponent and was now also fighting the great giant. I could hardly believe my eyes. I had known there was a great friendship between them, but I had never seen such a fight as the one I saw that night. They acted as one – as if all their movements had been rehearsed a thousand times and I shall never forget the harmony and coordination of their powerful strikes. What made it more incredible still was that they were our elders and by no means young men – and yet I could not imagine that any of our youth could have fought like that.

As the giant fell, a cry went up, and we knew they had taken a great loss. It was then that I saw their leader for the first time. He had neither the height nor commanding presence of he that had just fallen. He was a man of middling years with a greying beard and swarthy appearance, and when he and Elias looked upon one another there was a moment when time stood still: they just stood staring at each other in silence – was there a flicker of recognition there, I wondered. Then the man muttered a few words, Elias replied, and I strained to hear but could not. And finally, the man gave a signal and turned. It was for retreat. We had won!

~~~~~~

Elias gazed at his enemy of old:

As soon as I saw him, I recognised him immediately. It was he who had led that first raid on the High Town all those years ago and now, as I witnessed his grief, I could see that he had sent a much loved subject (probably his own son) the mighty Logan, as a false 'envoy' to try to overthrow us once again. But he had not understood our ways then and he did not now. Back then it had been revenge, but now, what was the motive for their attack? Was it wounded pride at having been rejected? In any case, the death of Logan had been a great blow and had broken him. We both had lessons to learn: lessons in greed, pride, but also in misplaced trust. We had misunderstood them, and they had underestimated us. Few words were spoken between us – he had spoken only to say that this was the end….and that we would never see them again. Then he had given me that look of denial, and finally the signal to depart once more. We could have followed them as they retreated but I was not prepared to lose any more men in a battle of retribution. Of course, I knew his words could be hollow and that he might well return again to avenge Logan's death, but I could not strike down a man on that surmise, not while he retreated, not following his loss. It was not in my nature; it had never been in my nature….

It was only after they had gone that I started questioning my culpability in letting this raid happen in the first place. How could I have been so stupid and trusted them so implicitly when they first arrived? Why had I let Njall invite them to look around and not suspected them more? Was the marriage proposal part of the ruse to find our weaknesses or had they really taken offence from rejection? At least we had not left Larna or our precious daughter to their mercy. Well, for now it was time for a parting of the ways. More threats may lie ahead, but we would do our utmost to be ready. We would certainly have to reassess our night watch. Still, I had to hope that maybe in the future we, or our children, might look back and find a way for reconciliation. Perhaps….

Several men and women perished in that raid and the grief was compounded by the utter decimation of Highton once more, as had been the outcome of the last raid, when Marte was but a baby. All that remained was stone – the roofs and cherished belongings, all were destroyed in the blaze. It was a catastrophe not helped by the awful realisation that we had all been duped by our raiders. If there was one consolation, it was that we still had a King, though he had been wounded and his life lay in the balance once again. Janmat and Per worked tirelessly as did the other one of Janmat's apprentices who had not left for foreign shores and had since been summoned back to remain at Highton. Most of those still living had now lost relatives in the raid or the great sickness, and the atmosphere was laden with sorrow. Questions were asked once again why our townships should have had such different outcomes – why Highton should be the first target for destruction, and they had a point in this. We were all beginning to see how our townships should have more equal status, as Lowton had been in a position to help not only in the raids but for the duration of the great sickness too, but had been spared much of both tragedies! This argument would certainly need to be addressed. The fact that Lowton remained the smaller and humbler of the two townships did not mitigate the circumstances; we were the favoured ones on each occasion, and enough was enough.

Roslin and Marte dedicated their time to caring for the wounded and (as had happened after the great sickness) our township became a sanctuary and practically doubled in size due to the homeless. Others were tasked with rebuilding so that at least the able-bodied might return to their homes. The organisation alone was exhausting, and with autumn well underway, we had scarcely any time again to prepare for the coming winter. This alone was a cause for grave concern but the spirit of my friends and family never failed to spur me on. Even Marte, who had seemingly had no cause to carry on living, had thrown her life and soul into her work once more and I had to admit that was one good thing to have come of this tragedy. There had been times I had truly feared for her life and begun to give up hope that we would ever have the old Marte back again. She certainly seemed to have found her old energy, even if there was still a reserve and a sadness about her. I shuddered to imagine what they would have done to her if she had gone with Logan and hoped that it was not this that she dwelt on.

Larna too had survived the raid – thanks to Eddval! He had found her and taken her off to a place of safety – no one knew where - but they had mysteriously reappeared shortly after the retreat totally unharmed. He had obviously sworn her to secrecy as to how they had escaped, but as it gave Njall such joy to see his sister unharmed, I let that rest for now – there were too many other issues more pressing to worry about, but I would get it out of him one day…. somehow…. The fact that he had disappeared at such a time of crisis was just as I would have expected though - he was so like Wilfrid sometimes! Yes, now I came to think of it he was more and more similar: watchful, brooding, calculating and always looking for the chance to better himself with the least personal risk. And this had been just such an occasion! What a strange coincidence that Wilfrid had done something similar all those years ago at the first raid on the High Town – taking Mira to a place of safety! That was what Eddval had done and received nothing but praise for doing so, whilst leaving his own King's fate to chance. Larna's safety could easily have been delegated to another – though it was true Njall had tried to get his sister to escape with her handmaiden, but that girl had perished. I couldn't help but compare Eddval with Wilfrid – hadn't they both behaved in just the same way during a time of crisis! How strange that they should be so alike! And just as I suspected Wilfrid all those years before, I found myself suspecting that Eddval had had a hand in this too. Oh, why couldn't I trust him? Why couldn't I trust my own flesh and blood? Try as I might, I couldn't get that question out of my head. I knew I should let it rest and put it behind me, but I simply couldn't let it drop. Eddval's actions in the battle kept coming back to haunt me. The thought that I had ever considered him for Njall's second bothered me more than anything else. He had not been there at the crucial moment; he had not acted as second at all. If anything, that role had fallen to a doctor's apprentice who could never have aspired to such a role. Yet hadn't he fulfilled that role magnificently! Now why hadn't Eddval fought like that? He had always shown promise in training.

Fortunately, my mood lifted as I recalled Per's heroic role in the battle. Where had he got his strength? He had fought like a true warrior and roared like one too! I smiled for a moment as I thought of gentle, thoughtful, sensitive Per's transformation. I had watched him growing up and always admired him for his maturity and quick mind, but never expected to see him in such a light. Marte's playmate, who I could always rely on to look after and bring her back to us, despite her daredevil ways. Sensible, reliable Per, old beyond his years. Conscientious too – he had always served his master well and completed all his tasks appropriately. In fact, he had been Janmat's model pupil. Slowly, I began to appreciate what all these things were shouting loudly and clearly to me. Of course! Why hadn't I seen it before? I suppose because I had never seen him in battle before. I had never seen how brave, powerful, and selfless he could be in the face of death. Yes, it was clear to me now! Per should be Njall's second! Never mind that he had trained as a doctor, he could still use those skills within our community – he was without doubt the perfect fit for such a role. I had to speak to Njall at once.

Chapter 34 'A New Way'

Njall was taken aback for a moment, then he looked at me gravely; I knew what he was going to say,

"Elias, I understand what you are saying, and I must admit I have had thoughts like these myself. But you must be aware that this will only worsen the argument Eddval has with you already!"

"Of course I have considered this, he is my own flesh and blood, but Njall, you know as well as I do that you and Eddval could never work together – there needs to be a bond of trust between King and second and the two of you argue like children! Not only that but he took your sister's side rather than yours in battle – surely not the role of a second! He must know as well as we do that it could never work!"

"Then there is only one way forward as far as I can see," said Njall calmly and steadily looking me straight in the eyes.

"You will have to concede to him taking over from you one day as the leader of Lowton – as he has always wished…. Marte and Haiden could be his seconds."

I gazed at Njall and saw in him all the qualities I could have hoped for in a leader. The humility he showed in suggesting he should hand over half the kingdom to his 'rival' was incredible and yet I had always thought him capable of it. He was not stupid either. He knew there were risks involved in it – after all, handing over power to a rival could be very dangerous indeed, but he knew Eddval like I did. Content in achieving the position he wished for, he would settle down and work as honestly and as hard – in fact, strangely, as Wilfrid had when he had held the power in trust.

"Eddval should recognise that there is only one leader and that is you, Njall. Birne and I have simply directed Lowton for our leader. But what of this new young friend Eddval has made –

he seems to be lapping up every word that Eddval says to him...."

"Elias, I have every respect for you, and I will not do this without your blessing for I still believe that we act in partnership. As to Eddval, well yes, he may indeed be grooming that young man to be his second, but you and I have the power to invest in him or otherwise and we can set up the ground rules. You mustn't think I do not see the risk in suggesting this way, as I hand over power, but I do it in good faith and also in the belief that Eddval would make a better leader than a disgruntled second in command, or anything else for that matter! Moreover, we are divided as two separate townships with separate councils already. Look how Highton has fared so differently in both our recent disasters!" We both smiled at this, there had been so much controversy over this already and I knew this wasn't personal. "I believe this could work. It isn't fair that Highton should always take the brunt of any attack as the principality! Both townships should be ruled separately, and this could be the answer we've been looking for."

I was beginning to be swayed by his argument despite the niggling doubts I had about Eddval's character. It could work, especially if he and Marte were able to heal their rift and work together again. She had empathy for the people that Eddval lacked and could moderate where he might be too harsh. Eddval, on the other hand, had strength of character and leadership qualities. He was like Wilfrid in so many ways; Wilfrid, who had gone on to govern so well. When I spoke, it was with every confidence that Njall would listen to me and accommodate my wishes.

"Alright I will consider it, but on one condition, that he and Marte are able to work together again. I will start preparing Haiden for the role of second to that partnership."

Njall smiled, no doubt reassured that I had agreed to his proposal, "I truly believe it is worth giving Eddval this chance, and this might also be what Marte needs to get her back on her feet again!"

We exchanged looks. I wondered now whether he simply wanted Marte better for her and my sake, or whether he might have a stake in this as well? If the latter were the case, there was no doubt in my mind that he would have my blessing.

~~~~~

Marte threw herself into her new challenge:

Nothing prepared me for the events which were to follow the raid. Of course, I couldn't have expected life to go back to normal – after all, our township had become a sickbed again for the wounded and a sanctuary for the needy, and we were all frantically busy rebuilding lives and homes. There was scarcely time to prepare for the oncoming winter, though Father did what he could. I hadn't expected Njall and Eddval to get on any better but at least they didn't quarrel over me anymore - hardly surprising, as I knew I had become a shadow of my former self. I thought I would never win my place back in Eddval's heart - and secretly I was glad of this – but Njall seemed to have distanced himself from me as well. Where before he might have actively sought my attention, he deliberately kept at bay and seldom spoke to me. However, as the days went by, I felt he wished this weren't so. I was sure he still wanted my friendship, though maybe he was afraid of me after my illness. Maybe he thought I might be afflicted like poor Anye.

When I heard what had happened with Eddval and Larna, I had wondered whether Eddval had secretly harboured a desire for her. But it soon became clear this was not the case when she returned to stay with us, following the fire, as his attentions seemed directed elsewhere these days. Leif was younger than Eddval, and still lived with his parents, but I did wonder whether Eddval might be trying to impress him in that way of his. The boy seemed to be enthralled by him and whenever I saw them together at meetings, I sensed a relationship forming between them which eerily reminded me of ours. It scared me to think of it – had I been like that? Hanging on his every word? I hoped and prayed that it was not the case, not because I ever wanted to be back in Eddval's favour, but because I feared for Leif somehow. He was so young, so vulnerable....

Father and Njall took every opportunity they had to hold private talks with one another, and we sensed that something might be afoot. Eddval became ever more mistrusting and resentful of the attention Father bestowed on one who was not his flesh and blood, and the tension mounted the longer it went on, with only the weight of work to be done to diffuse it. They only spoke to one another at Council now and always in a detached, formal way that belied our family ties. At last, all was revealed one clear, crisp evening when we were summoned to a gathering around the fire at our homestead. This was out of the ordinary as we knew Eddval preferred to keep his own company, or that of his new friend, and he was never invited to our dwelling now. We knew something was afoot and yet we had no idea what was to come. I suppose I never expected Njall to be so magnanimous, nor that Father could ever have relented. In fact, I believed Father had turned yet further against Eddval, not just for my sake, but for another reason that he did not care to divulge, no matter how hard I tried to wheedle his thoughts out of him. Per and Janmat were there too, and I assumed that we were gathered together as testament to their great fortitude in the disaster, and yet I sensed there may be more. And so, we sat there facing Njall and Father and awaiting goodness knows what.

Njall talked for a long time about honour and integrity, being a true subject to the people, and that what he was about to say would go forward to both our Council and the Highton Council before it was finally agreed. Now we knew this was more than a thank you, though Janmat and Per were indeed congratulated, and then came the bolt from the blue. Per had been called to his side and thanked personally as had been expected, but rather than an amulet or other award of bravery, Njall got out the beautiful sword that had once belonged to King Edvard of old.

"Per, you will probably recognise this as the sword you were given to fight with at the battle of Highton. You fought bravely and without concern for your own life to defend mine, so now I give it to you in recognition of this. I would also like to give it to you to use as my Second in Command of Highton. This may come as a shock to you as you have not trained as such, nor feel it your place, but both Elias and I believe that this position should be yours – should you wish to accept it."

Per looked dumbfounded. This was a great honour of which he should be deeply proud, but he had certainly not expected it, and I wondered whether he would accept, though I didn't know whether he really had any choice.

"Eddval, now I come to you and Marte – will you please stand. It is in accord with your Father that I have decided to ask you and Marte – should you both agree – to work together as joint heirs to the governance of Lowton. This would be a new position to which I know you have both long aspired. It will be built by Elias for you to take over in due course, when the time comes. I give this to you on condition that you will work towards this role together. This will be a joint role and that is not negotiable. Haiden – please stand." Haiden stood, also bemused that he should be included in matters that normally superseded him. "You will be prepared to take second in command to Eddval and Marte."

Eddval looked from Njall to Father incredulously. He had not expected this either, but I detected a gleam in his eye as he glanced at me. There was no doubt he would take this new deal to get what he had always wanted. Even if it entailed swallowing his indefatigable pride to work with me!

There was silence for a moment as all took in this news, then

Njall spoke again.

"Now I will give you all time to consider what I have said. I must add that none of these roles will be forced on you – that is why I have spoken to you openly before announcing this at Council. I will give you a day to consider my proposals and you may speak to me about any wishes or concerns you might have."

As he left the room with Elias, we all stood speechless for a moment. There were tears in Mother's eyes. For the first time I thought how I had never truly appreciated Njall's true character before. I had always thought he was rather vain and proud of his superiority to us, though in truth he had never really behaved like that. Instead, he had always asserted his authority in a quiet and self-assured way. Now he was doing that again and giving us a choice! A real choice to negotiate and refuse what he was proposing, but what a choice! He was offering to Eddval – his rival in so many ways – equal status (albeit shared with me) which was something he had always wanted yet had seemed so unlikely to achieve. It was truly incredible! And not only that but he was offering me – a woman – a position of power for the first time in our history! No wonder there were tears in Mother's eyes. What would Council make of it? Per's eyes were shining too as he came over to me. Eddval noticed him move and was also by my side in an instant.

"I can't believe this…. I can't accept this…."

"Oh yes you can," cried Mother and Janmat together.

Per blinked round at everyone, then back to me.

"Marte, if he really believes I can be his second then I will be proud to do it, but I have a condition as well."

I thought at once he would say that he should still be allowed to practise his profession, but he did not….

"I will do it if you and Eddval agree to this partnership, and you resolve whatever parted you in the first place."

He took my hands and I felt everyone's gaze on me. But I only looked at one, one whose eyes were so filled with hope that I couldn't refuse. And as I gazed into those eyes I felt as I had done before he had left for battle, that feeling deep within, and it gave me hope that my old life could be restored once more, and at that moment I definitely wanted to live again.

Chapter 35 'A Burden Shared'

That winter was mercifully mild, and the dark nights and days did nothing to dampen my spirits. There was to be a new way forward – divided, it was true, but united in that all seemed happily reconciled. Per had agreed to be Njall's second and had moved to Highton. But though he had moved away to be with Njall, strangely, the act of division seemed to have brought us all closer together. More consultation was necessary now between our townships, and these visits continued throughout the winter, only to be briefly stopped by two heavy bouts of short-lived snow.

Eddval and I found that we could manage to keep on speaking terms, though he still kept a very watchful eye on me when Njall was present. It was strange for we were hardly reunited as of old, and yet his controlling ways seemed to have reasserted themselves once more. He never asked me to come and live with him again – and I would never have done so – but I might as well have done. I could only assume he saw each call for my attention from another as a threat to our new alliance.

It wasn't until the following spring, when the first buds were on the trees and the sun was beginning to entice the first flowers into opening, that Njall asked me to walk with him. He had arrived early for a meeting of the Council for once and deliberately picked a rare moment when Eddval would not yet be present. I felt my cheeks burning as he spoke. At once I wanted to say yes and no – if Eddval were to hear of this it would spark his jealous possessiveness, and there would be a scene, we both knew this – and yet Eddval had no right to be jealous of me – I was his sister – he should want what was best for me. And surely this was what was best for all of us. I looked into Njall's eyes and saw there an affection that I could return. He had proved his worth to us all; he was a good man. I could love him – perhaps I already did, well, I wasn't sure, but I certainly admired him. I smiled back – I wanted to walk with him. I wanted to find out how he felt about me. Again, as I had felt years ago, I was flattered that I should be the subject of the King's attentions. I really believed my illness and its cause were behind me now, as we strolled together by the brook.

"So how do you find your new vocation?"

"I have never felt happier. It is truly what I want." And then I added, fervently, "we won't let you down Njall – we are just so grateful to you for giving us this chance. I know Father has had his doubts about it all along and yet I feel sure you have made the right decision."

"As I said before, it was never my intention to go against your father's wishes. On the contrary, I have his approval, you can be assured of that. Your father only wants the best for you both."

"He has to think of the people as well and I know he has doubted our capability. I do hope we have done enough to make him think otherwise."

Njall looked as if he was about to reply to this but then he seemed to change his mind,

"And tell me Marte, how have things been between you and Eddval? For this partnership to work, your old differences need to have been put behind you. Do you believe you have succeeded in doing this?" I noticed that he hadn't asked me what these were – but maybe he was hoping I might volunteer that information.

"We are working together just as well as we always imagined we would – surely you can see that for yourself."

"Oh yes indeed, outwardly you appear to be collaborating very well, but are you friends again Marte? That is what I want to know. There really shouldn't be a rift between brother and sister, particularly two as close as you once were."

And There Were Giants

"No, really, we're fine now. You have nothing to worry about."

Njall frowned and was quiet for a moment,

"We were all very worried about you for quite some time. I understand I should feel indebted to my brother Valdis for bringing you round from your illness."

Now it was my turn to frown. This conversation was not going the way I had hoped. He was probing too far after all.

"Njall, did you really bring me here to go over what is in the past? I think not. Surely it would be better to talk about the future."

He smiled. This was as far as he was going to get on that subject, but he seemed satisfied that my troubles were truly behind me.

"You're right. It would be far better to …." He trailed off as we rounded a bend in the stream and up ahead two heads became visible above the undergrowth. It was no surprise to me to see Haiden and Patrisia – we had stumbled upon two young lovebirds without a care in the world. Njall took my hand and pulled me aside so we were not observed. It was suddenly very awkward yet very funny indeed to be in such a situation – should we go back the way we came or walk on ahead as if we hadn't seen them kissing? It suddenly made me giggle, and Njall saw the funny side of it too, but no doubt mindful of their embarrassment, he guided me back along the way we had come.

"Well now that's news to me. How long has that romance been going on behind my back?" he whispered, "I can still remember them trailing behind us as kids, with their noses running, trying to keep up with us. I can't believe how time has passed!"

He looked at me suddenly and I felt my heart start to beat faster. Was this it? Was he going to kiss me? He edged a little closer, his eyes never leaving mine, when suddenly there was a shout lower down the riverbank. Was that Haiden? No of course not, they would never intrude. It had to be Eddval, and sure enough, there he was, running up the path.

"Where are you two going? People are starting to gather, and they are asking where you are? Mother sent me to find you. She said you were heading this way.... "

I didn't believe a word of it but privately resolved to ask Mother later.

"I was just asking Marte how she was after her long illness," Njall replied coldly. The two of them glared at each other for a moment and I felt the old rivalry begin to flare up again. Strangely I felt numb – detached - as if I couldn't be part of it all anymore.

"Yes, and I said I am fine now," I said bluntly, "and so you should both be glad." And off I went – back to the meeting, where I could be happy again.

It wasn't until the evening when we were all quietly working by the light of the fire that a thought struck me, which made my blood run cold. What if Patrisia saw me with Njall and started thinking about what she had seen that night? She was young then, a child, but now.... I shuddered. Everything would fall into place – my split with Eddval, my illness, my near departure. She would think back through it all and understand! Thoughts started playing on my mind, goading me this way and that, forcing me to envisage different scenarios, all leading relentlessly to a disclosure of the truth, until it was half-way through the night, and I still hadn't fallen asleep. It was cold outside and only a sliver of moon would light my way, but I had to walk to clear my head. It was becoming unbearable. How would Father treat Eddval if he knew what had happened between us – they were enemies already! How could Mother still love me? Njall would recoil in horror from me....and as for Per.... It had started.... all over again..... the misery. I was spiralling down, down, down, down, *again*. I had to get out, where didn't matter.

There was the small problem of the watch by the gate, they would never let me pass again with my history, I knew that, but as per their training, they were more concerned with keeping the enemy out than keeping us in, and I quickly slipped out unnoticed, after throwing a stone over the wall and diverting their attention. Once outside, the sheer physical act of walking did help my anxiety a little, for as I walked, I realised that I had two options available to me now. Either I ended this misery and shame once and for all, or I confronted it head on by speaking to Patrisia and telling her the truth. Could I do that? I stopped and thought for a moment, I was nearing the brook now and it shone black and silver in the hazy moonlight. It was so beautiful, I had to go nearer…. What if she told Per – could I live with myself then? Suddenly I realised that this would be the worst fate of all. My mind tried to imagine Per's face as he heard the truth and as it did, so I felt my legs buckling under me as if to topple me into the river. It looked so inviting, it was escape, so painless….I so wanted to fall and be enveloped in its cold embrace….

That was strange…. just a little further up, two great trees were casting their shadows over the water. I realised where I was. The trees straddled the riverbank and met over the water. They hadn't all those years ago when we were children, and I had dared them all to cross it. I remembered Per's face, his words to me, how he had encouraged me despite my foolishness…. I fell to my knees. Might he forgive me now? Why should he, what had I ever done that was worthy and good? I could think of nothing, and the water seemed so close now, licking and lapping at the bank, inviting me in…. But I tore my eyes away and gazed up at those great solid trees, so gnarled and black and strong as if they had been standing there since time immemorial. If I climbed once again and fell that would be it, the end, there was no one here to save me…. But if I were gone, I could never defend myself from Patrisia's story

– for she could surely explain everything…. he might never forgive me for taking my own life – he hadn't wanted me to risk my life then, and when I fell, he had been the first by my side, he had still cared…. No, I had to face him, I had to face them all. But first, I had to face Patrisia, she had to know the truth.

Somehow when I woke up, I found myself back in my bed at home. How had I managed that? The sun was high in the sky – I had slept well into the day. Had it all been a horrible dream? No, it had been horrible, but not a dream – and it was coming back to me now – I had simply managed to reach a resolution and dragged myself back to carry it out. The watch had been surprised (and then relieved) to see me return when they had not seen me leave. Mother was at home and eyed me warily as I emerged from my bedchamber. Her concern was obvious; she had seen so many relapses in Anye that she knew better than to believe I might be cured myself. I did my best to allay Mother's fears and to get myself through the day, until I could speak to Patrisia alone, and finally the opportunity arose. As I led her away from the township, I could tell she sensed this was something serious; I wondered if she guessed what it might be about.

We walked together in silence, Patrisia glancing over at me from time to time. We were over the summit of the hill and out of sight, by now, of Lowton. But it had started to rain, and I spotted a place where we had hidden as children under an overhanging rock. We darted underneath and she smiled nervously at me, trying to break the ominous silence that reigned between us.

"Marte, I know something is troubling you, but I don't know why you have brought me here. If there is anything I can do or say, anything at all, please tell me…."

I stared at her intently, I had rehearsed what I was about to say over and over again since I had woken that morning and yet I hesitated. There was still a way back, it wasn't too late. I didn't have to say anything….

"If this is a secret, I promise I won't tell a soul."

"Patrisia, you don't know yet what the secret might be. You can't promise anything until you know."

Patrisia looked alarmed now. Again, I wondered if she still had no idea what I was about to say and whether I should be saying anything at all. But then her words made up my mind.

"Now you're scaring me Marte. We were all so worried about you before, when you were ill. It nearly destroyed you and we feared the worst. Surely now if you feel you can confide in me then it would at least lighten your load. I might even be able to find an answer to what is worrying you so much. Please, Marte. You know that Per couldn't bear it if anything happened to you."

"What makes you say that?" I had not expected her to say this, but I really had to know,

Patrisia looked at me coyly and thought for a moment.

"Because he loves you of course…. we all do."

A wave of shame swept over me again and Patrisia looked concerned once more. She could sense that I was wavering, on the brink of something.

"I don't know why you have chosen me, but I swear to you upon my life that I will not let you down…. Alright Marte, let me make a confession to you. I have always looked up to you. As children we all admired your strength and confidence in all you did. You were a leader then and you are a leader now. Look at you – poised to be the first woman to become a leader in our homeland! You can't let that go, I won't let you, you must continue and fulfil your destiny…. I believe in you Marte."

I stared at her now, the tears beginning to well up in my eyes.

"You have no idea, then, how weak and stupid I have been!"

Patrisia wrapped her arms around me and hugged me tight.

"Just tell me what it is that you are so unhappy about. I am sure we can put it right together. Please give me the chance to help you. For both our sakes."

I looked into her eyes and saw Per there. I remembered my resolution. I pulled away from her and sat down. She immediately sat facing me and took my hand. I didn't pull it away....

"That night.... when your mother was ill, and you came to fetch me...." I searched in her eyes for a moment, "do you remember that night Patrisia?"

And then she knew exactly what I was about to say. Clever, clever Patrisia. I will never forget her words as she spoke next. She wouldn't let me say any more, she knew what it was doing to me.

"Marte, you were not weak or stupid. I always thought it odd that Eddval should be so jealous of you. It is <u>he</u> that has been weak and stupid, but he doesn't feel it as you do. Oh, Marte, I am so sorry you feel the way you do about this, you mustn't. You were so close, and you didn't want to disappoint him. But I know in my heart that it was Eddval's doing and not your own. I am right, aren't I?

Well, I hadn't really thought about it like that before, but it was true that Eddval had instigated everything and I had gone along with it not to upset him, certainly at first.

There were tears in Patrisia's eyes now – tears of relief.

"I felt sure I could help you before, but now I know what this is all about I am certain! Marte, none of this was your fault and you mustn't blame yourself.

"Then who is to blame – Eddval? Patrisia I didn't stop him. I...."

"No, because you didn't want to upset him, and you were under his power.... Eddval, is the way he is. He wants to own people, possess them – like he wants to own Leif now. He hasn't given up on you, but now he has a new quarry. It is just the way he is. "

"So, you don't blame him either?"

"It is not that I don't blame him – it's just that I know that is the way he is – and that Leif should be warned, in case he finds himself in a similar situation to yourself."

"Oh, I can assure you I spoke to him earlier – and he thinks me quite mad. But Patrisia, could you carry on if you were living with this burden? Would you be able to work with him every day and carry on as if nothing had happened?"

"I'm not you and I haven't even thought about it, but I do know this. You have nothing to be ashamed of, Marte. You have done the right thing and broken away from his clasp.... He doesn't own you anymore. But one thing is for sure: now we know what Eddval is capable of, we must be wary of him and take nothing for granted. He may have a new subject for his attention, but you are not free of his jealousy by any means, and neither is Leif.... You must be careful Marte, but you have so much to live for, so much to give. I know you do not feel ready to share this with anyone else right now, but in the future, take strength from what I have to say, you will find it protects you. Your friends and loved ones will not hold it against you I promise you that."

I looked at her now – this young girl – she had always been so much younger than us – the baby of our clan – never seemingly old enough to do anything – well I had never appreciated her as much as I did now. True, she had been like a pillar of strength, caring for her ailing mother, but now she was here for me too. Why had I ever mistrusted her? Why had I thought she would be my undoing?

I threw my arms around her and thanked her with all my heart. Now I had found a true friend – one who had surely saved my life.

Chapter 36 'Revelations'

Had I been wrong to believe it was my fault? Well, I wasn't entirely blameless. On the contrary, I still felt I had been weak and easily led; but I hadn't been the instigator and I had put an end to it. Now that Patrisia had finally put my mind at rest, that part of my life was well and truly over. I could live again without fear or recrimination. I was absolved. I was free! The joy and relief must have shown in my face because it was reflected in everyone I met. I wanted to get involved with the upcoming festival, I had thoughts and ideas again and my old energy came back from nowhere. Even Eddval noticed that the old me was back again and, though he was none the wiser why this should be, the atmosphere between us relaxed at last. Father and Mother couldn't have been happier and spoilt me rotten, and Haiden didn't begrudge the attention I received one bit. It was wonderful, but best of all was the realisation that I had found such a dear confidant. The difference in our ages didn't matter anymore, Patrisia was now my best friend. My duties lay at Council and in my training with Eddval, but Patrisia and I now shared much of our spare time together, as she was often at our house in any case to be with Haiden. And when Per would visit too, with Njall, these would be some of the happiest times I had enjoyed in a long while.

At last the much-anticipated day of the Sheep Shearing Festival arrived and Patrisia and I were busy making preparations amidst the general excitement. Of late, it had been held at Highton in the main square, in order to bring our two communities together and, despite the fact that we were to be separate townships again, Njall was keen to keep it that way.

It had been two years since my last festival, and so much had happened to me since then. I couldn't wait to see how the men would look. The tradition that the men must be clean shaven for the occasion always transformed them, as it was the only time they were beardless or cut their hair, and it made them look so young and handsome. But also, I was thinking how this might have been the occasion for my life to have been transformed. Sadly, it could never be…..

The youngest men appeared first, and dear Haiden looked no different really – he was still a boy and yet he and Patrisia were like a couple already! Looking at them together, I couldn't help feeling how immature I felt compared to them and yet I could have been betrothed and with child by now as many girls my age were. Larna was soon to be betrothed to a dashing young man from Father's and Birne's training camp. In fact, all the girls I had grown up with were spoken for – I alone stood out for being on my own. And why? – well my illness had obviously had something to do with it – but that was over now, and I had thought myself to be free, free of Eddval's power over me. And yet I was not entirely. Our partnership depended on our working together and how could I continue in that role if I were married to another – the ruler of a separate kingdom? Not only that but I knew that I came between them, Eddval and Njall – a source of conflict between our townships. I was trapped once more in an allegiance not only to Eddval but to Father, and the people as well. Was I not the first woman to take on such a role? I couldn't let them down and I never would. It hadn't been easy making my feelings known to Njall, but he had understood, and we had parted amicably – actually before we had really embarked on a relationship together. Indeed, I was surprised it had been so easy for me. It had simply been the right thing to do. So now here I was, surrounded by family and friends, and yet I couldn't feel more alone, more set apart. Had I chosen the right path, or had it been chosen for me?

The clouds had been building all day and by evening there were a few tell-tale spots of rain before it began to fall – in torrents! Larna's ceremony could no longer be held before the people in the open air, so the festival itself was postponed until better weather and the ceremony became a much simpler affair, under the cover of the Great Hall, and the celebrations were confined to immediate family and friends. I had thought that the storm would clear the air, but I felt stifled that night as I sat there listening to the laughter and singing. No-one had a care in the world – they were all caught up in the joy of the occasion and yet all I could feel was eyes on me, watching me or judging me. I wanted to get up and run back to the sanctity of home – but I couldn't – it was raining so hard outside and I would surely be drenched; moreover, we had all been offered a bed for the night so I could not escape.... The feeling of being trapped got worse and worse. Then I felt a hand on my shoulder. It was Per.

"Come on, we're going."

"Where? Outside? It's pouring with rain, we'd get soaked, or struck by lightning!"

"Not where we're going. I have something to show you...."

There was singing now and dancing. The mead was flowing freely as we slipped out, seemingly unnoticed, though I felt sure there were eyes still trained on me. We were back at the entrance hall, standing before a closed door. He took my hand, opened the door and led me through. From the dim light of his candle, I could see there were more rooms leading off into the distance.

"Where are we going Per?"

It wasn't that I was afraid, I could trust Per, I always had, but I had only ever been in the main hall of this enormous building before.

"You will probably sleep here soon, but I have something to show you. Something that will surprise you."

We followed the great thatched ceiling, lofty overhead. These rooms were on the same grand scale and as luxuriously appointed as the Great Hall but were obviously more intimate living quarters. The sounds and lights from the feast were becoming quite distant now. Per held his torch up high to light his way as we passed into yet another room in total darkness, far away from the hustle and bustle of the servants' quarters and the Great Hall – the largest room of all.

"This was the old King's bed chamber. The stone held strong in the raid, only the roof perished. It was whilst they were restoring it that they found this."

He moved towards the wall and to my astonishment pulled out with relative ease not one but two boulders from the wall leaving a gap big enough to stoop and pass through. Amazingly the stones all around remained intact.

"Come and see, we can sit in here awhile…. we should talk."

I followed him, intrigued, and to my astonishment he led me through the narrow gap and set the torch burning in a corner of a confined little space just big enough for two. He pulled back the stones and we were secluded from the world in complete silence, just the two of us in a tiny stone cell. "How do we get out?" I felt suddenly alarmed.

"Don't be afraid, the stones just push out again, they are much lighter than the rest. You can leave at any time."

"Was this a hiding place, then, that no-one knew about until the fire?" I whispered still in awe at this discovery.

"Yes, it only came to light quite by accident during the rebuilding. Only Njall and I and a few others know of it. Why it was here is quite a mystery, but we believe it was created after the first raid by Wilfrid. There was a heavy wooden chest before it until the fire, but of course that was destroyed."

There wasn't really room to stand comfortably, so we sat for a moment and Per smiled at me, obviously delighted that I was as taken by this discovery as he had expected me to be. Now that I had a proper chance to look at him, I saw a Per that I hadn't seen for a long time. A much younger Per, a boy again, on one of our adventures. I felt my heart quicken as I thought of it – we had shared so much together – so much happiness. A wave of warmth and security enveloped me – I was safe with Per; Per would never harm me. But there was also a thrill too – that we were in this place – a place few knew about. And here we were away from everyone, away from all those eyes…..

He paused, then took my hands and said gently,

"Marte, are you alright? You looked so unsettled earlier, is there something worrying you again?"

That was the frown of old when I had said or done something silly again, and Per was there to pick me up and make me better! Why did he do that? Why did he care about me?

"You know Per, I'm so glad you brought me here. How did you know I needed to get away? It was too hot and noisy down there and now I feel so much calmer. I can't thank you enough…"

"You've no need to thank me Marte. I'll always be there for you, you know that."

"You and Patrisia, you've been such good friends to me, I don't deserve you."

He looked at me for a moment, I could see he wasn't sure what to say next. At last he said,

"Marte, this governorship of Lowton you share with Eddval, is it really what you want?"

"Why shouldn't it be, do you think I shouldn't because I am a woman?" it was me that was frowning now, all defensive.

"No, I am just wondering whether you are happy, that's all."

I hesitated for a moment; there had been too many lies, and I wasn't going to lie to Per.

"Per, I must be honest with you. I have chosen an allegiance with Eddval because it is what is best for him, for me and for the people. You may think this role was handed to me, but I have had to make a choice: Njall proposed to me, but I refused him because I had made this choice – to be true to my destiny as the first woman to hold a title in this land and…."

"because you owed it to Eddval?" he interrupted.

"Well, yes, that is true – I owed it to Eddval, because they were his great plans of which I was a part."

"Umm. Yes, Njall told me of this…."

"There is something missing though, something I long for but I'm not sure I can ever have."

"Is it regret that you cannot be together with Njall?"

He had spoken quickly and was now gazing at me intently.

My answer too was out quickly before I could think about it.

"No, I do not want that…. I always thought I did, I thought I should want to be Queen but, in truth, I don't think I am sorry it is not possible…. In fact, I'm not sure what it is I really do want." I was beginning to feel hot and stifled again. What was I saying? What would he think of me rambling like this, with no clear purpose?

Per gently lifted my chin up so that I was looking at him.

"Marte, do you think I could make you happy?"

My heart stopped. Then suddenly I wanted to laugh and cry at the same time. What was happening here? What had he just said?

And There Were Giants

Tears began to roll down my cheeks, I couldn't speak, I was lost for words and lost altogether to a tumult of feelings, but I knew then what should have been clear to me all along, and I nodded, through my tears.

Per simply held me close and for a while we sat there together, listening – to silence – until the muffled sound of Mother's voice broke through it, calling for me as if she were far, far away.

He lifted me up and said softly,

"Time to go back now. Marte, only you can decide what you want, but if you choose to have me then I am yours, and I will follow your lead just as I always have done. I have never wanted anyone but you."

And with that he pushed the stones away and we were out of our sanctuary, and back to the glare of the lights.

Chapter 37 'Possessed'

I could hardly sleep that night. Of course, these were unfamiliar surroundings, and my bed was far from comfortable, but it was the thrill and excitement of Per's words that really kept me awake. How incredible that I had not seen it all before, not recognised that we were meant to be together all along! Every time he had gone, I had yearned for him and not realised why. Perhaps we had been too like brother and sister for me to feel that we could be any more to each other, and yet I had let myself become my brother's lover! Yes, I could finally look back at it now and not recoil in horror, thanks to Patrisia. Now I could be strong, and yes, we could, we must be together now. Finally, with this triumphant thought in my head I did at last begin to drift, exhausted, into an uneasy slumber only to be woken again by strange sounds…. or even stranger dreams…

There is a curious, dark hole in the mountainside up ahead – I must look inside – and as I move towards it, I feel as if I am being drawn irresistibly towards the entrance of a cave I didn't know was there before. Once inside, I don't look back, I just keep walking, on and on; but the further I walk, the more I become aware that it is sloping down, down, down into the earth. Slowly my eyes become accustomed to the darkness, and I begin to make out there is a shadowy, cloaked figure up ahead. Is it leading me or am I following it? – in any case I notice that it turns every now and then as if to check on my progress, for indeed it is getting ever darker the further we descend, and the shrouded figure appears to be holding the only light. The further we walk, the further my feet seem to sink into the soft, dusty ground until I can scarcely feel anything there at all and it is as if I am walking on air. The cave seems to stretch on forever, becoming colder and colder the further we walk, and I begin to feel that I may be gaining on my 'guide', getting closer to wherever we are going. Finally, the stranger comes to a standstill, and I see that we have reached a stone wall. In the eerie, blue half-light, I can just make out strange, indecipherable markings inscribed upon it. Then, in the gloom, I glimpse a door opening in the wall. The figure stoops and leads me into what could only be a tomb, for there is a headstone set within. Suddenly, I am seized by an overwhelming sense of doom and desperately I try to turn and escape back up the way I have come, but the figure checks me and compels me towards it once again, and as it does so his features are slowly revealed. Under the hood he has matted, unkempt hair that falls over a furrowed, weatherworn face with eyes so bright a blue that I realise that they were the only source of light. Those eyes – they are surely Eddval's! – and yet surely not for the features are Wilfrid's – but the face is grotesquely melting now and changing…. it has transformed into…. the face of Eddval! As I stand transfixed, gazing into the eyes of this monster, I realise that the spectre has almost imperceptibly raised up a sword – he is about to make the blow that will end my life and cast me into the hole that now gapes before the headstone! I close my eyes – this is to be the end of me, I can do nothing to stop him…. Then, a hammering on the door thunders through the oppressive silence. It gets louder and louder and more and more insistent. The spectre is perturbed, possibly even fading, and I think, for one fleeting moment, that I might be able to escape after all, then, to my enormous relief, the door bursts open and Per is standing in the doorway, brandishing his sword, the one that Njall gave him. At the sight of it, the Eddval/Wilfrid figure recoils as if in horror. Per must know that this is the moment to strike for he rushes forward and plunges his sword deep into the spectre's chest, and as he does so, the spectre falls back into the hole before the headstone that was surely meant for me. I scream as the earth closes over the face, for it is now Eddval's, and it is swallowing him up, closing over his dying body as it melts away from view. Per and I are plunged into darkness, and we clutch at each other, horrified by what we have seen, but intent now on finding some means of escape for surely we are saved?.... And yet a distant sound of laughter sends a chill through our hearts once more. We realise, with horror, that it is the spectre who is laughing at us as he rises once more from the dead, rising from the grave. He has no wound now, he is whole again, invincible, and there can be no escape from him after all. He grows and grows until he is towering over me, clutching at my shoulders, pulling me inextricably towards him…. there is no escape, he will pull me into the grave with him ….. now he is shaking me…. why is he shaking me? why is he calling my name?.....who is that?…. is that a woman's voice?....

And then I woke up….

"Marte, Marte, you must wake up! You've been having a nightmare!"

I forced my eyes to open. It was Mother. She looked drawn and tired. I looked around me and saw Anye and Patrisia also looking anxiously at me.

"Where am I?" I gasped, for everything looked unfamiliar in the grey light of dawn; my dream was still vivid in my mind, and I felt as if I could still be in the cave.

"We are in Highton staying the night with Njall and Larna, dearest one. You gave us quite a fright – you were screaming and clutching at the air as if you'd seen a demon!"

"I believe I did! Or was it just a horrible dream? It seemed so real! Oh Mother, Anye, I'm so sorry I woke you. Please go back to sleep. I'm fine now. I probably drank too much mead, that's all…."

Mother looked unsure. She put her arms around me for a while and muttered something about this room bringing back bad memories and evil spirits, but she wouldn't elaborate on this when I asked her and said she would tell me in the morning. And so, as the sun began to rise, we fell asleep again, reassured by the onset of daylight, and I dreamt no more.

We all slept well into the next morning, and found that we woke to a beautiful, sunny, bright day. All the fears and horror of the night before had dissipated, as had the storm, and yet their memory was still foremost in my mind and Mother's words also. I simply had to find Per to tell him about the dream in which he and Eddval had featured in such a frighteningly vivid way, but first I had to ask Mother why she had thought there were evil spirits in the room – the room with the secret….

I listened with wide eyes as she told me a strange tale:

"Marte, long ago, when you were but a toddler, we came to Highton to celebrate Mira's birthday. All was well at first, until I was suddenly taken gravely ill with…."

"You, not Anye?" I interrupted,

"Yes, I know I am never ill, but it was very like Anye's sickness, and yet Anye was quite well, as she usually was in those days, and took you and Per on the picnic which had been planned. Mira brought me to this room and laid me down on her bed and bid her servant to take good care of me. I remember becoming more and more sleepy until I could scarcely open my eyes and then I cannot definitely remember anything else. But I know I was in this room, and I know that when I left it, I continued to suffer from a grave sleeping sickness, which only left me a few days later. There was one legacy from this illness though – a dream which haunted me for quite a while…."

"Was it the dream about being in the raid that used to wake Father sometimes?"

"No, it was slightly different from that one and yet similar too: I was being led into a dark, enclosed space by a giant who meant to harm me."

I gasped as I heard this - it sounded so similar to my dream! But I willed Mother to continue without interrupting her,

"Marte, I have told you that long ago, when I was but a child, I was abducted by King Edvard and Wilfrid when they were raiders. And you know what happened consequently – they agreed to live peaceably and put an end to the raids. But Marte, there is one detail I haven't told you. When they found me, my father had hidden me in a space between two walls where he believed I would not be found.

I gasped again. Mother looked at me puzzled.

"Marte, what is it – you look as if you have heard all this before?"

"Mother, your dream is almost identical to the one I had last night! And not only that, but there is a space behind that very wall! Per showed it to me last night!"

And I moved over to the wall and pushed the stones aside – albeit not quite as easily as Per had done – and Mother stared at the hole that they uncovered. Slowly her face began to glaze over and then she clutched my arm,

"Marte, I remember something. Yes, I remember, I was being carried towards that very hole in the wall. Someone was carrying me there and speaking to me, telling me something. But I couldn't see or hear properly, I was too sick…."

"Can't you remember who it was or anything else? Did you go inside? Perhaps if we went inside it might help you remember more?"

Now she was looking at me intently again and took my hands.

"I'm sorry, but I could never do that…. You see, when my Father hid me in that space, he closed me in, and I was absolutely terrified and not just because of the raid. You don't know this about me Marte, but I have a horror of being closed in – I cannot bear it. It was because of that fear that I was discovered and brought to this land…. I couldn't bear being in there, and then I heard Mother and I tried to get out, and so I made a noise – and they found me."

And There Were Giants

How strange that Mother had a fear that I hadn't known about before. And even stranger that she should have had such a similar dream to mine – after being in this very room! We all knew that Mother had had nightmares following her abduction from her homeland in that raid, but this particular dream was exactly like mine and I hadn't directly experienced a raid – only witnessed its aftermath. Still, it was a real and ever-present danger and perhaps that was why we dreamt this way – as a warning …. Shivering, one thought struck me however – if this was a warning, why should my brother Eddval and Wilfrid, who was dead, feature so strongly in it as forces of evil? Also, why did Mother think she had been hidden behind this wall too? We pondered this puzzle some more and concluded that it must be her mind confusing the two catastrophic events that had befallen her: the terror of the raid and the seriousness of her illness. Moreover, Anye confirmed that Mother had been found on the bed, when they had returned on the picnic, just as they had left her, but in such a profound sleep that they could not wake her for days. The servant confirmed she had not stirred while they had been away.

We were soon all together in the Great Hall again and I was reunited with Per. But this wasn't the moment to talk of the events of last night – there were still too many ears and eyes – so it wasn't until we were preparing to leave that I snatched a few moments alone with him. Of course, you can guess where we hid – the only place where I felt we were safe from being overheard, though I felt distinctly uneasy within its walls now.

At first, he thought he had a simple explanation for the similarity of our dreams – they were indeed a premonition of imminent danger. But the fact that both Wilfrid and Eddval featured in my dream as the enemy made him pause for a moment. He looked at me seriously, then started to ask me questions that made me feel distinctly uncomfortable.

"Marte, have you ever wondered why Wilfrid used to visit your mother in private?"

"Yes, I did always think it strange, but then she said he always admired her speeches at Council and wanted to redress the wrong he had done her by destroying her home and taking her away."

"Yes, but as children I always thought that Eddval and Wilfrid were alike in some way. And now I think of it they did have the same blue eyes…."

"Per, what are you saying? Practically all the people here have blue eyes except for me and Mother!"

"I'm sorry Marte, I do not wish to offend you or your dear Mother, but Eddval's lust for power – perhaps it was instilled in him by Wilfrid. After all he used to speak with him sometimes." Then he looked at me,

"Marte, why do you think I featured in your dream? Why was it I who had to protect you from Eddval?"

This was the question that worried me most of all. I knew I loved and trusted Per and so it would be he who would come to my rescue, but why had Eddval (or indeed Wilfrid) become an evil spirit from the dead? Why was he trying to kill me? True he had done little to help me whilst I was ill but surely he would never wish me dead? Nevertheless, an uneasiness began to creep into my mind: my newly discovered love for Per – how would this affect our governorship? And more to the point – he had never seen Per as a rival for my affection before – how would he react to this? Per could see from my worried look that I could see the significance of my dream now.

"I have been led to believe from all who love you that it was a rift between you and Eddval that caused your illness. But I think there is more to it than that. Ever since we were children, Eddval had a hold on you that not even Njall could break. Until I went away, I truly believed this to be benign and indeed that he would protect you no matter what, but when I returned, I saw that the opposite was true. That he could destroy you too,

Marte, if you did not submit to his command. I believe this dream is a warning, but not of a raid, it is a warning of what Eddval could do to you if you crossed him."

"But what more could he do to me now? He has fulfilled his great ambition and found another upon which to place his affections!" I cried.

"Indeed, he has," Per raised an eyebrow at this last remark but chose to ignore it. He had something else on his mind.

"Marte, have you thought any more about what I said to you last night?"

We looked at each other and I saw so much love there and felt I had so much to give.

"You were right to think I was unhappy. I have been torn apart by allegiances, but my heart is still intact, and my head is still strong. I do love you Per – I don't deserve you, but you have always been there for me, and I have never truly appreciated how much I have always loved you."

"As a friend or…." he couldn't say it, we had been friends for too long, but then words weren't needed anymore….

Chapter 38 'Unrest'

Mother could see it at once. She had suspected the night of Larna's wedding, but on our return, she couldn't wait to ask me.

"Marte, am I right in thinking things have changed between you and Per?"

I smiled at her shyly, "Well, yes I suppose you are right. Why now and not before I do not know – I suppose we just didn't realise it before."

I could see by Mother's face that she was absolutely delighted, but that there was something holding her back.

"I don't suppose you've told anyone else have you? Eddval doesn't know does he?"

"No, but the way he was watching me last night, I'm sure he must have guessed." I didn't exactly say this with conviction and Mother didn't look convinced either.

"Well, think carefully how you tell him and make sure you tell him before he finds out from anyone else."

"Yes, of course Mother, but are you pleased for us? Do you think Father will be pleased?"

"Yes, child. We have always been fond of Per and Father has nothing but admiration for him. I am sure you will be very happy together." And now she hugged me tight and stroked my hair. "Just be careful how you put it to Eddval. Have you thought how this will impact on your governorship of Lowton?"

"Oh Mother, Per says he would never get in my way and says I must continue in my role."

"But Marte, think about this carefully, what if you have a child? What of the line?"

"We would care not for the line – Per has no claim and neither would any child of his. Also, Eddval could govern alone for a while – surely he would like that – to be sole governor – and it wouldn't be for ever. You still speak at Council, and you had us."

"I was lucky to have a good man and you are lucky too, Marte. Never lose sight of that fact. "

I thought ruefully how it had taken me so long to realise it.

"No mother, I won't forget…."

But then I fell to thinking about our shared dream again and the spectre who had looked both like Wilfrid and Eddval at once….

"Mother, I need to ask you something, I know you have said that Wilfrid wanted to make amends for the wrongs he did to you but why did he take such an interest in Eddval? He seemed to be championing his ideas and spurring him on – did you not think so?"

"Yes, he always took a keen interest in Eddval, in fact I have often thought that it was because they were so alike."

I looked at Mother as she said this, and I knew at once that this fact had always surprised her as it now did me. Then she looked at me frowning, "You can't possibly think that he could be Wilfrid's son? Marte, how could you believe I could ever have any relation with my greatest enemy – even if he did reform in later life? I could never have done that to your Father in any case. Now stop these evil thoughts at once. This dream is bringing evil upon us all – you must stop thinking about it and…." But she was cut short as the door swung open and Eddval marched in and stood glaring at us in that disarming way of his.

"What is going on? Why are you in here? What's going on?"

"We were just talking," said Mother warily, then she turned to look at me; was I ready?

"Yes…. Mother, would it be alright if Eddval and I had a few moments to talk alone?"

Mother glided out looking very troubled. I felt sorry I had ever brought up the question of Eddval's father, but at least my mind was at rest on that issue if nothing else…. And now, this was my moment to confront Eddval. He glared at me, obviously aware that whatever it was, it was something I was reluctant to say and therefore that it probably affected him in some way.

"Well, are you going to tell me or not?"

"Now Eddval, you mustn't think that I have gone back on my promise – I will still govern Lowton with you one day and make you proud to share that responsibility with me."

"Why should I question that?"

"Because of what I have to tell you…. You may think it could affect our future plans, but it needn't, please be assured of that."

I paused – he continued to glare at me suspiciously. I wondered, now, if he had any idea what I was about to say – had he not guessed after all?

Finally, after an interminable pause, I whispered, "I have fallen in love with Per and he with me. We want to be together."

Eddval looked at me incredulously for a moment. Then to my surprise he started to laugh – oh that laugh – it sent shivers down my spine! I had not expected this reaction at all, and he continued like this, his manner now in complete contrast to the suspicious glower of before,

"You can't be serious Marte! You and Per? Not in a thousand years! I don't believe a word of it! What could you possibly see in him? That spiritless, wheedling idiot – do you not remember Marte? – he was always the one to bow out or complain – he couldn't stomach anything! And now you profess to love him? Ha? I know, it is because you can't have Njall, so you have to have someone – anyone as long as it isn't me!" these last words were spat out venomously, but his apparent good humour soon returned,

"Well, it won't take you long to see your folly. Of course you don't love him – well not more than your own brother!" and with that he stormed out, dashing my hopes of any reconciliation. He had denied our relationship possible and yet it would surely only be a matter of time before he saw the evidence with his own eyes. And then I would be stupid to think that he would accept it. I felt totally crushed by his treatment of me once again. How could I ever have thought he loved me when he behaved in this way? It was beyond my comprehension.

Eddval might not believe it, but it was true nevertheless; Per and I had fallen deeply in love, and we were very, very happy. Before long, Per confessed to Njall and I to Father. Njall was by all accounts as surprised as Eddval had been, but at least he acknowledged it and apparently took the news with good grace. Father was as happy as Mother, and though he could see there might be repercussions on my role and Per's, he did not appear concerned. In fact, his only concern, like Mother's, was for Eddval's reaction and he was not pleased with what he heard on that front.

"I am not at all surprised to hear this, but I will talk to him - and to Njall. I can imagine they are both feeling aggrieved – just expressing it in their own very different ways!" he added with a twinkle in his eye. "But do not worry Marte, together we will work this out. I will personally see to it."

But before he could, our affair was overtaken by far more pressing matters. A disagreement between neighbours, which had been but a minor squabble to start with, had escalated into a major dispute and Council was called upon to deal with it. No sooner had I heard what it was about then I wondered if I could take any useful part in it.

Malia, had been betrothed to a man from her village and been living with him for some time, when she had met and fallen in love with another from Highton. Of course, her husband was much aggrieved and held the other man and his family responsible for stealing his wife's affection away from him. Such cases were not uncommon. Both parties would be heard and then judgement passed – usually in favour of the wronged husband, as they had sworn themselves together. However, in this case, as I tried to hear their case impartially, I felt myself impossibly torn between the wronged husband and the two unfortunate lovers. I knew I would be called upon to pass judgement along with Father, Eddval and the elders, and yet I simply couldn't. (Strangely I felt too emotionally involved in their plight to be able to judge one over another, it seemed impossible to resolve – and yet I had never really known any of them).

As it happened, I was never called upon to do so. Matters suddenly took an unexpected turn for the worse…. the young lover was suddenly taken ill and died. The immediate assumption was that he had been poisoned, and suspicion soon fell on one of his adversary's family! There was uproar that this should have been possible during a hearing where both parties should have been protected! Fighting broke out between the families and suddenly we had a major incident on our hands only to be compounded by the fact that the young girl was to take her own life shortly afterwards! Our judicial system was severely stretched, and I began to feel afraid:

afraid for what this would do to our community, and afraid for what could yet happen, as people took sides and the fighting spiralled out of control. Whilst the men did their best to quash the uprising, I fell to thinking how we had failed Malia and her lover. It appeared that he had been murdered but was this really the truth? And she had felt strongly enough to take her own life! I shivered as I thought how close I had come to that irreversible fate.

It took a call to arms from the warrior camp before there was any semblance of order again and the case continued to mushroom in size. As we tried to pick up the pieces and keep up with events, I began to recognise something about myself for the first time. Surely, I wasn't capable of being impartial, nor of dealing with judgements of this kind; this was not where my strengths lay! I supposed I was too close to it all in my own life. One thing I was sure of, though, was that I must take heed - for love could indeed be a very destructive force!

Despite my self-doubts however, Father insisted that I heard all the judgements and gave my views. Somehow, he still believed in me, that I might have something valid to say in all of this. My first thoughts were regarding the affair that had caused the conflict in the first place. Had it been so very wrong for Malia to fall out of love and in again? What if she had been allowed to go – what then? Could that perhaps have prevented all this bloodshed? As to the judgement, all I could see was that enough punishment had been handed out to both families by this tragedy as both sides had lost two lives that they valued so much. Furthermore, I needed proof that the young man had been murdered, and none had been found. Could he have taken his own life? There was no telling. And as it happened, no further action was taken against the families, but for those who had taken sides and fought before justice had been passed, and peace was eventually restored between our communities. Also, I was glad to find that Father and Birne heeded my concern about the cause of the conflict, as henceforth both parties were heard at Council, and 'partings' were less one-sided than before.

For some time, though, my relationship with Per was hidden from view by this crisis, and Eddval seemed too busy and embroiled in law enforcement to take any notice of us. Unlike me, he took the case and each fresh disaster in his stride, apparently completely detached from the human tragedy involved, and for once, he worked well alongside father and Birne in reconciling the families and their communities.

At last, there came the time when we could announce that we were to be betrothed, and that the ceremony would take place at the following festival. Soon the news was on everyone's lips and eclipsed the horrors of Malia's story; they were, of course, all wondering why I had not chosen to be Njall's bride. This speculation was, no doubt, a source of great irritation to the King himself, but he never showed it. Instead he agreed to let Per leave his service to return to his duties as a doctor in our village and took a man in his service as his second instead. How I wished that Eddval had been as gracious towards me as Njall, though it was true we had never been as close.

After that, I noticed that Eddval was relying more and more on his right-hand man, Leif, and that he was distancing himself from me once more. Though I was relieved, I still wondered whether he had started to hate me again for refusing to continue our illicit affair, or at other times I wondered whether he might be plotting to install Leif alongside himself instead of me. I didn't know whether to be happy that he had found another upon whom to bestow his affections or not. One thing cheered me though - he had been in such denial about Per that perhaps he was not really that concerned about it. Also, I felt sure that Leif had no reason to be as unhappy with Eddval as I had been. There was no reason for them not to be together, and I believed, then, that this was what both of them needed.

Try as I might, I could no longer find the original enthusiasm I had first had for my alliance with Eddval. Maybe it was the trial and the terrible tragedy that followed, maybe it was the fact that I wanted so much for him to be happy and that I believed that Leif might indeed be a much better partner than I, or maybe I was just too afraid of him after the way he had treated me – why I did not know – though I did wonder whether the answer lay in that dream of mine.

Chapter 39 'Denial'

Whenever a festival approached there would be a crescendo of activity and anticipation, but Eddval remained impassive and seemingly unaffected by it all. I still hoped this was proof he had accepted my love for Per; after all, when Father had spoken to him about the implications of our union he had made hardly any comment at all – he had even reacted as if it were not true, as before. My relief over this was short-lived however, when one clue, one new snippet of information, made me doubt his indifference. He had confronted Njall.

There was something significant about Eddval's sudden appearance out of context at Highton. Per decided to find out what had brought him there:

It was so unusual to see Eddval out of his domain, his stronghold, that I felt compelled to follow him. Why had he come here to Highton? There was no meeting scheduled to take place, only the usual, frantic preparations for the forthcoming festival, and he was not here about that surely?

I did not have to wait long for an answer – Njall was waiting for him in the empty reception hall at the Chamber. He only had his new second with him, who happened to be a good and trusted friend of mine.

"So, you have come. I thank you for giving me some of your time at such a busy moment in all our lives. What is it that is so pressing that you need to see me now?"

"Njall, you cannot believe, any more than I do, that this is a true union between them. It is a ruse to undermine our chain of command and I sense there is some foul play here. Only a matter of a few months ago there was talk of a union between Marte and yourself, Njall. And what became of that? If she can discard you so easily, then what chance has this marriage of going ahead? Not only that, but Father ordained him as your second – how can you let him go so easily? You would do well to keep him by your side and prevent this shambles of a marriage from taking place."

"Eddval, do you truly not believe that Marte has finally found her match? Then you are deluded, and I am certainly not going to pretend it is falsehood. Do you not think that I would have had it otherwise? All my life I felt I must be destined to take Marte as my bride, and all my life I thought it was you who stood between me and my prize. Now, you might think that, in my power, I have the right to exert my will over her – I am, after all, King of this realm and can choose who I like. But no, in the end I have chosen to accept that another was more worthy in her eyes than me and I do accept that, Eddval, for her sake. And you, as her brother, if you truly love her, then you would do well to do the same. You may think you have the power to stop her from marrying, but that is not a brother's right whilst your father approves. You have no hold over her other than to protect her best interests! If she has chosen a worthy husband, then it is for you to uphold that decision.

"You know as well as I do that he is no worthy husband!"

"Eddval, answer me truthfully, would it be any easier for you if you believed he was? What if she had chosen me – would you have accepted that any better? You must let her go Eddval, she is not yours to keep, she is your sister to love and protect, but that is all."

For the first time I could detect that Eddval was becoming really angry. Up until now he had been calm and self-assured, but suddenly his temper flared up and he virtually spat at Njall,

"You are beginning to sound just as weak and contemptible as him! Well, we will see who is truly strong enough to deal with this situation!"

And with that he stormed out of the chamber, straight past where I crouched, luckily unnoticed.

I couldn't own up to having been a witness to this, so I waited until Njall had left before I stood up and saw Gabor looking intently at me.

"If you ask me, which you probably won't, this spells real trouble, Per. I would watch that Eddval like a hawk. There is something not quite right about him in the head – he is too pumped up with his own importance to see reason, and I wouldn't trust him. Watch yourself Per!"

"He has always wanted to keep Marte for himself – this is nothing new Gabor. The only strange thing is that he confronted Njall about it but has not even deigned to look my way. Thank you for your advice my friend, I will heed it. Please do not breathe a word to anyone that I was witness to this."

"You have my word Per. You have always treated me well, and I would be happy to serve and protect you, but if you will listen, I will say one more thing…"

"What is it? Don't worry, you will not offend me…."

"It is this. I do not believe that you or your future wife will ever be safe in this land whilst he lives here. Either you or he must leave…. the sooner the better…."

I was taken aback for a moment. I had not expected him to speak so bluntly! Or indeed so wisely.

"You feel we should leave? And go where? Our families and all that we have ever known is here and I would not wish to leave my mother for good ….Besides, Marte is heir to the governorship of Lowton, she would never leave."

"I know. It wouldn't be easy, but I feel sure it is the only way. He is dangerous Per, you must see that. He is not of right mind when it comes to Marte. Please forgive me, if I have spoken out of hand, but I am a plain-speaking, honest man and I do so from the heart – as your friend."

I admired Gabor his honesty and courage in speaking so boldly. Indeed, he could be risking his position in so doing for my sake.

"Thank you, my friend. I will not forget what you have said, and I will speak to Marte of what I will say are my fears. We are both bound to secrecy in this, and you know me to be a man of honour, as I know you are. If Marte and I must leave to protect our future, then leave we must, but in the meantime we must be vigilant! And I know I can count on your help in this."

"Of course."

Chapter 40 'A Storm Brewing'

It was a balmy night outside but oppressively hot in my room. Tradition was that Marte and I were not to see each other the night before our betrothal, so I was back at Njall's once again, where the ceremony would take place the following day. Marte had remained behind in Lowton with her family and would come up by great procession in the morning. After all the excitement of the preparations, I now felt rather lonely, having retired early, and now missed the encouragement and companionship of my family. Still, I was not going to spoil the best laid plans for anything. Njall and Gabor were close by, and everything was prepared and ready. I reached out for the drink that was by my bedside – how kind and attentive everyone had been. The drink tasted a little too sweet for my liking, so I laid it down again. But then, I reasoned with myself, it was a draught to help me get to sleep and, given the importance of the next day, I must sleep well. I was just about to pick it up and take another sip when a sound outside the room made me jump – strange that anyone should be abroad at this time of night. Then, there was a knock at my door – it was Njall.

"Sorry to disturb you – were you asleep?"

"No, I couldn't sleep either! I am delighted to see you."

"I just came to wish you all the very best for tomorrow. I haven't forgotten that you nearly gave up your life to save mine and now I will be able to see you made the happiest of men tomorrow. It will bring me great pleasure Per."

"Thank you Njall. I, too, wish to see you made the happiest of men one day. You have always been so good to me and to Marte."

He smiled. "Yes, look after her. And don't let that brother of hers get in your way! He cannot accept that she is not his to keep!"

And There Were Giants

We smiled at each other for a moment. It was so good not to be on my own anymore, for in truth, I was feeling a little nervous. Then, suddenly, I felt a cramp-like feeling in my stomach. It gripped me and twisted my insides so that I cried out in pain.

Njall was immediately by my side.

"What is it Per? What's wrong?"

The pain subsided, and I looked back at him puzzled, until it suddenly gripped me again like a vice, making me retch.

Njall stared at me in horror for a moment, then he was at the door calling for help. Gabor was there in a flash, took one look at me, and was off again immediately to fetch Janmat. I was by now retching and convulsing over and over again, my body contorting in agony, and as I did so, all I could taste was the sickly sweetness of the draft I had sipped. How had I not suspected it? – I should have recognised it at once! I had been poisoned in the King's own household! Could this be Njall's doing? Was I going to die?

By the time Janmat had arrived, I had been sick several times and was weak and confused. As the retching continued to wrack my body, I felt my mouth on fire and a bubbling chalky white foam exuded from me. I knew I had to expel this evil from my body – and that Janmat would give me a drink to help make this happen. If only he could do it in time! He poured the draft down my burning throat and for a moment I felt its soothing effect before I felt my body forced to purge itself once more. Janmat continued to administer the draught, but it was a while before the waves of nausea finally began to ease and I was left, utterly exhausted, yet still alive – just.

Everyone had tried to crowd into the room by now, family and friends had all arrived, but Janmat would not let anyone in at first. It was important that the drink be held carefully as evidence of the crime, and no-one was allowed near it. Of course, Janmat had only needed to smell it to pronounce it to be the probable cause. Had I taken any more of it, I would have surely died! How lucky that Njall had interrupted me.

And then, as the night drew on, and my near dance with death appeared to be over, all eyes fell on Eddval – he was the main suspect now as he had the greatest motive to poison me, and he had to account for himself. No sooner had he arrived with Marte than he had been immediately seized under guard's arrest. And his reaction was entirely to be expected,

"How dare you look at me as if to accuse me of this? I am innocent! Just because I disapprove of his alliance with Marte does not make me guilty of this crime! What kind of justice is this that rules a man to be guilty simply because he is the most likely suspect! What proof have you that I had any hand in this? Show me! In any case it could just have soon been him!" and he pointed an accusing finger at Njall who stared back at him as appalled and as shaken as Marte.

Recent history had taught us to be careful to accuse without evidence, and it was true that Eddval had been nowhere near Highton that day and had trustworthy witnesses to prove it. Moreover, we had all known he had not been interested in the pre-nuptial celebrations the night before and had declared he would not come to our betrothal either. He had been summoned from a gathering at Lowton and had been there all along. Furthermore, his friend, Leif, had not been near either, as he had been at the gathering too, along with his parents and siblings. No-one had seen either of them leave. As to Njall, he had not retired but had been with his sister and her new husband up until the time he had come to me, so had not been near the draught either.

So where had the drink come from? Well, it had been prepared in Njall's household by a longstanding and loyal family servant. She had served the family well since Edvard had ruled and had been the only servant to survive the fire and the plague, which had destroyed so many lives. She had prepared the draught, as she usually would, for members of the family or guests, and had taken it to my room and left it there. She swore, under oath and on her own life, that neither Njall, nor anyone else had instructed her to poison the drink and admitted quite freely that she had prepared it herself. The herbs and preparation area were quickly inspected but nothing untoward was ever found, either there or anywhere near. It was and remains to this day a complete mystery how the drink came to be poisoned.

As the prime suspects in the case, Eddval and the servant were to be put on trial. Njall, in his wisdom, declared that he should be declared a suspect too, though I knew in my heart that he had no part in this. I had agonised over what had happened that night when he had entered my room and come to the conclusion that, if this had been his doing, he would have checked to see I had drunk from the cup; yet he had not even glanced at it, until I was taken ill.

As Eddval stood in the Great Hall of Council, it was plain for all to see that he was not only convinced of his innocence but very, very angry.

"So, you have found nothing. There is absolutely no evidence against me and yet I am still blamed. Well, I tell you this: in all honesty I have wanted to be rid of him – yes, I admit it! I never approved of his marriage to Marte, and I believe to this day that it will bring harm to the alliance that we have worked so hard to achieve. But, and I am willing to swear this before the gods and the people, these have been my thoughts only and not my actions. I have had no hand in this deed, and you cannot blame me for it."

Eddval was then questioned on every detail. Witnesses, who had been with him that night, were brought forward and all evidence considered. It thus became apparent that there wasn't a single shred of evidence to link him to the crime, bar motive, though many still believed that he must be the perpetrator. And the clearer this became, the angrier Eddval was that his trial should continue, and almost inevitably, much of his anger was directed at his own father. It was shocking and horrible to see.

Njall's trial had much the same outcome and though he was held in more respect – not only for his high standing in the community - he took pains to object if he thought he was having any more favourable treatment than Eddval.

And what of the servant? Again, the great hall was searched from top to bottom and the poor woman was interrogated over and over again. She had not been alone when she prepared the drink and had only gone up alone to deliver it. There had been no-one other than the servants and our party in the Great Hall that night and all swore upon their lives, with great fear and trepidation, that they had had no part in it.

At last, after several days of fruitless searching and deliberating, it was concluded that Eddval could have had no part in the poisoning, and that he was a free man once more. Yet Eddval couldn't let it rest. He now had a grievance: that he had been wrongly accused of a crime he had not committed, and that grievance he held against his very own mentor, the one he should have held most dear and true – his own father. For in Eddval's mind, his father believed Njall's word over his! No sooner was the trial dismissed than he turned on him,

"Someone has set this up, this whole affair! I have been used by someone and you, my own father, you have done absolutely nothing to defend me! No, on the contrary you have been only too happy to join in the attack! I know we have not always seen eye to eye, and I know you have never approved of anything I cared about, but you could at least have stood up for your own son in this – my worst hour! Did you really believe that I could have poisoned Per? Well, I had hoped that he might be persuaded to leave again – after all he was quite happy to go away before – or that Njall might have come to his senses at last - but not this. And now that my reputation is in tatters, who should be standing up for me, but will you? No! I'm sure you would rather I was dead or had never been born!"

Elias looked utterly lost for a moment; perhaps Eddval's words were too near to the truth.

"I am sorry you have not found in me the father you felt you deserved. It does seem we have been too quick to accuse you in this case, and for that I must wholeheartedly apologise. But hear this Eddval. This has been a warning to us all, not least to you yourself. You must now accept what is yours, and what is not, as must we all."

"And so, do I still keep my position as future Governor of Lowton?"

"No-one has found any reason to prevent it, but we all must tread carefully from now on. No-one can deny that a great evil has been committed – by who remains a mystery – but what is clear is that we must remain vigilant, and respectful."

"So, you are saying I must 'tread carefully' as you might still prove me guilty?"

"No, I am not saying that at all Eddval, do not twist the words as they leave my mouth. I am merely pointing out that you must now accept Marte's betrothal and try to protect her and her future husband."

"You cannot hold Marte's illness against me either. She brought that upon herself, and yet you have always blamed me for that too."

"Eddval, I can understand why you feel so aggrieved now, but you must listen to what I say. I do not want to prolong this ill-feeling between us anymore. We must agree to listen to each other and accept one another, but above all to honour and respect each other and the happiness of those around us. And that is all I wish to say on the matter."

Eddval did not look satisfied with this hasty conclusion. Instead, he looked as if he wanted to carry on arguing, into the night if necessary, to get his father to back down and admit to some kind of ill treatment or wrongdoing. But he was never going to get him to do that! Elias was wise to Eddval's methods: he often twisted arguments so that the fault lay with his father, when in fact it lay with himself. Neither father nor son would concede to anything in this latest impasse, and so the ill feeling continued to fester and grow between them. Eddval could not stop goading his father and though he tried not to, Elias resented it more and more.

Mother had another of her attacks and Patrisia, Roslin, Father and I took it in turns to watch over her. This had been another of life's mysteries – why she should suddenly be afflicted like this, out of the blue – and yet I had begun to see a link between life changing events and the onset of her symptoms. I wondered whether her deep sleep could actually alleviate some of the stress of what was happening around her or helped her to cope with it in some way. Patrisia and I fell to discussing this and then to the controversy that concerned my poisoning.

"In your heart of hearts, do you believe Eddval to be innocent or guilty against you?" she asked suddenly.

"I believe him when he says that he would like to see me dead, and I also believe that he did not poison the drink himself. However, I feel he may have had a hand in it somehow – even if it were to influence another to do it."

"But he, Njall and the servant swore under oath, and upon their lives and before the gods, that they had had no dealings with one another."

"Oh, I am sure that is true as well. Though I have no proof of it either, I was convinced by what the servant said, and there seemed to be no relationship of fear or collaboration between any of them. But I still think we have missed some vital clue, that there was someone under Eddval's direct or indirect influence who did this – but we may never discover the truth."

"What of Leif then?"

"No, I do not even believe that Leif or any of his family had anything to do with this. They are good, honest, hard-working people; they wouldn't risk everything to have a hand in a deed like this, and I don't believe it of the boy either. True, he is besotted by Eddval, but we know they were with friends and family right up until the time Eddval was summoned…. Somehow it is all too obviously Eddval, and yet not possibly so. I am as mystified as anyone, but one thing's for sure – I am by no means safe here."

"What do you intend to do about this then? What if it happens again? How can you protect yourself?"

As I saw the fear in her eyes, I knew I couldn't keep her in the dark – I had to reassure her somehow.

"Patrisia, I am going to tell you something which must not leave this room. Do you understand?" She nodded, apprehensively. "I have thought long and hard about this and have not taken this decision lightly, but Marte and I – we…. we are intending to leave, once and for all – to start afresh where no man bears us any grudge. Neither of us is safe here, certainly whilst this mystery remains unsolved."

The tears rolled down her cheeks as she threw her arms around me,

"Oh Per, that it should come to this!"

But she did not try to persuade me to stay. She knew it was the only way forward for us now.

"Must it be a secret?" she whispered, "what of mother?"

"I know it would be so much better to say goodbye to her properly, but he must not hear of this, and the fewer that know the better. He would gladly be rid of me, but the loss of Marte would infuriate him further. We must not breathe a word to anyone, Patrisia, not even Mother and Father, I have only told you and Gabor, and you may both be able to help when the time comes."

"Of course." She replied sorrowfully.

Chapter 41 'Portents of Evil'

There was to be one final voyage before the winter shutdown, and Marte and I were to take it! We had publicly announced that we would be betrothed in a simple family service during the midwinter solstice rather than wait for the following spring and, under the circumstances, everyone thought this to be a wise decision. Of course, no-one knew of our real plan, except my sister and my trusted friend. The four of us were due to meet at sunrise, when Marte and I were to make our way to the port. There, we were to make ourselves known to the boat's crew. Marte had told them to be prepared for a last-minute cargo which was to be used as a welcome gesture for trade. However, they were to discover that very morning not what, but who that cargo was to be! It all seemed so simple, so fool proof. What could possibly go wrong?

That night I kissed Mother goodbye for what was to be the final time. Perhaps it was best that I was gone when she awoke once more – then there could be no regrets, no tearful goodbyes I thought. But as I kissed her, she opened her eyes; I seemed to have that effect on her. She had been sleeping for the best part of three days now and it was as if she sensed something was afoot. Once she had taken water, and looked about her she cried,

"Per, what has been happening?"

She always asked this now, but this time it took on a new poignancy, a new symbolism, as if she already knew the answer,

"Nothing much has happened, Mother. The trial has been dismissed and there has been no conviction – we are all still as mystified as ever." Suddenly her eyes glazed over, and I feared for a moment that she might be going to relapse into a fit again, but then she cried out....

"Now how can that be? When I have seen it with my very own

eyes!

"What have you seen Mother?" I asked hesitantly; for Mother usually woke from a total void; her mind would have been resting for however long she had been asleep. We always had to fill her in on all that had happened – as if she had been dead to the world.

"It is as I say, I have seen it all – I know how it happened!"

"Mother, you are not quite over your illness. Rest a while longer and then we can tell you…."

"Per, neither you nor Marte are safe whilst Eddval reigns here!" she cried out suddenly,

"No, I fear not Mother, but we have an armed guard day and night…."

"You must leave this land and not return…."

I stared at her in shock. Mother would never say that surely?

"He will not rest until his son is free to rule as he pleases."

She had been staring out in front of her, her eyes shining as she spoke these words but then she turned to look on me wide eyed – as if she had seen a ghost!

"You must leave at once and not return!"

"Mother, do you really want me to leave? Mother, Mother…."

But Mother was looking down at her hands now, which were shaking, and did not appear to hear me. All at once she shook her head, rubbed her eyes, then looked back up at me.

"Mother, I don't want to go…. I don't want to leave you!"

She looked puzzled. "Where are you going then? I thought you were going to stay here now you are going to marry Marte!"

It was then that I realised that this was now my mother, and that I had not been speaking to her before.

"What's happening…. tell me, what have I missed whilst I've been asleep?"

That night, I couldn't sleep for thinking about what had come over Mother and what she had said. Well, first of all, I had never seen her like that – it was as if she had become another person entirely! And then who was the 'he' that would not rest until 'his' son could reign as he pleased? What did that mean 'could not rest'? if this was about Eddval as the son, then she had surely been talking about Elias – why could he not rest?

I wanted desperately to share this strange turn of events with Marte, but she needed to sleep as much as I did. We had to be up at dawn and then we would have a long day ahead of us. And so, I eventually drifted into sleep and began to dream….

Despite the blue sky, there is a chill in the air and storm clouds are gathering up ahead. The picnic things are strewn everywhere and there is the sound of children laughing – I am a child again myself and by Mother's side, playing with Marte. We are having so much fun that we do not notice the gathering storm until the first few drops of rain begin to fall. There are just a few drops at first but then they intensify, and as they fall, I notice that they are splashing into Mother's drink and Roslin's drink whilst they talk and laugh as if nothing is happening, and they keep splashing and splashing until the cups are overflowing. The berry juice flows a golden pink, but then I notice it darkening in colour, slowly but surely, until it suddenly dawns on me that it has become the colour of blood!

I was so shocked at the sight that I momentarily woke up and gazed about me…. There was a plaintive call outside and I wondered if it was a creature of the night or one announcing the coming dawn, for there seemed to be a grey light coming from somewhere. I shifted uncomfortably and tried to make sense of what I had dreamt, but then fell back almost at once into my dream world....

This time I am on a ship with sea birds screaming overhead. Marte is by my side, and we are rowing full tilt into the wind, her hair is being buffeted around her so that her face is hidden from view. Suddenly, her hair is swept away by a gust, and I see that she is agonised, terrified; she is pointing to the front of the ship and is trying to tell me something, but her words are being snatched away by the wind. I turn to look to where she is pointing, and there stands a tall, dark, shrouded figure at the prow of the boat, gazing out to sea. With its back to me, I cannot make out who it could be, but it is huge, and I wonder that I have not noticed it before. I feel compelled to watch this distant figure, who is neither troubled by the strength of the oncoming wind nor the swell of the sea. But the wind is dropping now, and the birds' calls are becoming more and more distant. Marte starts to fade into a swirling mist and as this happens the figure begins to turn, so slowly as if to be practically imperceptible. When at last it is facing me it is blurred and shadowed by the great cape – who is it? I recognise him somehow through the mist – the eyes shine through it – then I know – it is Eddval, only Eddval has such blue eyes, but no, there are deep lines on that face, the nose is wider, the mouth thinner, it isn't Eddval at all, it is a warrior from long ago, a seafarer...... then I remember that face – it is Wilfrid's! Wilfrid who once governed but was slain by the plague that also took his wife, Mira. It is he who is taking me away, and now he is smiling a cruel, vindictive smile. He wishes to destroy me.... he is all powerful, and I have no strength in my body. I am puny, pathetic, helpless.... The figure grips me by the shoulders and – surely, he is going to toss me to the mercy of the waves? I must fight him – I must stay on the ship – I must escape, for Marte's sake – but he is shaking me now.... shouting at me.... the face is fading...

~~~~~~

And There Were Giants

Marte's relief, that Per was waking from a nightmare, was short-lived:

My first thought was that Per was suffering from the same affliction as his mother, for he was writhing uncontrollably and there seemed to be no waking him. But just when I thought I had lost him to the deep and impenetrable sleep, he awoke and sat up gazing at me, his face and body drenched in sweat.

It was then that he told me of his dream and of his mother's words, and we sat there facing each other, in full knowledge of what danger we were in. That dream again – of Eddval and Wilfrid! The warnings were loud and clear, we did not need any more motivation to go, and yet this latest premonition did not promise us safety in our journey across the sea either. We were in the grip of a living nightmare and those around us were unable to protect us. There seemed no way out, no real solution, but our minds were made up – we had to leave and hoped that this was indeed the right decision.

Shivering, we hurried down to the jetty, the anxiety of our peril still fresh in our minds, and found that preparations were already underway for the voyage, though it could not have been long after first light. I was glad that the men were so efficient and well prepared for our journey, for I wanted nothing more than to put as much distance as possible between Eddval and ourselves. All I had to do was introduce Per and myself as the final 'cargo' for the boat – of course this was not what they would be expecting at all, but they would be sympathetic to our story – and urge them to leave as soon as practically possible. But as we approached, old Siegfried greeted me with an air of conspiracy about him that troubled me slightly.

"We are all set – your colleague has handed me the cargo, and we will shortly be ready to set sail. Would you like to speak with him?"

Per and I glanced at each other, dumbfounded. What was this?

What cargo? What colleague? Per was the first to speak now – I could tell by his frown that he was worried, though he spoke as convivially as he could,

"We had not expected our colleague to be here as well at such an early hour. He has already handed you the cargo then?"

"Yes indeed, the last of the gold is almost on board. We will take good care to deliver it to Valdis – you can be assured of that. The message will be delivered so that he can acknowledge the gift and return when the time is right. "

This was too much. There was something going on here that we had had no part in, and I was suddenly convinced that we must return to Lowton at once – that here, after all, lay the danger that the dreams had warned us of. We must go home and think again.

But it was too late. Just as I was about to speak and prepare to make our escape, who should appear out of the jetty cave - but Eddval! A chill struck through me like a lightning bolt.

At the sight of us he paused and frowned for a moment, then came striding over.

"Whatever are you doing here at this time?"

It was Siegfried's turn to look surprised as he looked at our shock and Eddval's anger.

"Your sister has assisted you well in your plans Eddval – and I know you would never act without her – why do you criticise her now?" he asked.

Eddval ignored this and his face did not turn away from mine. He was searching my eyes closely and I shrank from his stare. Then his lips slowly began to form into the merest of smiles as he realised why we were there.

"I don't think you have loaded all the cargo that was meant for this ship, Siegfried." He said finally, still glaring at me, "You have before you more cargo…. Per, I believe you are going to take Valdis' place are you not?"

Now Old Siegfried looked at Per in surprise. He had not been told about this part of the plan.

"But you were to be betrothed to Marte! Surely you do not mean to leave her before the ceremony has even been sealed?"

This was addressed to Per, but Eddval chose to answer for him, before he had a chance to open his mouth,

"Oh, there is time for that yet now, isn't there Per? Valdis has established himself so well abroad; he needs someone to take over his business. One day Per will return with a whole fleet of ships, won't you Per?"

"No, I would sooner fight you than leave now," answered Per, finding his voice.

His retort cut through the air like a knife.

"Well, you will regret that," sneered Eddval, but his eyes were shining. He sensed an easy victory, and possibly (the chill raced through me again) an easy way to be rid of his adversary.

"No!" It was I, trying to stop them, whilst desperately racking my brain for another solution. Now Eddval himself barred our escape.

"Marte, you cannot possibly think that now I have the chance to kill him honourably I would not do so!" cried Eddval his eyes fixed menacingly on Per.

"Eddval you've got to stop this!" I cried, "I am not yours to use as you will, you do not own me, if anything you share power with me, and I will not allow you to fight him. You have no good reason."

"I am fighting him because he wishes to take you away from that very role you speak of – the role you share with me. I will not have that – he can go but you cannot. If he does not go alone then he must fight. And you," he was addressing poor Siegfried now who had no idea which way to turn. "You are my witness in this. I have every right to bar my sister from leaving the kingdom with this felon."

There was a pause. I wondered whether Per would back down and plead with Eddval or even agree to succumb to his will. But then he drew his sword.

"So be it! I am ready."

Eddval looked pleased at this. So, he thought he would be exonerated if he killed Per. Well I would not allow it. I threw myself in front of Per and held out my hands.

"Over my dead body."

Then Per did the bravest thing – he took me by the waist and handed me back to Siegfried saying,

"Whatever happens you must deliver her safely back to her parents. Should he win then she must not be left alone with him. I declare this to be a fair fight – you are the witnesses."

A crowd of Siegfried's men had gathered by now and he had addressed them too. We knew already that Per would not beat Eddval – he lacked the depth and years of training. There was no way he could fight Eddval, who had been originally groomed to take over the Warrior Foundation and had been its star pupil. But there was nothing more I could do. To stop him now would mean he would have to leave me alone and would ever be a coward in the people's eyes, and I could not wish that fate on him either. He had to fight as he had declared it a fair cause.

And so, the fight began. I couldn't bear to look. At one point there was a gasp, and I was forced to turn back, thinking Per was already lost, but he had just taken a blow and was bleeding. The tears were pouring down my cheeks and yet I was powerless – yet again at Eddval's mercy – and not only that but I had brought Per, poor, innocent Per, into this trap too. It was my fault once more. At this realisation, I recalled the dark days, when I had been wracked with self-loathing and crushing guilt. Was this my destiny, then – to bring shame and despair to those I loved? Would Eddval destroy me too? He had almost done so before. Yet there was perhaps the faintest glimmer of hope, for I had survived, and he had not vanquished me nor Per in my nightmare.

All at once, I heard the distant thud of horses' hooves and my heart leapt. One of the men must have called the alarm, and sure enough, over the top of the hill, and as quickly as the stony, steep descent allowed them, came Father and alongside him Birne, Janmat, and shortly after, Mother. But the two of them did not stop for one instant; they just carried on relentlessly, Per bleeding quite badly now from the cut across his arm. Then, there was the sound of more horses and Njall appeared with Gabor and his guards. All stood now as witnesses, but no one intervened, no one did anything except watch, watch as powerlessly as I did.

Chapter 42 'A Free Spirit?'

At least he could have felt no pain as he fell, simply the anguish of defeat. And I was to be a widow even before I could become a wife! Eddval was triumphant – wallowing in his own glory – and at that moment I hated him with more intensity than all the misery my life had given me up until then. There could be no reconciliation now, no joint governance. This rift could never be repaired. He hated me too and he hated my brother Haiden, indeed anyone who had questioned his will – was that not why he had tried to lure back Valdis? The three of them: Njall, Eddval and Valdis would rule over us and we would be slaves to their will. Was that not Wilfrid's wish from the grave?

Empty and utterly devastated, I sank to the ground. Per had died needlessly because of me. I was the cause of so much wrong in the world…. It was in the hushed silence that followed, as all stood and beheld Eddval as he gloried in his victory speech, that I sensed the slightest of movements across from me on the ground where Per lay. Then, to my utter astonishment, I saw his hand close once more over his sword. He was still alive! I let out a whimper, which I quickly tried to stifle in sobs, and fortunately no one seemed to notice. Then Per slowly and tentatively began to get up, first to his knees, then even more slowly to his feet. He must have been knocked momentarily unconscious, and was now unsteadily making his way towards a shocked, then leering Eddval. We were all expecting him to fall again, and no-one more so than Eddval. But, like me, he had not seen Per in action during the raid; he had not seen how he could call on an almost superhuman inner strength when it was needed. No, he had not, he had chosen not to be there, so Eddval simply waited there for him to trip and die finally; but in defiance to us all, he didn't. He summoned that strength from somewhere – was it from the gods watching over him? Was it from love for me and the family he would leave behind? –and launched his sword at Eddval with all his might. It landed with such an impact that all heard its blow. It had lodged itself right in his chest, half-way up to the hilt. I was back in my dream! The cloaked figure was sinking now, staring in an agony beyond reason at his attacker. The look of utter shock and astonishment on his face will stay with me forever – he had completely and utterly underestimated Per. Both of them were by now on their knees, exhausted and spent. But as Eddval fell to the ground for the very last time, I still had to force myself to believe that Per had indeed found a way to defeat Eddval – where none had existed. There would be no last laugh from Hell. And that he had won fairly, there could be no denying that.

~~~~~~

They gave him a royal burial, but many questioned why. I suppose Mother, Father and Njall were too racked with guilt over his trial to allow any less. It was not so much sorrow we felt as we buried him that day but a mixture of guilt that we had never been able to live up to his expectations and desires, and relief that we no longer had to suffer his resentment. For a while, I feared that he may return to haunt me from the grave as he and his father had done before, but Per assured me that he could not, for his was an honourable death and the gods would never allow it.

Per had been gravely injured in the duel – his arm, though badly scarred, did eventually heal – but the blow to his head brought on a similar illness to that of his mother's, though fortunately never as acute. Yet he remained alive! The gods had answered my prayers! It took a long time to heal the physical and emotional wounds of that day but, after a bitter winter, the spring brought us new hope and happiness on the occasion of our betrothal, which we could now celebrate with everyone.

I never have been truly free of Eddval though. I still feel his eyes watching me, disapproving of this or that. But though I never felt this more than the day I was betrothed to Per, nothing could take away the happiness I felt – my restless soul could now settle, at last.

Printed in Great Britain
by Amazon